Choice, Set Free
Book 4

The Tae'anaryn
&
The Enchantress's Chrysalis

By Dr Joseph Ireland, PhD.
"Dr Joe"

The Tae'anaryn *and* The Enchantress's Chrysalis

Choice, Set Free 4: The Tae'anaryn and the Enchantress's Chrysalis
Copyright Dr Joseph Ireland 2018. Edited by FM.
Published by Dr Joe www.DrJoe.id.au

National Library of Australia Cataloguing-in-Publication entry

Author:	Ireland, Joe
Title:	The tae'anaryn and the enchantress's chrysalis
Series:	Choice, set free. Book 4
Imprint:	Dr Joe
ISBN:	1st edition 9780992329426 and 9781727758856
	This edition: 2nd 9780645899931
Date:	1st 15 October 2018, 2nd 3rd July 2024
Pages:	264
Size:	140mm x 216 mm (5.5 x 8.5 in)
Spine Width:	14.834 mm
Weight:	333 gm
Target Audience:	Primary school age. "Middle fiction".
Subjects:	Individuality--Juvenile fiction.
BISAC:	YAF000000 Young adult fiction
Dewey Number:	A823.4 F IRE
Lexile Number:	750

                    By Dr Joseph Ireland "Dr Joe"

About the author

Hi, I'm Dr Joe: philosopher, educator, storyteller.

I am a science education specialist, based in Brisbane, Australia, which means I go about trying to get children (and teachers) to understand how to create knowledge through science. I have a lifelong passion for philosophy (particularly epistemology) science (as a social phenomenon) and fantasy literature, having written award winning games for the Living Greyhawk campaign setting. I enjoy spending time with my wife and family, attending church, and in challenging people in what they think and in what they think about what they think. I also play flute.

The Tae'anaryn is a thinking book – designed to challenge readers young and old to consider the world they live in. Fantasy novels are a great way to teach, allowing us to explore worlds beyond our reach, to meet people beyond imagining and to take a piece of that experience with us when we return to everyday life. That is what I hope this book will do for you. I hope it will take you on a journey to meet ideas and individuals you might never have the opportunity to meet in any other way. Learn more, discuss, disagree, converse. I hope you enjoy *The Tae'anaryn*.

Sincerely,

Dr Joe Ireland.

More wonderful titles by Creating Science & Dr Joe:
Choice, set free.
Delightful high fantasy for the thoughtful young reader
    1: The Quest of the Tae'anaryn
    2: The Tae'anaryn and the Wizard's Apprentice
    3: The Tae'anaryn and the Paladin's Squire
    4: The Tae'anaryn and the Enchantress's Chrysalis
    5: The Tae'anaryn and the Spear of the Troll Prince
    6: The Tae'anaryn and the Khozmoh Djinn
    7: The Tae'anaryn and the Voyage of Imagination's Dawn
    8: The Tae'anaryn and the Crown of the High King

Engaging science fiction adventure with real science!
Space Chase 1: Arrendrallendriania
Space Chase 2: Elizabeth
Space Chase 3: Daniel
Space Chase 4: The Mechanizer
Space Chase 5: Moiya
Space Chase 6: Pancake

Dragon Riders of Pearl
Because Dragons…
Dragon Riders of Pearl 2: Seven Worlds
Dragon Riders of Pearl 3: Return of the Plague
Dragon Riders of Pearl 4: Rage of the Dragonmen
Dragon Riders of Pearl 5: Twilight of the Giants
Trilling young adult science fantasy adventure.

The world's best D&D campaigns – The Wolf in the Sky, Balor's Blade, Quill Versus the Lost Academy of Angelfall, and Hidden city of the Exiles

And do not forget – Creating Science, hands on science experiments and activities for everyone! And Dangerous Science, science to blow your minds.

                    By Dr Joseph Ireland "Dr Joe"

Choice, Set Free

The Tae'anaryn
&
The Enchantress's Chrysalis

When soft the caterpillar,
Spins her cocoon,
Patience waiting not amiss.
Soon the butterfly,
Will emerge,
From this sacred chrysalis.

Annadaria Greens'holm, 313 CY.

By Dr Joseph Ireland
"Dr Joe"

Dedicate

For the angels I helped to raise

5,8 1 14,5,99,61,6 5,12 1 8,9,1,26,26 26,2,40,3,50

By Dr Joseph Ireland "Dr Joe"

Table of Contents

Table of Images

 By Dr Joseph Ireland "Dr Joe"

Main Characters

Kialessa. The main character of the story. She is a tae'anaryn, a race with a demon as one parent. She has red skin, small horns, and a tail. She is beginning to establish her reputation in the small kingdom that begrudgingly accepts her.

Darrix. One of her best friends, a paladin's squire.

Piex. Another best friend, a wizard's apprentice.

Posk. Kialessa's good friend, a mentally disabled half troll boy with exceptional physical strength and agility.

Allastassia. A talented enchantress, and the most popular girl at the college.

The kingdom of Lenmer'el

Going to school inside a castle means the students get to meet the kingdom's highest authorities often, and at times, even the king .

King Dunnkan. The kind king of the nation. His closest advisors and personal bodyguard consist of:

High Captain Bon Shur'e. The captain of the king's army and the strongest and most skilled warrior in Lenmer'el.

Lord Cour De'Feur. High wizard of Lenmer'el, an elf. National expert on all things arcane, including the sciences of magic and alchemy.

Lord Grudon Fletcherson. The king's steward, in charge of running the day-to-day affairs of the kingdom, a human.

Lady Jacinthia Stonehall. A dwarven priestess of the Eternal, the highest religious authority in the kingdom.

The College of Lenmer'el

Kialessa is beginning to notice, and make friends, with some of the other 60 or so students at the college.

Aolith. A lesser noble, a princess, granddaughter of king Petr's cousin. A capable warrior and educated sage.

Dale. Son of a local Duke, Dale is known for his tough demeanour and, at times, brutally effective tactics.

Doreth. A soft-spoken dwarf, cindersmith and priestess.

Federach. Powerful earth priestess and daughter of the dwarven ambassador. She tends to be brusque, can be a little underhanded at times, yet at other times overly idealistic.

Natasha, priestess of Lumos. A cervitaur (half reindeer). She was sent by her people of the northern woods in order to strengthen the alliance with the human kingdom of Lenmer'el, and to learn their ways. She hates wearing dresses, and loathes carrying people on her back, but puts up with both for the sake of the humans… occasionally.

Marchan. The son of a lesser noble and merchant prince, Marchan is the only other capable young wizard at the college. He is 17 years old.

Rude boy, the. A boy around Kialessa's age, the son of a local duke. Small in stature and fond of picking fights and insulting others, especially with Kialessa. She has never bothered learning his name.

1 Federach priestess of Mya, Natasha the cervitaur, and young noble Aolith

 By Dr Joseph Ireland "Dr Joe"

Glossary

Abashed – ashamed and embarrassed

Aberration – something different from normal

Abrasions – scratches and grazes

Archetypal – stereotypical, the ultimate example of something

Chrysalis – a change or a creature undergoing such a change, such as what a caterpillar undergoes in order to become a butterfly

Cyst – a lump, and usually not a good one

Emphatically – determined and forceful

Existential – dealing with what it means to exist

Exuberance – full of excitement

Fleet – short lived

Impediment – something that blocks a goal

Imperious – kingly, in charge

Insatiable – a hunger that is never satisfied

Jeunes – an Elven word for 'young ones'

Magnanimously – generously and nobly

Nascent – beginning, just starting to grow

Nimbus – a cloud made of light

Nuptially – a made-up word meaning "marriage-like"

Obeisance – worship and loyalty

Paramount – highest importance

Primordial – from a time before 'ancient'

Proficiency – skill and ability

Provincial – i.e., not from the city but the provinces nearby. Also, a little insulting as it often indicates 'uneducated'.

Scintillations – glistening lights

Substantiality – more than enough, i.e., very real

Sufficient – good enough for the task

Tumultuous – noisy and rowdy

Vividly – in a way that produces strong images or feelings, i.e., 'life like'.

Winnowed – slowly and carefully shaped or sorted

Enchantress / Enchanter – a being that is able to wield magic innately, entirely by personal talent (as opposed to wizards who must study carefully). While Enchantresses often need nothing more than force of will, they may also use words, gestures, or material foci such as a wand or ring. While they like to claim their working of magic is effortless, without practice or cost, evidence would at times disagree.

– Humdug, dwarf scholar.

 By Dr Joseph Ireland "Dr Joe"

The Chrysalis

People change. You will learn this.
High King Malkom.

Thunder rumbled in a storm-drenched sky, as though speaking dark mysteries from deep within the first true storm of summer. The warm air had been growing heavier all day, now the gathering darkness burst with life giving rain. Kialessa held Allastassia's offered hand, and they looked out at the rain from the stone archways of the college in reverent wonder. Neither said anything for a long time.

'I wonder when it will stop?' Kialessa asked.

'I hope it never does,' Allastassia replied, her voice soft and dreamy. 'It's so beautiful …'

They listened to the clatter of rain on stones, polished over a century by countless caravan wheels. A single flower, a buttercup, hung its tired head against the wind. Soon it, too, would drink up the rain, and brighten the world with its brilliant white petals.

2 Kialessa and Allastassia watch the first true rain of summer

Kialessa felt safe, finding it nice to be able to stay under cover while such a downpour took place within arm's reach. 'You like the rain?'

'Oh yes, there's so much magic in the rain!' Allastassia sighed, and weaving an enchantment her eyes sparkled.

Kialessa knew it well, for it opened her eyes to see the magic in the world: the inaudible words in fire, the symbols written in every stone, the power found in new falling rain.

'It washes so much more than dirt aside,' Allastassia explained, waving her hands In mystic gestures just trying to explain a world Kialessa could not see. 'It feeds the flowers, and every little raindrop has a tiny rainbow hidden inside. It's *amazing*. Oh, and look, two little fairies!' she said, and pointed excitedly through the driving rain.

 By Dr Joseph Ireland "Dr Joe"

Kialessa stared as hard as she could, but could see nothing unusual. 'How can you see them?' she asked.

'They're invisible, but they cast such shadows against the magic of the rain … those fairies live inside the fountain at the upper end of the king's court. Not too many people use that garden, so they're left to themselves to play. When I was young we used to chase each other all the time. Now they usually just ignore me. Fairies are like that.'

Kialessa watched as her friend's eyes followed the invisible creatures around the corner, sighing to herself as they went. It wasn't always easy to be Allastassia's friend – she was extremely talented, and deeply competitive. But then there were these rare moments when she was simply… nice.

It made Kialessa sigh too. 'I wish I could see the fairies whenever I wanted,' she confessed, cuddling up against her friend as the occasional drip made it past the slate eaves and onto their clothes.

'You can if you want to!' Allastassia said, eyes wide with enthusiasm. 'Wizards unlocked the secrets of this enchantment long ago. I learnt it from my mother. They have it all down in a little spell they make all the apprentice wizards learn. If they ever let you study to become a wizard like Piex, they'll teach it to you.'

'Me?!' Kialessa said in disbelief, 'I can't even read properly, how am I going to learn Dragonspeech and whatever it is that wizards write in?'

'Actually, you learn faster than anyone I've ever met, except Piex. I've never seen anyone learn to read so fast.'

'But I'm still *ages* behind you,' Kialessa insisted.

'Yes, and catching up very fast!' Allastassia gave her an affectionate, one armed, hug. 'I'm sure you could learn another language or two if you wanted to.'

Kialessa was surprised, and amused. 'Well, maybe next year.'

'Magic is not so hard to understand,' Allastassia claimed.

'It's everywhere, in everything. It's made by everything, and makes everything happen.'

The air suddenly twingled around the golden-haired enchantress as, without a word, she commanded the unseen magic all around her. Dancing lights like living sparks of magic flowed around her hand. Then, always willing to show off, she put her hand out into the downpour. But instead of soaking her hand, the raindrops just didn't seem willing to hit it. Her hand was as dry as ever.

Kialessa grinned, impressed.

Allastassia laughed at what must have been her genuine smile. The enchantress waved her hand in the rain, yet still it stayed dry. The puddles on the ground nearby rippled with her invisible power.

Kialessa wasn't sure how she did that. There was magic about, that was undeniable, yet Allastassia always made it seem so easy, so natural.

'That's amazing,' Kialessa admitted.

'That?' Allastassia mocked with a happy smile. 'That's nothing!'

With a rich and generous laugh Allastassia sprung out into the rain. It was falling all around her as she swished her boots through the puddles, yet not a drop landed on her hair. Allastassia kicked up great fans of water, higher and higher as though they danced with her to music Kialessa could not hear.

It was amazing, but Kialessa was sure Allastassia's concentration would slip or that she would and go sprawling into the puddles, 'Don't Allastassia, you'll catch your death of cold!'

But saying so only seemed to provoke the young enchantress even more. She never did seem to keep rules she didn't like, and she could always convince the adults to change them. Allastassia spun around in dizzy circles, laughing and dancing with the rain that could not touch her. The ground seemed to drum with her racing heartbeats. Then, with a

 By Dr Joseph Ireland "Dr Joe"

majestic gesture of her hands, a gutter full of rainwater lifted to become a thin sheet of cascading water, like a window. Allastassia laughed, and whipped the entire path clean of water to create another wall.

The ground seemed to be thrumming with music Kialessa could almost share in. It was beautiful, it was amazing. It was a concert of rain and magic just for her.

'That's wonderful!' Kialessa said. 'Now come inside before we are late and the headmistress is displeased!'

Allastassia's expression abruptly changed. She looked angry. 'No!'

Raising her hands the wind and water in the field swept quickly around her like a rising tornado. Allastassia laughed, but it wasn't the pleasant laugh of friendship like a moment ago. It was a cruel laugh, the thrill of someone becoming distracted with too much power.

Kialessa's heart began to race. The change had been so sudden, so unexpected. Something was coming over Allastassia; was she controlling the magic, or was the magic controlling her?

Kialessa stepped out into the deluge, trying to get her friend's attention, yet Allastassia spun and danced in a torrent of ever spiralling wind and rain that pushed Kialessa back under the archway. Allastassia didn't even notice. Unexpectedly there was an enormous clap of thunder in the sky above, and Allastassia laughed a shrill, power-hungry sound Kialessa had not heard before.

'Come inside, before you get hit by lightning!' Kialessa shrieked in fear, but the wild winds tore the sound away as soon as it left her mouth.

And Allastassia only laughed more. 'What's the matter Kia, *afraid* of a little lightning?'

She waved her hands towards the sky, and it responded with a chorus of thunder, great threads of lightning weaving themselves among the clouds.

Kialessa fell back, gulping down her fear. She'd never seen

Allastassia manifest such power, and apparently, neither had she. She looked surprised, but then continued. She formed the lightning again and again, bringing it closer and closer to the ground.

'Allastassia, stop! Think about what you are doing!' Kialessa begged.

'What are you so worried about?' Allastassia mocked. But then spoke in a soft whisper that magically conveyed to Kialessa's ear as though they were standing in a silent room together, 'It's only... *lightning*!' Allastassia's voice chilled Kialessa's neck, and in the next instant a white shaft of light split down from the sky and into the ground. For an instant they were both blinded as the world turned white in the light of the raw power held in the enchantress's hand. The noise shook the castle from one end to the other.

Kialessa screamed.

Allastassia was speechless. She looked at her hand. 'Did... you just see what I did?' She said, oblivious to how the rain was now soaking into her hair and clothes. 'I was ... holding lightning. I was *holding lightning*!' and she raised her hands to do it again.

'Allastassia, stop!' Kialessa begged, trembling with surprise, 'You've stopped thinking. You could hurt somebody!'

For a moment, Allastassia stood there. She looked like she was having an internal battle between hurting her friends, and holding lightning once more.

'You're... frightening me.' Kialessa told her, hands clutched together.

Something must have reached her then, for Allastassia stopped and became aware of how wet her clothes had become. She looked around, hair plastered to her forehead, then looked at her hand as if confused.

The sky exploded with thunder once more, and Allastassia shrieked with fear, cowering in the rain. Kialessa ran to her side but the enchantress refused to move. She simply looked up, her eyes filled with a profound sense of power and weariness. She looked like she was battling to keep her eyes open.

'I… held… lightning,' she whispered, and fell into Kialessa's arms, completely asleep.

Kialessa screamed for help, her loud voice cutting through the thunder and the rain to rouse the lazy castle guards. They seemed bitter to have to brave the cold wet in their armour as they carried Allastassia back inside.

But before she went to join them Kialessa cast one look at the ground where Allastassia had been – a great gash, the size of her fist, permanently carved into the solid stone by the lightning that an ambitious young enchantress had held.

***

'It's called the "chrysalis",' Piex, the wizard's apprentice, explained to them all. They were in the dormitory of the girls and Allastassia was lying like the archetypal damsel-in-distress on a silk sheet dyed angel-pink by her own unconscious magic.

Piex continued, 'It is the moment when an enchantress, or sometimes a sorcerer, begins to come into their full power. It's a delicate time. Drensage, scholar of Fae'merel, believed they were to be kept with mild herbs and gentle words. He believed if such didn't exercise control they could sometimes become so caught up in their growing power that they expend an entire lifetime of magical energies in a single act. It destroys them from the inside out, consuming them with their own magical fire.'

'Really?' Kialessa asked.

'Indeed,' Piex expounded, 'it is called the shattering, the shattering of the chrysalis. This change must be managed. It must be slow. Mild herbs and gentle words.'

Rain still thundered in a darkened sky. The priestess was present, checking on her, adding prayers. It was night, so Kialessa wasn't sure what Piex was doing there. Yet since Kialessa had indicated that magic was involved the wizard had been promptly summoned, and it seemed that Piex was again engaged in a late-night study session with the sagemaster.

Piex stood by the edge of the doorway, careful to not **actually** enter the forbidden dormitory of the girls. It was a rare, even an impossible privilege for young Piex to be in this place, yet he was on official business as the wizard's apprentice and thus was allowed – almost welcomed.

Another student pressed some flowers to the overflowing pile that had accumulated around Allastassia in the single hour since she had been here.

'Will she be all right?' Patsi asked, voice trembling.

'Kialessa?' Allastassia suddenly muttered.

She ran to her side, and Piex might have joined her but for a stern glare from the headmistress.

'I held lightning …' she muttered, and returned to sleep.

'She has spent her strength,' the priestess explained. 'She will be fine with rest, a night at least. I expect her to return to full vitality by morning.'

Kialessa could not hide her relief, blinking away the tears that seemed too ready to spring from her worried heart. 'That is good. But please, tell us, will it happen again?'

The priestess looked at the wizard, who shrugged, and sat himself down on a chair. He picked up Allastassia's hand to check her pulse, using his other hand to study the invisible radiance that surrounded those who worked magic. He gave a questioning look to the priestess, as though she could read more in Allastassia's future than he.

Her stern dwarven features were difficult to read, but her brow was folded together in concern. She immediately dismissed the gathered circle of concerned friends to their own beds once more.

The wizard almost whispered, speaking only to Kialessa and the priestess, 'It is a good thing you were there this night, dame Kialessa. It is difficult for me to say at this early stage how this will play out. If it is the beginning of her chrysalis, this event

By Dr Joseph Ireland "Dr Joe"

does not bode particularly well, I'm afraid. It is clear that young Allastassia will need some help; good friends, and good advice, during this dangerous time of change for her. She is becoming a woman, adding the full powers of womanhood to the strength of a young girl's enchantments.'

The priestess pressed her hand to Allastassia's forehead. 'I will call for her mother; her own chrysalis was mild in comparison. A family member with similar experiences will still be well equipped to help this young one.'

Kialessa looked at Allastassia. She was the only child of the most powerful enchantress in Lenmer'el. She was surrounded by friends. She had held lightning, and Kialessa wondered what she, personally, could possibly do to help a young enchantress on the dangerous cusp of coming into her full powers.

'What do I do?' Kialessa asked them.

The priestess answered, 'Stay close, Kialessa, love her as a friend. That is all you can do at a time like this; when someone close to you must walk a difficult path that they, alone, can take. Do not carry her trials as your own, but care for her, help her see them through. She will be stronger at the end, and remember fondly all who stand by her at a time such as this.'

'Just… be there? Be her friend?'

'Indeed. Oh, Kialessa, never forget what a powerful thing simply being there for a friend in need can be!' the priestess promised her.

The Circus

Many privileges in this life are not for us, this is true;
none have access to every moment of reality.
Sagemaster De'Feur.

The priestess's words were true - the following day Allastassia was up again, all trouble long forgotten. The rain had stopped, and the sun lit the sky. By midday the college broke for lunch and Kialessa went with all the other students to the lower lawn. That meant Piex and Kialessa sat there, studying on the steps. Their good friend, Darrix the paladin's squire, was soon wrestling with the other boys. Allastassia was holding court with her devoted admirers, bringing the paper butterflies they made to temporary life. Their other friend Posk was nowhere to be found, but chances were he'd be along soon. It was Planasday, and combat training was on this afternoon. The five of them formed an unstoppable team that won so many times the tutors had taken to breaking their group up among the other teams, which meant making them face off against each other. But that was never any fun. Still, it was hard, physical combat after a week of intense study, and it was the day many students looked forward to most of all.

All at once people began shouting and running towards the edge of the lawn overlooking the field where the horses were kept, including Darrix's impressive mount and best friend; Mask, the stallion.

'What's going on?' Kialessa asked Piex.

'Don't know,' he replied, not moving his head from his book.

'Well I'm going to find out!' she said and jumped up. She raced to the far end of the field and pushed her way between the other students to get a proper look.

Out on the horses' field a dozen gaudy wagons, pulled by two slow moving posks each, were settling down in a semi-circle, unloading their gear. Three wagons carried strange monsters that looked quite dangerous, the wagons were pulled by even stranger beasts – a giant chittering beetle, a hulking minotaur, and a golden posk with dragon-like wings.

'Who are they?' Kialessa asked out loud, not caring who answered.

'You mean you don't know!' a voice teased. It was the young boy, the mean one. The one who teased her every chance he had. The one who'd stolen her paper when she was trying to learn how to read, the one who'd knocked down her archery target and accused her of missing. The one who was still the first to laugh at her.

The one she'd shot so many times with practice arrows during combat training they'd asked her to stop singling him out.

'It's the *circus*!' he replied to her annoyed silence. 'Didn't you know? There were posters all over town. Oh, that's right, you can't *read*!'

'I can read!' she shouted, not sure if she was angry at just him, or the way everyone shouted and jostled all around her. 'Just … not very well. Yet. But I bet I'll read better than you one day!'

'Yeah, right!' he sneered, and went away, no doubt to tell one of his friends how she'd failed at something again. He was such an immature boy, and it made her very, very angry.

But she didn't have time to simmer about that right now; it was a "circus". She'd never seen one before, and when someone had mentioned they were coming a few weeks ago she'd dismissed it thinking it all sounded pretty unbelievable. Seriously, using magic for entertainment? But these people were clearly dressed to entertain. Their clothes were impossible shades of orange and yellow, and they were quickly setting up large tents of pink and blue.

Kialessa's attention was drawn to a strange sight. There was a young girl, about her own age, dressed in blue. She looked quite human, but couldn't have been from the way she behaved. She was helping the giant minotaur put in the giant tent poles, but she didn't carry them around in her arms: she seemed to be carrying them inside her mouth. She would just throw her head back, open up, reach in, and pull out a tent peg the size of her own arm, time and time again. Kialessa had to wonder how many tent poles she managed to fit in there.

'Ewww,' another student moaned when she noticed.

Just then one man among the circus folk, whose nose was tipped red with a glowing ball, noticed them all and begun to juggle three tent pegs all at once. With an unfortunate crumble that set Kialessa and the other students into hysterics of laughter he dropped them all, one after the other, right on his feet.

Without warning someone began bashing a steel plate behind them.

'All right, *all right*!' It was the headmistress. 'Students, get *back* to your studies this instant. The circus folk need to set up and we can't have you watching over them every moment. Don't worry; they'll be ready soon enough!'

'Look!' someone called in belligerent excitement. Everybody turned back around and pressed against the fence.

The circus folk had attached an enormous copper ring to the

top of a tree stump they'd planted in the ground. They hooked many ropes from various wagons, and with a magical gesture by the woman who led them, the stump suddenly began to grow upwards like a magic tree. And as it pulled the mysterious ropes from the wagons, enormous sheets of fabric unfurled till a giant circus tent of bright colours and strong fabric was erected.

'Come, everyone,' the head mistress repeated a moment later, and they all sighed.

But Kialessa dawdled as long as possible, till the head mistress caught her by the shoulders. 'Come child, maybe if you do some chores for me, I'll let you have a copper piece and you can see the circus for an extra day?'

Kialessa looked up at her, and said nothing. Had the head mistress already forgotten she'd earned over a thousand pieces of copper just helping out; saving the king's life, foraging in dark wizard's towers, and helping paladins to slay demons?

Then again, maybe she is just too old to remember, Kialessa wondered.

***

Piex was standing on his tip toes, wand in hand, peering down into a young girl's mouth. His face a mask of such concentration, it denied the ridiculousness of the situation. She knelt there on one knee, head thrown backwards, mouth so widely open her jaw was visibly dislocated. And if Kialessa didn't know better, she'd say she was enjoying herself.

'Piex, stop that, you look ridiculous,' Allastassia complained. She seemed very uncomfortable with the whole situation.

'I think wizards look like that all the time,' Darrix said with a grin.

They'd been out, enjoying the evening breeze, when they'd stumbled into the little girl who could hold entire tent pegs in her mouth. Turned out she was yet another old friend of

Allastassia's. They met years ago, at the elf queen's birthday party or something. And it seemed Flower, as was the girl's name, softly spoken with a voice that sounded a little tense, loved being the centre of attention almost as much as Allastassia did. She was once more in the company of her friend, or pet

3 Flower and Ugly

 By Dr Joseph Ireland "Dr Joe"

minotaur, whose name was apparently "Ugly". He was massive, but never said a word. Flower claimed he'd lost his voice as a child in a sickness, and been cast out of minotaur society for it.

The girl mumbled something incoherent as Piex studied the back of her throat.

'We have no idea what you just said,' Allastassia protested. She was not impressed by Piex's insatiable curiosity at the best of times.

Flower clicked her jaw back into place, and stood up, smiling. She had an innocent looking face, round with naturally puckered lips, making her look quite young, yet mature at the same time. 'I don't mind, not really. I've spent my whole life with people staring at me. I am part of a circus, after all.' Then she gave a very gracious and elaborate curtsy.

Allastassia looked like she was about to change the conversation topic to something sensible; like weather, or nobles, or even perhaps about any other freak at the circus. *Anything* to stop everyone looking at the back of Flower's throat.

But Piex cut in, 'It's clearly an interdimensional rift, permanently affixed to a secondary soft pallet at the back of her mouth. Have you any idea regarding the physical dimensions of the space within?' he asked.

'We still have no idea what you just said!' Allastassia complained.

'Oh, I get asked that all the time,' Flower giggled. 'We think my "pocket" is the same size and shape as the rest of me, only inside… like I'm an empty me inside. We keep all kinds of stuff in there.'

Allastassia whimpered.

Even Kialessa found that just a little… odd.

Flower grinned, and did a professional curtsey the way she probably did every day when horrifying the locals with her bizarre and unusual talent. 'Oh don't worry, we clean up everything properly, and make sure there's nothing sharp or dangerous in there.'

'I think it's amazing,' Kialessa admitted.

4 Flower, circus performer, contortionist

Flower smiled. 'Still, skin that doesn't burn. I think *that* would be even *more* amazing!'

Kialessa smiled. She found herself beginning to like this girl, so very different from other humans she'd met.

Piex cut in before she could ask Flower how she knew about her skin . 'Have you any indication what might have caused this aberration in your otherwise normal human physiology?' he asked.

Allastassia groaned, flung her hands up in the air, and turned away.

Yet somehow Flower seemed to know what Piex was saying.

                    By Dr Joseph Ireland "Dr Joe"

'Yes. My mother, she's the ringmaster of the circus you know. Well many years ago when she had just borne me, and she and father were much younger, they tell me they saw a star fall to earth. So they ran and found a young star, shivering in the cold night. They picked her up, and cared for her for several hours until messengers from the King of Stars arrived and threatened to kill them all if they didn't give the star back right away! Well, once they saw that my mother was only caring for the star, the soldiers were very apologetic, or so I'm told. Anyway, the next night they get a visit from the Star King himself, and he tells them how grateful he is for saving their little star, because she was apparently a *princess*. So he tells them, (and Flower tried to imitate an adult male's deep voice here), "Just as you have protected and blessed my little one last night, so will I watch over and protect your little one every day of her life." Then he puts a little light, like a star, into my infant mouth, and the next day they find this tiny … other universe inside me.' Here she paused, like she was waiting for applause. But the truth of it was the five of them were far more aware than most of the magic in the world; weird things happened to them almost every day.

Flower stopped waving her hands around, and they fell to her sides, 'But to tell you the truth, I can't see what possible benefit having a hole in the back of your mouth does me, or my family. It's lucky we're in a circus… I don't know how my talent would help *save a king*!' she said, looking over to Kialessa meaningfully.

Again Kialessa wished she had the time to ask Flower how she knew, but Allastassia stood between them to comfort her, 'Don't worry, my friend. You'll see; you'll come into your full powers soon. Maybe you can breathe star fire like a dragon? Or swallow the whole *ocean* one day?'

'We tried both those things,' Flower muttered. 'Nope, it's just a silly, me shaped space that starts at the back of my throat and it's where we place the well-polished tent poles just to *freak people out*: just a circus trick…' Her voice trailed to a mutter, and

Kialessa could see why this bothered her. Kialessa knew what it felt like to be nothing more than a circus trick for other people's entertainment. And to be honest, it did seem like a rather weird and … somewhat stingy gift from the extremely powerful deity like the Star King. He was generally known for being far more generous than that – but Kialessa wasn't going to say that out loud.

Eventually Piex spoke. 'So… just how wide can you open the fissure?' he asked, more curious than wise.

Kialessa guessed what would happen before he did, and Allastassia had already covered her eyes.

'Oh, about this far,' Flower said with a mischievous grin, and then she flipped her head back till her upper jaw pointed upwards, dislocated her lower jaw, and grabbing it pulled it so far out she could have twisted over and no doubt stuck her entire foot inside her inhumanly gaping wide mouth.

Darrix gagged, Allastassia groaned, and Kialessa felt decidedly queasy. Posk, who had been ignoring them all up to this point, grunted in disbelief. The towering minotaur just nodded, and grinned.

And Piex, who had shown no emotional disturbance in the least, simple pondered out loud, 'I imagine that makes it rather easy to clean your teeth.'

'Flower!' A woman's voice screamed from the direction of the tents.

Flower straightened up, popped her jaw back in, and looked very guilty.

It was her mother, the ringmaster. 'Habol lost the trumpet chicken again; it's down at the fens. Quit showing off and go get it, please,' her voice was stern, but she had a broad, almost affectionate, grin on her face.

'Yes, mother,' Flower said, abashed.

'Can we help?' Allastassia offered, probably hoping Flower really wasn't in any trouble.

The towering woman glared at them, dismissing them with

a lordly nod. She had no real authority over them, Kialessa knew, so it was all an attempt at being important and funny at the same time.

But Allastassia and Flower ran off as fast as they could. It was time to hunt chickens.

***

It turned out to be very hard to lose something that wouldn't keep quiet, and the trumpet chicken proved utterly incapable of being silent. But it was fast. Frustratingly fast. It took them a good ten moments to finally corner it. Posk chased it into a pond full of long grasses, and Kialessa, who was hiding there, finally swept it up into the air. She had been waiting in abject silence among the reeds, even while the horrible little swamp flies bit her legs all over. But she had not made a sound, and now, she'd saved the trumpet chicken. Carefully she held it away from her so that it couldn't shatter her eardrums with its unnaturally powerful voice.

Flower cheered, and Kialessa handed the little trumpet chicken back to its owner, not much the worse for wear. 'Quickly now, the swamp flies will bite you!'

And with a squeal, she headed out to dry off.

***

But by the next morning Kialessa was covered all over with tiny, itchy little fly bites. It made it very hard for her to concentrate. But what complicated things even more was the level of excitement in the room. News had spread around that the king was paying for all the students at the college to spend the entire afternoon at the circus.

So today was a crazy day; and the tutors were having a terrible time getting everyone to focus. It would have helped if it was something interesting, like stories, or music, or athletics.

But it was the boring classes; spelling, and heraldry, and arithmetic. Everyone had to learn counting, except the ones that already knew like the noble children and Piex, who was doing something he called differential calculus which even most of the tutors didn't know anything about. The wizard had to teach him that.

But what made it a thousand times worse was that Kialessa was so itchy! She'd saved the little trumpet chicken. But now the marsh fly bites were red, and sore, and itchy, and combined with all the excitement of the day it was impossible to keep still.

So she was bored, and agitated, and her legs were covered in itchy red marks that were driving her insane.

It was almost lunch time, finally, and Kialessa was just getting a new slate from the tutors' desk when a boy's voice yelled out;

'Help, Pox!' he teased.

It was the rude boy again.

She looked at him angrily. She did not like being called a disease, especially one that could kill little children.

'Ooh! Keep away!' He shouted. 'You've a Pox! Pox! Pox!' He teased, and his friends laughed.

The tutor was too busy to notice, and the class very noisy.

'Shut up,' Kialessa snarled at him.

But he did not stop teasing her from his desk. 'Ooh, what you gonna do?' he teased, grabbing her sleeve to prevent her getting away. Reaching over his desk he made an unkind face at her. 'Pox, Pox, off ground when Pox is around!' he said, pulling his feet from the floor.

It made her so angry. She'd been helping people to find their pet, and now he was teasing her for it? What a dumb, stupid, immature little boy.

'Pox, Pox, demon girl is a Pox girl–'

He never did finish that sentence, for before she could really think about what she was doing, Kialessa smashed her slate on the floor and with both hands shoved his desk right into his

     By Dr Joseph Ireland "Dr Joe"

chest.

She must have pushed very hard, because he tipped right over and slammed his head into the cold stone floor, the desk falling right on top of him.

'Kialessa, what are you doing!' The tutor screamed even as the boy begun to cry.

'He … said I have a Pox,' she lowered her gaze to the floor. 'He called me demon girl.'

'Well,' the tutor argued, coming up to help him to his feet, 'your behaviour hardly befits an angel.'

The words hit her like a knife going into her heart. Tears sprang to her eyes. 'I'm sorry. He just called me names, I was so angry; I'll never do it again!' she promised.

'Oh look, he's bleeding,' the tutor commiserated over the boy's tumultuous weeping. 'Darrix, watch over the class, I'm taking him to the nurse.'

Kialessa fled to the window crying, burying her face in her agitation and regret. Allastassia came up then, and put her arm around her.

Kialessa knew she would not be seeing the circus today.

***

It was so quiet. Kialessa could never have imagined the classroom could ever be so quiet. It must have been because she was alone. Everyone else had gone to see the circus.

Her legs still itched, but it wasn't what hurt most.

She didn't know what hurt the most. Was it the steward's condescending remark about how **embarrassed** he was that he'd been protecting **her** from bullies not earlier this year?

No, not that, though he really does know how to put the guilt trip on. Kialessa was already feeling guilty, and didn't really need any help to feel bad about what she'd done.

Was it the detention, being left to clean the slates while everyone went to see the circus and patted the rude boy on his head?

No, not that either. She supposed she did deserve some punishment for breaking college rules. Everyone needed to be punished when they broke the rules, or no one would ever keep them.

So perhaps it was the angry and hateful way his father had spoken to her, questioning even the king's judgement in allowing a demon girl to attend college?

No, they all thought it. That was no different to any other day…

When she thought about it, what really hurt was that she'd lost her temper, and someone had been hurt. It was the one thing she couldn't forgive herself for. The one thing she didn't know *how* to forgive herself for. She'd lost her self-control, and someone had gotten hurt.

She'd tried to say sorry, but they had all stayed silent. It was so unfair, not a single word was said to the boy who teased her so much she'd lost her temper. He deserved punishment too, but Kialessa was just too wise to point that out.

They watched her every day, she knew. They couldn't miss the horns, and the tail that poked out from her dress and helped her keep her balance in athletics class. The rude boy's father had surely been only one of many parents that had expressed their concern about having a tae'anaryn at the college. But King Dunnkan was kind, and taught that everyone made their own choices about what they became.

Kialessa felt a lump rise in her throat. It was just that it seemed everyone around her expected her to become a criminal or something. When she did something right, it had to be absolutely spectacular before anyone even noticed, and when she did they seemed all surprised like it wasn't supposed to happen. Allastassia could sneeze and they'd call her a princess. Before they'd even trusted Kialessa to sit next to someone she had had to save the king's *life!*

And when she did do something deliberately wrong, like, for the *first time ever*, everyone was, "Ah yes, the tae'anaryn.

Well, what do you expect? That's just the way with tae'anaryl. You'd better beat her twice as hard; I hear they have very tough skins …"

She blinked back the tears again. They'd all be glad to see her cry. To make her suffer for, well, standing up for herself … sort of …

She sighed, and decided there was no point getting upset about it anymore. She'd pay her own way into the circus, or anywhere in life. Other people's issues about race and goodness were not her problems to take on. It was their problem; she could be what she wanted.

But it still hurt.

She placed another washed slate back onto the pile, dimly wondering what it would be like to have so much paper she never ran out, instead of heavy stone "sheets" that needed to be washed after every single time students used them. Kialessa was not made for washing things. Oh, she knew how it should be done; she'd started life washing dishes. But she knew if she ever wanted to be more than a dishwasher she had to exceed everyone's expectation of her. She couldn't just be **good**, nobody would notice. Because of who she was, and the kind of people tae'anaryl usually were, she had to be *exceptional*. Either that, or consign herself to being hated by everyone around her the rest of her life.

Be amazing, just to fit in, she huffed. It did not seem fair.

She *was* sorry she'd hurt someone's head in anger. Kialessa sighed, and pulled another stone slate from the pile.

Tomorrow, she could try again.

The Play

'*Never forget what a powerful thing simply being there*
for a friend in need can be!'
Jacinthia, priestess of Lenmer'el.

Trumpets sounded.

It was night, and Kialessa was finally released from detention, happy to have served out her time. Wanting to forget the unpleasantness of it all she rushed down to the circus. As luck would have it, they were doing a little extra today. They were putting on a play. She paid her own attendance for the entire stay with a silver piece from the purse inside her sash, ignoring the teller's stare and smiling at her anyway, ran in.

She had very little trouble finding Allastassia. Kialessa sat right beside them, right in the very front row. And to her delight, Darrix was there too. Posk was nowhere to be seen, and Piex was probably studying wizardry somewhere; probably the history of interdimensional pockets inside the back of people's throats.

'What's happening?' Kialessa asked.

 By Dr Joseph Ireland "Dr Joe"

'The epic saga is starting,' Darrix replied.

'What's a saga?' Kialessa asked.

Allastassia looked at her like she was joking, then laughed. 'Oh Kia, you're so very provincial!'

Kialessa had no idea what that meant.

'It's a performance, a play,' Allastassia then explained with a smile. 'They tell a story, using music and dancing and magic. There's fear, and laughter, and sorrow... have you really never seen a saga?'

'Never!' Kialessa said, yet with a smile. She supposed her mother had probably put on a bit of an epic saga whenever the king's guard turned up and asked for taxes though. She was really looking forward to seeing a professional saga! It sounded wonderful!

The trumpets sounded a fanfare once more, and the thick burgundy curtains appeared to pull back of their own accord from centre stage. It was set like a country scene, with rolling hills and wide grasslands. A woman was standing in the middle of that scene, dressed in an expensive looking travelling suit. She had an enchanting voice, just perfect for singing stories out loud;

'Folk and fair ones, from far and from near,
Draw nearer and listen, my tale to hear,
A story of heroes, sword savvy and true,
And damsels distressed, oppressed, and then who,
In need of a bright knight their freedoms declare,
From demons of darkness, and peril, to share,
A bright day of wonder, when darkness is done,
Hear tales so true, of the carpenter's son.'

The whole play was in rhyme, and most of it was sung, so Kialessa found it quite hard to follow. Thankfully, she had two good friends willing to explain certain bits. Probably the worst park was the demon, who had a huge red cloak and roared so loud that it made everyone scream. It slew people just by looking at them, which was a bit confusing since everyone kept falling over and Kialessa didn't know why till Darrix pointed it out. It was a pretty horrible demon.

Trouble for the demon was that it fell in love with a princess, played by a stunningly beautiful human girl who could jump as high as her own shoulders and turn at the same time. At any rate, the demon decided to kidnap the princess since it couldn't risk allowing her to see it, and it couldn't bear to be away from its love. Or what it *termed* to be its love, at any rate. Kialessa greatly wondered why they used the word 'love' to describe the demons' feelings when it was acting so cruel, a point she expressed to her two friends, who shrugged.

In the end, a carpenter's son, who also happened to be in love with the princess too, learns how to fight with a sword and challenges the demon. His love for the princess is so "great and true" that the demon cannot slay him with his heat vision, or whatever, so they go toe to toe in what was a fabulously well-staged battle scene. The two actors were really going for it with swords, scimitars, and battle axes, and all the while the audience cheered.

Naturally, true love won out the day, and the carpenters' son put his blade through the demon's chest and it stuck right out the other end. Kialessa had no idea how they pulled off that magic trick, but the demon died reaching out pathetically for the woman he couldn't touch, and they all felt just a little sorry for him. Everyone clapped as the love-struck couple kissed their way right through a scene change to their own wedding. The narrator shortly after ended the play:

'A story so true we have told you this night,
To tell it another way t'would not be right,
The princess and pauper, blissfully wed,
Toward clouded castles they nuptially head.
For though demons encapture, and strike at their foes,

  By Dr Joseph Ireland "Dr Joe"

Of this timeless truth 'tis sure everyone knows,
On earth, in the hells, or in the heavens above,
For there is no power, that's greater than love.'

People liked it so much they stood up to clap. They continued to clap for ten moments, and the poor actors had to come out two more times. They even made the princess and carpenter's son do the dance from the love scene once more. Apparently it was fairly common to pressure the actors in to performing their favourite parts again, which seemed strange but nice.

The clapping looked like it might go on forever, but then the huge minotaur Ugly, horns tipped with spikes yet dressed in a gentleman's vest, closed the curtain with surprising softness, and everyone left quite quickly after that.

***

'That was *divine*!' was all Allastassia could say, over and over again once they left.

'It was very good,' Darrix agreed.

'Guys! Wait for me!' It was Flower. She was grinning from ear to ear, which made Kialessa realise just how inaccurate that phrase was when discussing it in present company. 'My mother has given me permission to attend the king's college while the circus is in town. I'm going to be going to college for the rest of the season!'

She and Allastassia did a little squealing, jumping dance of excitement.

Darrix rolled his eyes as if to say, *As if we needed more of that.*

Kialessa smiled.

'So, did you like the play Kialessa?' Flower asked. 'What did you think of it?'

'I still don't get what that little man who kept hanging out with the carpenter's son was saying,' Kialessa complained. 'Why did he have such a funny voice again?'

'He was supposed to be a gnome, I think,' Darrix explained. 'He was there to make things funny.'

'He was pretty funny,' Kialessa agreed. 'But he didn't really do much against that demon, did he?'

'He's not **supposed** to,' Flower explained. 'He's the "comic relief", the guy they use in a play to make the main character look smarter and stronger, and to keep the audience laughing so they don't take it all too seriously.'

'How could you take **him** seriously?' Kialessa said. 'And the whole background kept rolling up and down. How'd they get to the castle again, were they teleported?'

They must have thought she was being silly, because they laughed, and didn't answer the question.

'I would *love* to be in a play like that,' Allastassia sighed.

'Bet you want the part of the Princess too?' Darrix said.

'Oh, only if it was what would work best,' she sighed. But Kialessa knew there was only one-part Allastassia would ever even **think** of doing if they ran a play. 'And you would audition for the part of the prince?' she asked him.

He laughed. 'I'm sure you'd organise it. But don't we need some sort of permission? It's their play, after all.'

'You mean we can't just come up with our own version?' Kialessa asked, somewhat surprised.

'Yes, of course,' Allastassia said.

'Actually, not if you plan to charge for admission.' Flower explained while Darrix nodded, 'the play belongs to them.'

'Whatever,' Allastassia interrupted. 'So, we'll just ask your mother first, Flower. Ask permission. I'll be able to get us permission.'

'But we don't even know if we want to do a play,' Kialessa worried for her enchantress friend. 'Do we know what's involved?'

But Allastassia wasn't listening. She was skipping away toward the circus once more. In moment, she'd located the bright orange, blue and red caravan of Flower's mother, the ringmaster, named after the central circle under the main tent where most of the circus acts took place.

5 Flower and Allastassia, avid students of the dance.

Allastassia was already knocking by the time they'd caught up.

'What's our story?' Darrix asked, no doubt wondering what they were going to say once the ringmaster answered.

'No story,' Allastassia explained.

Flower seemed to be hiding behind the wagon door.

'But–' Darrix began.

The door swung open, and the ringmaster was there, her hair flowing around her and her tight performance dress replaced with an elegant, yet comfortable tunic and leggings. She smiled at them magnanimously. 'Oui, two damsels and a handsome young man!' she crooned in her northern elven accent. 'Have you come to have us inscribe our names on some tree bark? I'm usually pretty busy this time of the evening, but I suppose I can spare this five moments!'

'No, no, 'Allastassia stumbled, a little uncharacteristic for her, unless it was intended to make her seem more endearing. 'Um, actually, we just wanted to tell you what a wonderful, magical, and **enchanting** play you all put on. I don't think we'll ever forget it.'

The ringmaster warmed to her flattery, and smiling, sat down on the steps of her bright caravan. 'Thank you, jeune femme,' she replied. 'It is one of our finer works, six months in the making. Perrol, my husband, wrote most of the music. Such a talented fellow,' she boasted.

'Did you create the script yourself, or base it on an older story?' Darrix asked, sounding interested, but probably still only worried about copyright issues.

The ringmaster smiled, 'It's based on an old legend from Apollia, one my grandmother taught me, and her grandmother taught her, from before living memory I suppose. Très bon, I'm glad you liked it. A good play can teach you things too; about trusting to love, and watching out for those demons! Nasty creatures!' she explained, and poked out at Allastassia who giggled delightedly.

Kialessa didn't laugh though. She thought demons looked a lot like tae'anaryl, and hoped the ringmaster wasn't referring to **her**.

'And the princess!' Allastassia gasped, 'wasn't she divine! Those leaps, and that …' she demonstrated, dancing around. 'What do you call it?'

'La Montouge,' the ringmaster explained.

'Oh, such a pretty name. I only know local dancing well, I'm afraid.'

'Then you should learn, you'd make a pretty dancer I think,' the ringmaster said.

'Do you think?' Allastassia remarked, eyes wide. But by now, Kialessa knew her old friend was up to one of her old tricks again. She was convincing someone to offer what she didn't want to have to ask for.

'Such a beautiful play!' Allastassia sighed. 'I hope I get to be in it one day. Wouldn't it be something if the youth of the college could perform it for our parents? They'd be ever so pleased.'

The ringmaster sat back, as though she'd just gotten an idea. 'Indeed,' the woman mused. 'And your parents would pay handsomely to see it all again… and if we…' Then she looked serious again. 'Plays are big projects, jeunes – young ones,' she explained. 'You'll miss many hours of your education…'

'Oh,' Darrix said, sounding unhappy.

'Oh dear!' Allastassia smiled, not at all sincere, and showing it.

Kialessa grinned. Missing hours at the college, what fun!

'Perhaps we can organise something…' the ringmaster sighed to herself, wandering off in thought. 'Go your way jeunes, let me see what can be organised.'

They walked off, Allastassia literally glowing with excitement. Flower ran up to them whispering and laughing with her.

Kialessa tarried a moment. Something was tugging at the edge of her imagination, like a warning from a bad dream. "Big project?" Wasn't a certain young enchantress supposed to be spending her time with mild herbs and quiet conversations?

But the others were already away, and Kialessa had to run to keep up. Allastassia was chatting with Flower as if the play was already a done thing. Soon, they said good night to Darrix, and went back to the girl's dormitory to break the exciting news to all the others. That evening they spent the whole time deciding who would be cast into all the lead roles, and even going so far as to consider who was going get talked into painting the backdrops.

'And, of course, you will have to play the demon,' Allastassia then informed Kialessa.

'What?' Kialessa scoffed, disbelieving. 'Just because I'm a

tae'anaryn doesn't make me a demon.'

But Flower agreed with Allastassia, 'You can play it so well! Just think how **amazed** all the little kids will be once they see how you can make your eyes glow without magic!'

'Oh, you've seen that,' Kialessa mourned.

The other two shrugged in agreement like it was very old news.

'Well, I still don't want to play the demon, just because I'm a tae'anaryn.'

'That's all right,' Allastassia explained, not to be deflated, 'You can play a demon, it's only acting after all. And you can fight for real, just like Darrix, oh, it'd be such a wonderful battle!' she said, holding their hands in her exuberance.

'I'm not playing the demon.' Kialessa said, releasing their hands, her eyes already glowing with annoyance. She'd learnt long ago not to say yes to every idea Allastassia had. She could be quite … self-serving at times.

'Sure,' Allastassia said agreeably, but Kialessa knew she was just thinking of another way to trick her into the part. Just because she was a tae'anaryn didn't mean she **had** to be the demon. If she was going to play a boy character why not play the prince?

Allastassia is probably just looking for an excuse to kiss Darrix, Kialessa mused.

'It's going to be a big project,' Flower muttered.

'Don't worry about it, jeunes,' Allastassia explained, mocking the ringmaster's voice. 'I'm actually quite good at getting people to help.'

Kialessa didn't doubt her for an instant.

Mild Herbs

'Doctor's orders, doctor's orders! It has to hurt if it is to heal!'

Daily saying of the headmistress of the children of the college of Lenmer'el, when insisting children with colic take a spoonful of bitter fish oil every evening, even when they complained it made them feel worse.

They waited in the darkness.

It was always this way with combat training.

The castle wizard, or more correctly his apprentices, would spend the whole week preparing some new challenge for them, designed by the college tutors. Usually it was fairly mild; capture the flag, avoid the swinging logs. The trick was in beating the challenge before the other teams did.

At least, it *used* to be a challenge.

Kialessa had to admit, her team did have several advantages. Darrix wielded the legendary blade Defender, presented to him by his master, the famous Paladin Tomin. No doubt the extra training and advice given by one of the most skilled and famous warriors in the country helped as well. Posk was just naturally strong, and Piex quite possibly the most talented and intelligent young wizard in the whole Great Kingdom. Just last week he'd overcome an illusionary goblin (they fought those a lot) without his usual enchantments – he'd actually neutralised the illusion itself. The other students had called it cheating, but the tutor had just laughed and allowed it. Kialessa had her magical sash, and a tail that helped her to keep her balance. As an extra treat they had Flower with them, who was such a nasty shot with throwing knives, and so incredibly flexible, no one could tell what she was going to do next.

And then there was Allastassia.

'We're going to win this one, I can feel it,' the auburn enchantress gleamed. Just this morning she'd accidentally conjured a pair of star jays from that auburn hair, but there were no unexpected birds to give away their position now.

'We're not supposed to be talking,' Piex whispered. He was a real stickler for rules.

'You're feeling very confident today,' Flower muttered to Allastassia. It was clear the acrobat loved combat training too.

'I can feel it, in my bones,' Allastassia grinned a very smug grin.

Kialessa loved working with them. It seemed the college tutors had agreed to Allastassia's pleading and let them choose their own companions for this tournament.

'It will be brief,' Allastassia boasted. 'I bet it's a "hold the high ground" again, we haven't had one of those in a while. Aolith and Federach will go for a ranged surprise attack, but I can handle their arrows with a sheet of ice spell my mother taught me. When Marchan tries to get Dale and Ridge to rush the ground, we'll send in Posk – he can take them both once more.'

'You know, there are another five teams out there,' Darrix muttered. Allastassia had only mentioned the lead team among the senior students. 'Any plans for Doreth, or Natasha?'

     By Dr Joseph Ireland "Dr Joe"

'The cervitaur?' Allastassia asked with apparent disbelief. 'Both command what little of the divine, as you do Darrix,' she said, clearly having given this some thought. 'Push through it this time; overcome their command with that faith you're supposed to have learned. But just in case, Piex, did you write out that scroll of silence like I told you to last week?'

'Yes,' he muttered.

'Good. Use it when the priests of faith cause trouble this time.'

Kialessa shook her head. Once combat started, no one took orders. They just worked together on the goal. If anything, they listened to Kialessa because her voice was the loudest, at least until Piex's silence spell took all the noise away – it was a very disconcerting feeling! But that was one of the benefits of having a wizard for a best friend, it meant someone who occasionally needed volunteers to practice on.

But combat training was very serious business. There were no prizes for winning, but people fought as though the pride was worth their lives.

She felt it before she saw it; the magical wave tingling past them before the lights went on. Sure enough, it was a "hold the high ground" battle again. Whichever team commanded the hill the longest would win.

And sure enough, Dale and Ridge charged. Marchan, the only other apparently capable young wizard, giving them cover with some very disconcerting fireworks that split the air with sharp cracking noises. The arrows that Aolith and Federach had loosed were already well on their way – Allastassia's whispering had no doubt given their position away. She was fast with her shield of ice enchantment, but Flower still had to dodge a flying arrow. Blunt arrows couldn't kill, but they sure did hurt!

Naturally, Darrix and the rest of them took a moment to take in the situation.

'Posk, charge!' Allastassia commanded.

He didn't move. Kialessa knew he wouldn't.

One of the other groups of younger students had taken cover by a stone pillar – probably a pile of wooden crates enspelled to look like natural stones. If Posk had rushed, he'd have to chance it past a hail of stones and arrows.

Posk grunted at a nearby hill.

Darrix interpreted, no doubt having the same thought anyway. 'We need to take the position by the tower of rocks or we'll never make it to the hill.'

'No, go!' Allastassia demanded. 'We have this under control. Look at this sheet of ice!'

'Can you do that on both sides?' Darrix asked, though they all knew the answer already.

He answered for her, 'Then we need to cover our flanks if we want to hold on to the high ground.'

He and Posk scurried as one, towards the hill, while Allastassia huffed. It was never Kialessa's official job to hold back and protect the casters, waiting for a key moment to strike with her whip or bow, but that was often where she stayed while Darrix and Posk ran off.

They followed them towards the hill, Allastassia's shield taking another two arrows with ease.

Kialessa watched that hill. The senior team had claimed it already, and no one rose to challenge them. It was as if they were all too afraid of the oldest, and second most capable, students in the college. But the senior students were currently trying to pepper Allastassia's team with arrows, Dale getting out his portable ballista. It was a cruel weapon for combat training, Kialessa knew from experience how it would knock you to the floor and take all your breath away. She wanted to get the team behind the hill quickly, but something about the senior team fascinated her… they stood, ready, facing them – unchallenged on the hill.

'Why isn't any other team trying to take the high ground?' Flower wondered out loud.

The revelation struck Kialessa, 'The other teams are helping the senior students. Whether they knew it or not, they are ganging up on us.'

A pace later they arrived behind the hill. Another team lay on the grass, the rude boy among them.

'They surrendered as soon as we arrived,' Darrix explained, and Kialessa could not but help grin at the cowardly boy.

'Next step, take the mound of rocks,' Darrix said.

'They've got a crossbow,' Flower explained. 'It's huge; it's going to get through that shield Allastassia.

She did not look pleased, but her eyes betrayed that she'd already realised that.

'How are we going to get through the gap?' Flower asked.

'A feint?' Kialessa suggested.

'It would be good if we could get close enough for Piex to use his starburst enchantment,' Allastassia said, taking cover behind the hill while Darrix and Piex looked out.

'Still can't turn yourself invisible, Piex?' Kialessa asked him.

'It's a lot harder than you'd think,' Piex argued.

'Well you can't run, Dale's got the entire gap covered, and I don't like the look of what Marchan has got planned,' Darrix said.

'We can't stay here, they'll win by default,' Kialessa remarked.

'We need a little something unexpected,' Allastassia said.

'Oh, like what, throw Piex over?' Flower muttered.

Posk grinned, and grabbed Piex by the seat of his pants.

Piex was too panicked to say anything coherent. 'Oh! No, no, no, no, not again!' he panicked.

'Ahh, I wasn't being serious guys,' Flower confessed.

'Don't forget your starburst!' Allastassia grinned.

'Don't forget to roll,' Darrix said with a smile.

Piex went screaming over, and Dale let loose his oversized bolt. It flew low, as no doubt of all the things he was expecting, he was not expecting a wizard to go flying overhead. The rest of them took the chance to run across, Allastassia's shield taking the arrow as Federach's aim ran true – it would have stuck Allastassia right in the centre of the chest, even if she was running at the time.

The second team of students were a little more determined. Piex took down two of them, blinding another, but he was barely holding off the other two. Just as it looked like they were going to knock him senseless with their wooden swords, he unleashed his golden shackles enchantment. Golden chains sprung from his hand and imbedded themselves in the stones and into the ground, pinning his opponents. It was an advanced spell, intended for full military operations. He was under strict instructions to use it with great caution, as with his deadly mage orb enchantments. There seemed to be a limit to how many enchantments a wizard could hold in their mind at any one time, yet he always kept it to the legal ones during college.

Then Piex sat down, it seemed he was out of spells for the day. It was clear he was getting tired.

Flower kept the senior students busy with a flurry of knives as they all took cover.

'We're going to have to rush the hill,' Allastassia told them.

'We can't rush that hill,' Darrix told her. 'Kialessa is right; it's thirty to six right now. Someone's going to have to draw their fire, Kialessa –'

'I'll do it,' Flower offered.

'No!' Allastassia demanded, clearly becoming annoyed that not only were they losing, but also that no one was listening to her, 'Kia's the fastest and most lithe. She can make it right around the hill and back again.'

Kialessa was less inclined to take that chance, 'They've seen all my moves,' she muttered.

Allastassia turned on her, an angry look in her eyes, 'Kia, trust me, you've got to-'

She immediately stopped talking, and her eyes grew wide. Just as she was swinging her shield around, someone bashed Kialessa to the ground with the flat of their metal sword right up

　　　By Dr Joseph Ireland "Dr Joe"

against her hip. The blow would have killed her if it was intended to.

She heard Darrix say, 'They're charging our position!' but couldn't make much sense of it as she hit the floor.

A young man stepped over her. It was Dale, magical waves of energy streaming from him as he stepped out of some kind of invisibility enchantment.

It seemed Marchan was, indeed, a more capable wizard that Piex was willing to admit.

Dale cracked Posk on the back of his head and turned to face the two remaining girls. Posk sat down; he knew when he was out of the game. Everyone turned to face Dale as the senior students came streaming down the hill towards them.

'Got you now, kids!' he gloated.

Kialessa lay there, clutching her side. It was an unnecessarily fierce attack he'd raged upon her. Perhaps it was in retribution for the way she'd tripped him several weeks ago in training? Or perhaps it was for the way she'd mocked him after he'd failed to hit her seven times with his bow, allowing Darrix to capture the flag last week? Perhaps he was just sick of losing to a half-soul.

Darrix tried to hold off the three senior students with only his sword and shield to help him.

Flower moved to help Kia, but Dale stood over her, menacing them with his sword.

'Did you have to hit her so hard?' Flower shouted.

Darrix cried out, either he'd taken a hit, or he was out.

'Let her help,' Allastassia demanded.

Without warning, Dale kicked Kialessa in the stomach with his heel. 'Last team standing gets the prize!' he gloated.

For a moment, there was stunned silence as Kialessa held her abdomen. It was never illegal to kick a student while they were down, but it was looked down on as cowardly and unnecessary. Kialessa was down; she wasn't trying to get back up. What did she need a boot in the guts for? It hurt so much she could hardly breathe.

At that moment there was a sizzling crack of electricity.

Kialessa had never heard anything like that before.

She looked up to see Flower ducking away – Allastassia was surrounded by a circle of lightning. Her eyes sparkled with their reflection, and she looked very angry. Without warning she took hold of her lightning, and threw it at Dale.

It blasted into his chest, doing real damage. He stumbled over Kialessa and fell to the ground, barely breathing.

'Then you'd better get out of my way,' Allastassia replied to Dale, her voice deep and riven with power. The illusion enchantments around the crates trembled and failed around her ring of lightning.

Through pain and dim fear Kialessa realised: Allastassia had just lost it completely.

Desperately Kialessa tried to say something, to call to her friend, to try to bring her back. This was *only training*.

Instead, there was nothing she could do but watch helplessly as Allastassia blasted the crates apart. Federach copped a large piece of wood, which couldn't seem to decide if it was a rock or not, and sat down. The small, bleeding cut above Federach's eye did nothing to stop her from glaring at Allastassia.

Aolith had the sense to try and shoot Allastassia, but her now floating ice shield deflected it. Allastassia threw lightning back and hit Aolith square in the chest. It seemed to be a little less deadly than the lightning that had struck Dale, but Aolith sat down none the less.

Every other student quailed.

Allastassia then began to *levitate*, effortlessly, her beautiful hair streaming dramatically behind her as she made her way to the hilltop.

She menaced up to Dale's ballista.

Kialessa tried to sit up, watching in surprise as Posk tore his own pant leggings and pressed them down on the deep wound in Dale's chest. The priests would heal the wound soon, but there was still a lot of blood.

     By Dr Joseph Ireland "Dr Joe"

Allastassia looked back at Dale, eyes wide as he watched her threatening his ballista. He shook his head fiercely despite being in real pain.

Raising her fists high, Allastassia obliterated the ballista with raw lightning. Laughing, the enchantress gloated. Then her face twisted in pain, 'Why wouldn't any of you listen to me!' she screeched with raw emotion.

'Allastassia, calm down!' Flower cried, but it only seemed to make the enraged enchantress even angrier.

'Not so easy to ignore now, am I!' she shouted, rising up into the air. Lightning flew from her, striking the roof of the hall.

Students scattered in all directions. None of them had the courage, or folly, to face her. The crackling of electricity grew, and suddenly deepened. Bright light coalesced in her hand, and it grew and lengthened, and Allastassia held it like a javelin.

Reaching deeper than she knew she was able, Kialessa found her voice, 'Allastassia!' The sound shook the dust from the walls piercing everyone's ears.

For a moment, the enchantress paused. When she spoke, her voice sounded in both Kialessa's ears, and deep within her heart. It was as if Allastassia was speaking inside her head, and Kialessa knew it would be difficult if not impossible to sort out which thoughts were really her own if Allastassia ever perfected this gift. *No one knows me. Why doesn't anybody ever listen to me?*

It made no sense, everybody listened to Allastassia all the time, she gave them no other choice! But to blindly obey her was a completely different thing entirely. Could she not tell the difference?

'Did you hear that?' Darrix said, helping Kialessa to sit up, his very touch imparting strength to her and chasing away the agony.

'Hear what?' Flower asked, her face full of worry and concern.

'I did,' Kialessa told him.

'Perhaps,' Darrix said, 'there's a *part* of her that feels

unlistened to. That there's something she's trying to say, but only now admits it even to herself?'

'Then she'd better sort it out quickly,' Flower said, pointing.

Even as they watched, their physical prowess tutor, the old gedzelai monk, mounted a pile of crates to face Allastassia. Along another crate Marchan stood, a lethal *Magus Spherae* glowing in his right hand. Then, through the door, two of the castle guards arrived. They moved swiftly and without fear, weapons drawn, to the base of hill where Allastassia floated.

'Stand down, young one,' the tutor insisted. 'You danger yourself, your future, and your classmates. Mild herbs, no danger.'

'I am SICK of mild herbs!' Allastassia screamed. 'I don't need them! I don't need quiet books and soft words! I need adventure! I need power!' and with that, she threw her deadly javelin at the tutor.

Somehow, he leapt right over it. A second later a rope, thrown by one of the guards below, tightened around the enchantress's ankle. Marchan shouted, but she ignored him. Just as she was about to electrocute the guards below he threw the orb at her. It blasted against her lightning ring, and it must have hurt, but she battled on. She levitated up till both guards were hanging by the rope. Arrows, sharpened and intended for war, sped towards her from the shadows, no doubt from the other guards. They would have struck her in the legs, but her ice shield kept Allastassia safe. Lightning seared the ground, as objects began to catch fire. Kialessa watched as the students fled.

Yet Allastassia battled on, holding her own against the chaos and melee. Then, with a clutching gesture, she raised up a small hill of grassy earth and dumped it back down again, a wave of destruction splitting the hardwood floors and toppling the pillars of the roof. But no light entered, as dark clouds gathered ominously above the building.

Her assailants pulled back.

Breathing heavily, Allastassia screamed. She didn't seem to

know how to say what she was trying to, and so screamed again.

She was beginning to sound like Posk.

Flower grabbed Kialessa's arm, and the world suddenly snapped back into focus.

'What are you shouting for Kialessa?' Flower begged, and then Kialessa was aware of how much her own voice was echoing Allastassia's own. Somehow, she was enchanting them all. That was when Kialessa began to tremble, for she did not know how this would end. If the king's guard arrived they would show little pity, and if any of the king's personal bodyguards arrived … Kialessa hoped it would be the priestess, for she was the most likely to show mercy. Kialessa clutched her hands together in impending dread.

Suddenly a cool breeze wafted past, reminding Kialessa of early spring. The air moved toward Allastassia, stilling the flames and lifting away the burning smoke. The ground trembled again, but seemed to settle back into place. Allastassia's lightning slowed, and she floated lower in the air. Yet still she screamed.

'ALLASTASSIA, STOP!' a truly compelling voice whispered both inside, and out.

'Lady Greens'holm,' Darrix whispered. It was Allastassia's mother, the most feared and revered enchantress in all the land.

Instantly Allastassia alighted to the ground, yet the lightning continued to surround her, her eyes still bearing the marks of lightning from within.

Flowers sprouted where the mother walked, blooming a moment later. Dandelions wafted in the breeze around her, and the ground turned about as though ready for planting in her footprints.

'What have you been doing?' Lady Annadaria Greens'holm asked in a soft, forgiving voice.

Allastassia looked around, chin held high. Then her mouth fell wide open, her eyes filled with tears as she saw the damage to the college training hall for the first time. The floor was shattered, the roof shot through with a dozen holes.

The lightning ring disappeared instantly. For a moment Allastassia just stood there, looking embarrassed.

Then she fainted.

***

Later Kialessa and her four friends, including Flower, waited in the infirmary. The nurse walked towards them speaking quickly. 'The enchantress will see you now,' she said. Her voice was curt and professional, though perhaps a little too quick, she couldn't seem to look directly at them.

She looks nervous, Kialessa thought.

They filed in. The large room was all but empty, except for Allastassia's veiled and luxurious bed. This was the royal infirmary room no doubt.

The enchantress's face was red and moist, she had clearly been weeping. Lady Annadaria was standing by her. Kialessa thought how gentle the mother looked, always the soft hand of rebuke, as Kialessa recalled from this past year.

Allastassia burst into tears again, and before anyone could stop her Flower ran to embrace her. 'I'm so sorry, I'm just so sorry,' she kept on saying, over and over.

'No one was hurt… permanently,' Darrix consoled her.

'Oh, but I smashed up the entire hall!'

'Well, yes,' Darrix admitted.

'Oh, they'll have that fixed in a half season,' Flower promised her. 'It's one of the … occupational hazards of working with gifted students.'

Little tears still trickled down Allastassia's face. 'Don't tell me they'll cancel combat training!'

'Oh, I'm sure they'll find another venue…' Piex muttered, though they all knew better.

Only Darrix had the courage to come out and tell her the truth. 'No, cancelled for the rest of the season. You can't believe how happy it made some of them.'

They looked over at Piex. He said nothing, since he was had already lost interest in the conversation and was reading the infirmary charts in the room, tutting in disagreement.

Posk took the silence as an opportunity to share his thoughts. He pushed past them, close to Allastassia, but she did not flinch. He looked up at her with wild admiration, making a throwing gesture with his arms as though he, too, wished he could wield lightning.

Allastassia turned her head, and could not look at him.

He moved into her line of sight again, and tried to say something. His face was sympathetic, but his hands were an imitation of her clutching gesture with which she had torn apart the hall floor.

'I guess he was impressed,' Darrix translated.

'Oh, I've made such a mess of things!' Allastassia mourned, shoving Posk aside.

'It's not a mistake if you learn from it,' Kialessa tried to say something helpful.

But it made Allastassia cry again. 'Mild herbs, no violence,' she promised.

Her mother sighed. She stood by the bed, patting Allastassia's hand. 'It's the heavy price we must pay to wield such power responsibly. I, myself, burnt down an entire fey grove – it took me a year to regrow it. But I'm glad we've put that behind us.'

'Behind us?' Allastassia looked upset.

'Indeed. I knew you would have to face an emotional confronting, of sorts. You have to embrace your full powers now, and that is a very scary thing. But don't fear what you are becoming Allastassia, for it is a wonderful, powerful, and creative change.'

'But will it always be like this mother? Am I to go mad three times in a season?!'

Lady Annadaria laughed gently, the sound of ancient

waterfalls from deep within timeless forests. 'Sometimes, it will be worse! But afterwards, you will be stronger. Just remember to look after yourself, and don't take it out on others – we all need kind friends and gentle words at times.'

Allastassia nodded, the picture of sincerity itself. 'Kind friends, and gentle words.'

'And mild herbs,' her mother smiled.

Allastassia smiled, and nodded in return, a beam of sunlight suddenly brightening the room.

Lady Annadaria Greens'holm smiled. 'At least that's put an end to that. I was worried about you, Allastassia, but now I'm sure we'll be all right. The elven sage-queen has called me to her summer council, and I am already late!'

Allastassia looked sad, but it was clear this was not news to her. 'You will leave the servants to take care of me?'

Lady Annadaria nodded, 'All of them, for what need have I of servants when nature herself grants my every wish!' She booped Allastassia's nose in play. 'I will be away until season's end. But I just know you'll be all right, my little summer blossom,' she promised herself, holding her daughter by the chin as tiny motes of light sprung to life as glittering butterflies around them, 'I just know you'll be all right.'

The Plan

Never bite off more than you can chew, or you will either choke or drool, both of which will have you looking like an idiot.

Jindalessa, shamaness queen of the troll hoards.

'It has been decided,' the headmistress announced to them all two days later, 'that the students of the king's college are going to perform "The Carpenter's Son". The purpose is to develop team building talents, presentation skills, and physical fitness through dance. All who wish to audition for the lead roles may apply this afternoon at the upper field.'

Allastassia led the girls in a squeal of delight.

Kialessa shook her head fondly. *So very good at getting her way,* she thought. But it still didn't shake that nagging feeling at the back of her mind. It wasn't who was going to play the demon, that didn't matter. And there was no doubt who would get to be the princess. It was … something else … something that kept slipping from her mind as soon as she almost grasped it…

***

Kialessa thought the auditions were brilliant, and really showed some of the skills some students had that weren't always obvious in battle and college training. Of course, Darrix got the role of the carpenter's son. Patsi, one of Allastassia's other close friends, got the role of the narrator. Kialessa, who didn't audition for anything, was part of the chorus because at least she could keep a tune.

But, much to everyone's interest, no one got the role of the princess.

'How is that even possible?' Patsi whispered, 'Allastassia is the only one who auditioned.'

'Now, go to, young ones,' the ringmaster said. 'We have a lot of script writing to do tonight, and I want you at your best. We are rehearsing each Planasday for the next half season –'

'What?' a student complained. It seemed at least someone would miss combat training.

'Hold your posks!' she shot back. 'I assure you we'll have more than enough work to tire you out, young misses and masters! Now, our work here is done till tomorrow. Away! All of you!' she shouted in a voice that permitted no disagreement.

They headed for their dormitory, a group of sorry friends soon clustered around Allastassia. They said virtually nothing till they got to the dorm.

And then the tears started.

Allastassia sat on her bed, surrounded by friends, tingling with magic no one could see. 'I don't get it...' she whispered. 'Why didn't I get the part?'

'I'm sure she's just testing you,' an older student muttered.

Allastassia looked out at her with tear filled eyes. The entire room felt tremendously sad. Kialessa watched as the curtains were magically bleached of all colours. Two other students began to cry.

'Oh, dry up, blondy!' a dwarven girl insisted. It was

Federach. Not the most gentle of souls, but she was brutally honest, a mean shot with a crossbow, and a studious priestess of Mya in training. She'd even broken Kialessa's arm in combat training once, and healed it right after. She studied with the priestess quite often even if they were of different deity. She spoke roughly to the fair-haired enchantress right now, 'Life isn't all about you!'

Allastassia looked at her, anger shining from her tears. Then her bottom lip quivered again.

'Oh please,' Kialessa muttered, and slipped out to find answers before the insults started.

She found her way quickly among the darkness of the circus tents. People there were easy to avoid. She worked her way up to the caravan of the ringmaster, which she appeared to have all to herself. Carefully, making sure to keep to the darkness, Kialessa stepped up onto the wheel spokes and tried to see inside.

It was lit with a small lantern, but even with the faint, flickering light it was difficult to see if anyone was inside. The night was quiet, the caravan even more so. Kialessa decided the ringmaster was out.

Briefly she wondered if she should just knock on the door, confront the Gentle and ask what was going on. But that didn't feel quite right. Whatever game the ringmaster was playing at wasn't going to be found out with direct questions.

Then she heard laughter coming from the main tent. It sounded like the ringmaster.

As silent as the night Kialessa ran around to the far end. She found a part that looked like the tent peg had slipped up, or not been put in properly.

Taking a furtive look around, she slipped herself into the darkness of the tent.

It smelt like a farm.

Specifically, the wrong end of a farm.

Holding her nose, she looked around. She was in a darkened

room, along with several of the circus animals. Most had blankets on their cages.

All except a little trumpet chicken. It was tied to a pole so it could scratch around in the dirt, and there was a little pile of straw so that it could sleep.

Except right now it wasn't asleep. It was wide awake, poking her with its trumpet beak while it made soft 'pop' noises.

She tried to shush it, and it seemed to get the idea. Carefully she picked it up and snuggled it back down into its bed, hoping it would behave. Begging with her eyes, she willed it to keep silent.

Kialessa sighed as it snuggled down.

She moved through the crowded room to where she could hear the ringmaster's voice.

The older gentle was talking to someone else, which was good.

A man was saying something, '… think the second act will need more focus. If we're talking children, they'll need more time than you've given them to rehearse.'

'I agree, but what are we going to do?' she said in her exotic accent. 'We're only paid up for half a season, and that's barely long enough to sort out who the real talent here will be.'

'Agreed, so why are you indulging this little side project? Haven't we got enough to do here already? We don't have time-'

'There's never enough time, chéri,' she said.

Kialessa peeked out of the curtain, and looking around found she could see nobody. But the tent looked huge from here, even larger than before. She stretched out, and to her surprise noticed Flower, not saying anything but clearly listening to the entire conversation. She was sitting on the arm of the massive minotaur, who seemed to have nothing better to do than to be a chair right now. He seemed a little uncomfortable, but looked like he would never move again unless it suited his acrobat friend.

The trumpet chicken hooted again, and Kialessa stared at it in frustration. She looked around, and noticed a tall side pole that led up and out of the small room where she was hiding. Maybe she could see who was talking from there? As silently as possible she crept over and begun climbing up.

Again the chicken hooted. Then bleated.

'Shut up, Nonker!' Chéri shouted. 'You're going to wake everyone up again!'

Suddenly Kialessa heard someone's footsteps rapidly approaching the storage room.

Her heart sank. This was never a good way to meet people.

'Sit up!' the ringmaster stated, 'she is here.'

The footprints stopped.

Then the ringmaster said in a loud, welcoming voice, 'Priestess! Thank you for coming! I'm so glad you could make it!'

'No trouble at all,' she said, though her voice sounded tired. It was the dwarven high priestess, personal attendant and bodyguard to the king. 'What matter concerns you?'

Kialessa breathed a sigh of relief, and thanked the priestess and her god for saving her. She scurried quickly up a nearby pole, a rather easy task with all her combat training. She found herself looking down at the centre ring from the darkened rafters. There, in the centre, was the priestess, back toward her, talking to the ringmaster. Flower was sitting there with her minotaur, looking polite but not really interested. In the centre of the ring a large table was set up, and on the table dozens of pages and parchments were strewn about, most likely papers for the circus or parts for the play. Kialessa couldn't tell.

And there, sitting at the table with a quill in one hand and a serious look on his face, was the clown who'd played the part of the gnome in the play. He'd been the one who'd dropped the pegs on the first day. He looked, Kialessa thought, uncharacteristically serious. She began to wonder if he was, perhaps, Flower's father.

The ringmaster sat on the edge of the table to speak to the priestess. 'I take it you already know about your little enchantress?'

The priestess sighed, 'We do.'

The ringmaster looked over at her husband, who looked back at her, brow furrowed in concern. 'Under normal circumstances I wouldn't mind her taking this part, she's the natural choice. And this, apart from the fact that this whole play is her idea. But her auguries are dark at the moment. I don't like it. I think she's putting too much stock in this play. To say it means everything to her is not unkind, but the truth is, she will get burned.'

Jacinthia, the high priestess, sighed. She paused before replying, 'What would you have us do?'

'It's a chrysalis, isn't it,' the man Chéri stated bluntly, like he was bothered by the news.

The priestess nodded.

And the ringmaster shook her head, 'And one so young!'

No one spoke. The ringmaster filled the silence once more. 'Misuri mei … mild food, no stress. And yet she wants to take on a play! This is not going to be good for her health. I want you to take her out of the play. I don't want her anywhere near it.'

Flower looked annoyed, as though she'd had this argument before and still gotten nowhere, 'But it's her idea!'

'And she has no *idea* what she's just taken on.'

'It will break her heart,' priestess Jacinthia counselled.

The ringmaster sighed, 'I know. But right now, she should take it easy. No surprises, no pressure. Mild herbs.'

Jacinthia shook her head, 'We told her as much, and while I understand what you are saying, and I respect your judgment. But we want to her to know she is needed, and trusted. She is keeping to her treatment as far as I am aware. I am sure she will not take this well.'

'Not half as poorly as if she does,' the man called Chéri said, not making much sense.

'Whom will you cast for the role?' Jacinthia the priestess asked.

'I want a senior student to audition. You can't have this role compromised in any way. It has to be your *best*.'

Again the priestess sighed, 'I think Allastassia *is* our best.'

'Your best, without the danger of setting this whole tent ablaze,' Chéri stated. 'She can write the first review, if you like. We'll give her the lead role in the chorus. It'll work out fine, you'll see. We just need someone she trusts to tell her this and convince her of the wisdom.'

Jacinthia nodded, and left.

The ringmaster and Chéri stared at each other.

'Now…' she stated, 'where were we?' swinging down to sit on his lap. Flower sighed and rolled her eyes, looking like she really was ready to leave now, and her parents laughed. Suddenly the insufferable trumpet chicken honked out loudly. It was out of bed, pulling on its rope, trying to get Kialessa's attention.

'Stupid chicken!' the ringmaster swore.

'Wait!' Chéri hissed. He stood up, and walked with astonishing silence and speed toward the storage room. Kialessa realised now it was the back room of the main tent. The fabric walls didn't go all the way up to the roof.

If he looked up, even once, he'd find her.

He opened the curtain, and slipped into the back room. He settled the trumpet chicken back down. Then, looking about in the dust, Kialessa heard him mutter something that took her breath away, 'A child was here. Recently… Flower, were you sneaking around for entertainment again?'

She shook her head.

She saw Chéri, silhouetted in the light. She was almost directly above him here. Kialessa pressed herself tightly into the rafters, trying not to feel fear.

She watched as his gaze followed her footsteps towards the tent door, then over to the pole she was hiding on.

Then his gaze moved slowly up the pole.

He looked right at her, looking right at where she was hiding.

She stared back.

Yet, strangely, he said nothing, but kept looking about as if he couldn't see anything at all. If he saw her, or noticed anything out of the ordinary, he said nothing.

'Chéri?' the ringmaster asked.

'Eh? Hmm, nothing I guess. Perhaps they were here earlier.'

'Well, he does want the best!' Flower's mother chimed, presumably referring to the king. 'I suppose they like a little challenge now and then.'

Chéri smiled.

'Come, let us away,' she said with a wave of her hand.

Running toward her, she draped her arm over his shoulders. He pinched her backside, and they walked out laughing. Flower covered her eyes and allowed Ugly to carry her out on his shoulder, protesting how much they embarrassed her.

Kialessa sighed with relief.

She was about to climb back down, but then realised if they really suspected someone was there they'd just be waiting for her to come out again.

So she waited an hour in the darkness, clinging to the rafters, wondering what had happened, and worrying about what was going to happen tomorrow.

     By Dr Joseph Ireland "Dr Joe"

Realisation

There are only ever two reasons to be angry; you are believing a lie, or you are denying a truth. Either reason is equally concerning.

Jacinthia Stonehall, high priestess of Lenmer'el.

As it was, Allastassia took it well. Very well.

Almost… too well, Kialessa thought.

'No, no, I understand completely,' Allastassia was saying with a smile. They were standing apart from the other students, just the lead roles. Kialessa was there too, because no one seemed to mind her there. She might not have been Allastassia's best friend, but she was a special associate, helping Allastassia with all her important projects like catching bandits, or rescuing chickens.

But not, it would seem, being in plays.

'Now,' the ringmaster seemed to be repeating herself, 'you understand. It's not you personally, not at all.'

'Oh, I know,' Allastassia said with a smile. 'The priestess and I had a good talk.'

'It's that I think this role needs to be performed by someone taller, with a little more experience. I have a special role for you, little one. I'll need someone to help run errands to make this play work. You won't have anything to worry about except making sure you're nearby when I need you! Aolith will be playing the role of the princess.'

'Oh, of course!' Allastassia gushed. 'That's fine with me. Aolith, you're so pretty. You'll do just right with this role.'

Everyone was perfectly silent while Allastassia smiled.

'You're sure?' the older girl asked.

'Absolutely!' Allastassia told them.

Aolith shrugged. 'Fine, gets me out of combat training anyway.' Aolith was a capable fighter among the senior students with a large measure of respect, and a young noble in the king's court. But she had a pretty face and strong features, pale skin and dark eyebrows, which the headmistress promised were vital for being seen during a play.

'But that was what makeup was invented for,' Patsi had protested.

The ringmaster nodded, and everyone disappeared to help set up for the first reading of the play. It was a busy day, and people seemed honestly excited about something so different from battle or study.

Kialessa was about to turn back to Allastassia when the air suddenly tingled around her, a static discharge of electricity slithering up the auburn enchantress's arm.

Something she seemed completely oblivious to.

'Um, Alli?' Kialessa asked.

'Absolutely…' Allastassia said. Her lips were frozen in her usual perfect smile, but her eyes simmered with danger, 'No problem … no problem at all…'

***

Three weeks slid by without incident. Just as Flower had

been permitted to study at the college, so the circus was expected every day to teach the unique skills only they could provide. At first it was everyone, but after a few weeks the ringmaster had winnowed the group down to about half of the most talented students. They were to practice after dinner, which was unusual, and while the training was only supposed to go for an hour it usually went late into the evening. The difficult and demanding routine was beginning to show, and most students were falling far behind the ringmaster's high expectations. And now, in spite of Kialessa's still aching muscles, the ringmaster insisted it was time to learn how to throw knifes, and to juggle them safely.

While smiling.

The other students managed quite well, but it was clear Kialessa had the gift of aiming; she was almost as good as Flower. Four hours later and she was the only one still enjoying trying to hit a pin head at ten paces, and the only one who occasionally managed to do it. It made her feel proud.

It was more fun than watching the subtle and insistent way in which Allastassia was slowly taking over the play. She was supposed to be helping, taking it easy. But she was not. Slowly, one job at a time, the ringmaster was allowing her to take on every responsibility. Kialessa didn't know if Allastassia had her under some enchantment, or if the woman was simply very busy, but she was still worried.

For example, it was Posk's job to pull the curtain and backdrops, between scenes and at the beginning and end of the play. Perhaps Allastassia was inspired by the minotaur who accompanied Flower everywhere, or perhaps the heavy curtains really were too much for anyone else to open, but the enchantress had decided it was Posk's job.

But he wasn't very good at it. Twice he broke the cord as he opened them, not knowing when to stop. And most times he had to be found, distracted and absent, usually watching the performers practicing with wide eyed enthusiasm.

Kialessa was beginning to dread rehearsal.

***

Allastassia screamed.

Everyone in the area froze as if their lives depended on it. It was rehearsal night. Most of them looked around furtively, hoping to find out what had upset her now, and probably hoping it wasn't them.

As if on cue, a green half-troll boy stumbled across the lawn in front of the outdoor stage, chasing a moth.

With impressive restraint, Allastassia called her play leaders together. 'He can't do it,' she said. 'Not like this. I mean, we even give him a bell but he's too busy enjoying himself to pay attention.'

'He does get distracted easily,' Aolith agreed.

'Piex,' Allastassia ordered, talking to the backstage manager she had literally bullied into the job. 'You have good concentration,' which was an understatement, Piex's concentration was legendary. 'How do you do it?'

'I am not surprised it is difficult for him,' Piex muttered.

Everyone waited for him to explain. He put down the book he was trying to read while organising everyone that worked behind the scenes. He was quite organised, as a wizard should be. But he also considered using those skills to help arrange a college play beneath his dignity, and that he was doing everyone here an enormous personal favour just by showing up.

Like most wizards she knew.

Piex sighed. 'I have found these magical devices most helpful,' he said, pointing to his head. 'Have you noticed? Apprentice wizards pass their fourth test by constructing a wizardry hat. Sewn into the rim is a simple metal headband enspelled to improve concentration, and intellect. Now, it's never been done, but I can think of no actual reason why you couldn't try giving him my old one. I'm using the headband sagemaster De'Feur forged years ago since he now uses the greater headband he won by defeating my evil uncle Tobiuus. Now he lets me use his regular headband. I suppose we could try getting my old wizardry hat – he lends it out to the other students often.'

'How much does he charge?' Darrix asked, though Allastassia looked like she would have gladly avoided the question altogether.

'No charge, for wizards at least. I wonder if he'd let a non-wizard use it? I suppose so, the scholars have been known to…' Piex mumbled himself into silence.

Allastassia grabbed Piex's hand and was already off towards the castle.

'Shouldn't we?' Flower asked as if to indicate they should follow along.

Kialessa looked at the ringmaster, who shrugged her shoulders and waved her off. Calling Posk to join in, she, Flower and Darrix ran after Allastassia and Piex.

They found the wizard in his study.

He was tracing light blue runes in the air, summoning them out of clouds he formed with his own breath. Kialessa didn't know if it was a serious spell, or just practice, but she decided it wasn't appropriate to ask.

When at last he'd finished his task he swept the runes onto a sheet of parchment, and looked at them satisfied.

'Sufficient,' he proclaimed.

'Paramount proficiency, Master!' Piex congratulated him with words so unnecessarily big Kialessa took a moment before she realised they were still Emerellian, not Dragonspeech.

'Sufficient,' the master insisted. 'And what adventure do you young ones seek today?' He asked with a suspicious glare, but with a playful grin.

Allastassia spoke up immediately, 'If you will, good Master Wizard,' she curtsied her finest. 'We seek your indulgence to borrow a small trinket. Posk is so very important to the play, you see, for only he can move the curtains at the right time, and that alone. But he is so very dim. I don't suppose we could impress upon you–'

'You wish to borrow the lesser wizardry hat?' The wizard scowled.

Allastassia blushed, but did not back down.

The old elf stood, and looked over the half troll boy with imperious severity. 'Are you sure he is the only one you can work with?' he asked.

'Quite, good Gentle,' Allastassia claimed.

Flower nodded her support.

The wizard sighed. 'With King Dunnkan on your side, we are all at our honour to contribute all we can to make the play happen. The whole project is against my better judgement; you youth can learn more studying numbers! But as I am not King, I will loan you, for rehearsals only, my students' hat. But you must return it when you are done, you understand!' he glowered.

'Y... Yes, sir,' Allastassia stammered.

The wizard looked at her kindly. 'I don't mean to frighten you, young woman.' He explained, 'I only wish to impress upon you the cost of such a device. Two thousand gold coins, a lifetime's wage for a servant, though I know your parents spend that in a week. You must not lose this trinket, at any cost!' he insisted.

Promising their best to comply, Kialessa was glad when he didn't seem to insist on any binding magic. None of them wanted to be turned into a toad, and in her case, again.

The wizard removed the hat from one of the many, many drawers in his desk, and without any ceremony at all, placed the stuffy old hat on Posk's head. It readjusted instantly to fit him.

The wizard looked at Posk seriously. 'Now understand, young boy,' he lectured with more detail than any adult had ever bothered using to the half-troll, 'you must not lose this hat ever, ever! And you must return it every evening, do you understand?'

For a moment Posk just stood there. Then, in a voice so clear it startled them all, he said, 'Yes.'

Kialessa was amazed. Posk spoke six words, and "yes" was not one of them. It was usually a grunt with a sort of a nod.

Posk looked around, a glint of clarity showing in his eyes that had never been there before. Then he noticed them.

'Darrix,' he said, clear and confident.

'Good evening, Posk. How are you feeling?' Darrix replied.

But Posk only smiled. Perhaps he had no words to reply with yet.

'Piex,' he said, turning to the half dragon, tasting the word with his mouth for the first time.

'Well said, Posk.' Piex smiled, a little at a loss for words.

'Kialessa,' Posk smiled broadest of all, and struggling for words uttered one more, 'Tauira… friend!'

She couldn't help but hug the big half-troll boy. It was an amazing moment. For the first time ever, they were hearing their names from his lips. He smiled again, but then took on a serious expression as he turned to Allastassia.

'Stassi… stasis…' Posk struggled. 'Stassia?'

Allastassia was livid, but did her best to hide her indignity that of all of them, hers was the name he still could not speak.

It made Darrix laugh, and they went back to the play, hoping that this would fix everything because Allastassia, in spite of every piece of advice, was clearly becoming more and more stressed as each day wore on.

***

The next day, Kialessa watched as Posk's silhouette filled the doorway of history and historical lore class. The room fell silent, as the tutor gasped.

Posk hadn't taken off the hat, not even for a moment. Wherever he went, he looked around, trying to touch and see everything. He seemed to be studying everything with great interest; from the words the tutors used, to the fact that everyone had shoelaces and could tie them up as well. What was truly unusual, however, was that he was now insisting on coming to class. He was usually found with the tutor of the younger students, when be bothered to turn up at all. The history and historical lore tutor no doubt looked nervous as she remembered what had happened last time he was here.

Looking around, Posk seemed nervous.

'Posk, come in!' the tutor said, her voice trembling.

He looked around until he saw Kialessa, then ran in with his knuckles on the floor. He sat beside her, pressing up against her and almost throwing her out of her seat.

Positioning the stylus and slate, ready for writing, he pulled the hat down tight. He sat up straight and tall, and watched the tutor with great intensity.

The class was silent. Yet something about his sincerity seemed endearing, and just a little funny to Kialessa.

'Good Posk,' she told him, adjusting her seat and patting him on the back.

For the first time, ever, he did not reply with, "Good, good". He just sat there, staring at the tutor with unbreakable focus.

The tutor sighed, and got to work.

It took everyone five moments to get used to the fact that Posk was there, but eventually they did. They sat there, listening to the tutor. What was really impressive, however, was that so did Posk. Ten moments in, the tutor began to write on the board with her chalk. She was describing the hundred-year war between Emerel and Nomer'el, which actually only went for ninety-nine years, before they even had those names.

Posk watched in complete fascination.

While the tutor talked, he began to sketch, in what would have had to be the worst handwriting ever, and with a stylus held in his fist instead of three fingertips, the word 'Emerel.'

In a much more Posk-like fashion he ignored the tutor and pointed to the word, grunting loudly.

 By Dr Joseph Ireland "Dr Joe"

'Emerel,' Kialessa explained.

He pointed, and grunted again.

She didn't know what he meant. 'Emerel Posk. It's the word for Emerel.'

He looked confused.

'Emerel,' Patsi joined in as the tutor just watched on. 'You know, the massive nation north of this one?'

Posk looked really confused, and pointed at the word again.

The tutor came up them. 'It's a word Posk. We use them to convey meaning. Look, here is how you write you name, POSK.' She wrote the word and pointed at him.

He pointed at himself, looked puzzled, and wrote a single stroke on the slate. 'Posk?' he asked.

'Oh,' Piex stated, looking over from his reading, he'd been ignoring the lesson the whole time. 'That's the troll pronoun for "me". I didn't know he wrote troll.'

'Well, that might explain some things…' the tutor muttered. 'Here Posk, here is how you write Kialessa.'

As the word scrawled out on the slate tablet, the tutor sounding out each syllable, Posk shouted with surprise. 'Ki – ah – less – ah!' he muttered in utter amazement. He touched his lips and said it again, spelling out every sound.

'Perhaps he's only realising sounds can be represented by letters, since the troll script is highly hieroglyphic,' Piex suggested. 'They use one symbol for an entire word, you know.'

No one knew what Piex was going on about, but Posk was ecstatic. He ran to the front of the class and banged the board. 'Ex!' he shouted, 'P – ee - ex!'

The tutor smiled, and wrote his name.

Posk was amazed that they shared the same first letter. He even tried to write it out himself, but it was barely recognisable. Bouncing on both feet at the same time, he kept trying to learn. He insisted on learning more names, including the tutors.

'Stassi… Alli…' he struggled. The tutor wrote her name, and Posk smiled, touching each letter, but not daring to say it out loud once more.

Then he ran to the window, and pointed to the sun. 'Stassi… sun…' he grinned.

They burst out laughing, but he didn't seem to mind.

Allastassia, however, was silent.

'Seems our blossoming enchantress had scored herself another suitor,' Patsi teased her.

Allastassia was silent a moment, then dismissed the whole thing with an, 'Oh, *please*.'

'Let us hope Serros shares your sense of humour!' the tutor joked, possibly referring to those in history who had offended the gods by comparing themselves favourably to the divine.

'Though I could understand if he agreed!' Patsi laughed.

But Kialessa didn't. That was not the sort of thing you joked about if you wanted to keep on the good side of some extremely powerful beings with a reputation for being fickle, and vengeful.

Everyone laughed again as Posk banged for Darrix's name and spelling. He was in an ecstatic state of glee. He made them name everything in the room. The tutor endured it for a good ten moments before making him return to his desk, but he was a lost cause now for all his excitement, it would seem, at *finally* understanding *why* they were putting symbols on slates.

He ignored the rest of the lesson, and took to writing their names again, and again, and again.

Especially, "Allastassia".

     By Dr Joseph Ireland "Dr Joe"

The Clock

Never judge a man, by how he treats his betters.
For those he must impress, and serve with words and letters.
But watch and see the truth; his deeds an honest hymn,
Of how he will treat those, who can do naught for him.
415th Saying of the irrefutable sage of Venterrin.

Two days later it was Planasday. Posk always knew when it was Planasday, and without fail he turned up to join in the battles and competitions of the afternoon. He didn't seem to notice it had all been replaced with a play, however, and did his best to move the curtains on cue with the hat's help. When it came to college, simple things were what Posk was good at.

So it was a bit of a surprise when he noticed the clock.

Kialessa and the others were having a morning tea break that Planasday when he burst in, a frazzled tutor for the younger children hurrying in behind.

'No, Posk, put the clock back please!' she begged.

'Not him!' Allastassia mourned, and her friends giggled.

He ran right up to Kialessa. He always did. He shoved the

clock right under her nose and grunted in a happy, curious way.

'What's up, Posk?' Kialessa asked.

The tutor scurried up. 'Oh, I was teaching them about time and showed them the clock,' she stated, a little out of breath. 'And as soon as I showed him the clock he became all curious about the ticking noise. So I took off the back to show him the gears, and it's a little internal spring clock that uses one of those new spring things instead of a pendulum and he just won't let me have it back now.'

Posk was shoving the clock in Kialessa's face. He was giddy with delight. They'd pulled off the back of the clock all right. Inside, there were dozens of gears and little springs and pullies. It was a fascinating machine, but very, very small.

'Mrrrmrum!' he chortled in delight.

'Yes Posk, it's a clock.' Kialessa smiled. 'Now we need to put it back.'

But he wasn't content to do that.

'Apparently,' Flower laughed, 'He's just discovered the most amazing thing in the universe and needs to show everyone.'

'Perhaps he has not yet connected the clock with its humanoid origins?' Piex explained.

'You mean he doesn't know we invented it, that he thinks it just turned up and organises us all?' Darrix translated, walking up with some of the other boys. Posk happily shoved the clock into his face and pointed in great excitement at the little cogs, keeping the wizard hat close on his head.

By this time, several of the youth from the college were gathered, and Posk was lapping up the attention, thrilled at the discovery of a little clock. The tutor was flustered. He was showing it to all of them one at a time, taking great care to point to the little machinery parts within. Then, sitting right in front of Allastassia so that she couldn't *not* look at him, showed it with great interest and sincerity to her.

'It's just a clock, Posk,' she said with a sneer.

He shook his head as though he actually understood, and with incomprehensible muttering pointed to the various parts as though confidently trying to explain it to her.

She rolled her eyes. 'You like the little clock? Here, look at this!'

Perhaps she was tired of all the attention he was receiving, or perhaps she just really was a highly talented enchantress, but with a wave of her hand she magically projected a translucent and fabulously life like image of the clock up into the air, dozens of times larger and able to display every single moving cog and spring in intricate detail.

Everyone oohed in amazement, even the lights seemed to dim in the area in respect to the image Allastassia conjured without effort. Posk pressed his face right up to it, comparing it carefully with the clock he held in his hand, greatly impressed.

'Well, does that satisfy you Posk?'

He grinned.

But Piex shouted as though he'd only just found his voice. 'How did you do that!?' the young wizard demanded to know.

Allastassia harrumphed, 'It's not like it's very hard, I've been able to do it since I was six you know. Actually, not even my mother can cast-'

Piex pushed his way to the front, toppling a student in his enthusiasm. 'Go in closer, show us how far it can g-go in,' he ordered, eyes fixed on the image.

And Allastassia, ever willing to be the centre of attention, obliged. One gear grew in size and detail until the tiny scratches and pits on its surface were visible.

'More, more!' Piex ordered.

'It's not that easy…' she muttered, concentrating.

The scratch grew till it filled the entire floating image, and then it didn't look like a little scratch at all.

'It looks like a mighty chasm,' Darrix wondered.

Students oohed. The scratch did look like a giant had taken a huge stencil and scratched a mountain range into some bronze ground. Everything looked very different at that size.

'Can you do skin?' Piex asked. 'Or the leaves of plants?'

'Well of course I can, I imagine,' Allastassia boasted.

Suddenly Piex grabbed her hand and scattered the image.

'We have to take this to the Loremaster immediately!' He shouted like he was suddenly part of the castle guard. He dragged her up protesting. 'You don't know what you've just done here. We've been trying to make a spell like that for centuries!'

He continued on as she let him drag her away. Her friends laughed, and some sighed as the mystic vapours of her miraculous clock dissipated.

But none sighed deeper, or looked longer, than a profoundly disabled half-troll boy Posk.

***

'Apparently, they're all making a great fuss about it now,' Allastassia boasted after they returned for lunch. Everyone was used to Piex skipping class because he knew it all anyway, but Allastassia never did. This time, however, she was busy with the wizards. She had been made to cast the spell three, four more times for the sagemaster and his apprentices, who had then set about trying to decipher the arcane lore that made seeing into the very small so easy.

'Apparently,' Allastassia continued, 'it's something those wizards haven't been able to figure out for a while now, yet I managed to do it in my spare time as a baby.' She sighed with a contented grin.

'You're very proud,' Darrix smiled.

'Am I?' she pretended to be innocent. 'Perhaps, but it's not often we enchantresses manage to pull one over on those bookish wizards. They're usually the snobby ones with their "You might be able to do it, but we **understand** it". Humph!'

It was the afternoon now, and the students were chatting

while they prepared for another rehearsal.

'We do understand it,' Piex argued, drawn easily into her argument. 'A concave **and** convex scrying lens! You seem to have broken several rules to do what you do.'

'Maybe you just have too many rules,' Allastassia said with a very cheeky grin.

***

Another week slid by, and Kialessa watched Flower arching her back in a perfect backflip on the high beam. She was very good.

Everyone clapped, and the acrobat motioned toward to Allastassia.

The enchantress stood on the beam.

'No cheating this time!' Flower demanded with a smile.

Allastassia ignored her, but Kialessa grinned. She recalled how Allastassia had previously managed a successful backflip only after accidentally conjuring so much magic that her feet and hands had left beautiful star trails of glistening light. It had looked amazing.

Flower came to sit beside Kialessa, leaving Allastassia to achieve this alone. The room was noisy, other students were there practicing the skills the circus taught, such as skipping through hoops or jumping ropes. *Boring things* thought Kialessa. Flower was much more advanced, and as if to prove it, she didn't only skip back to her seat, she did a one-armed cart wheel and then landed in the splits, sitting down beside Kialessa and Patsi in some amazing twist that didn't look at all comfortable.

Her minotaur didn't even notice, he was standing by the beam and ready to catch people who fell off.

'Why does he never say anything?' Patsi asked Flower.

'He's so terribly dim-witted,' Flower answered. 'It's a wonder he can understand even simple instructions.'

Kialessa wondered about that reply; it had not been what

flower had told her on the hillside the first day they'd met.

Kialessa heard laughing, and looking over saw some other students gawking at Flower's odd pose. Flower ignored them, and watched Allastassia walking on the beam, trying to build up courage.

Kialessa watched Flower, completely ignoring the mocking students.

'Flower,' Kialessa wondered, 'how do you do it?'

Flower sighed, leaning in to speak quietly. 'You worry too much about what other people think, Kialessa. Who cares if they don't like you, or like you? You're still a wonderful person, that's what matters.'

'You make it sound easy,' Kialessa complained, then added, 'I'm glad we are friends.' She knew it was a great risk to label someone else as her friend, without asking first. But it seemed to be the right thing; Flower was very kind to her.

Some of the other girls joined them on the seat. It seemed They had overheard them.

'Look,' Aolith explained, 'even the worst man on earth can find himself surrounded by friends. And the best man on earth is going to make enemies that hate him. You just need to know you're doing what's right, because while someone will love you for it, someone else is going to hate you for it.'

Kialessa wasn't sure about what to say regarding that.

Flower kept looking out at the other students. 'People like us, Kialessa. We stick out. We can't simply blend in. We force people to make a choice to love us, or hate us. What matters, I guess… is do you love yourself? Can you live with who you are?'

Kialessa thought about that. 'I don't mind who I am, but not everyone can accept that.'

'It's that way for anyone,' Aolith told them. 'Even normal people.'

Flower shrugged, but did not disagree.

Kialessa turned to face Allastassia. 'Then how do we help

someone who's having trouble accepting who she is? Who places all her hopes and dreams in other people performing a play "just right"?'

'I don't know,' Aolith confessed. 'It's not always very easy to avoid getting dragged into her issues, she's so intense! She should just chill out, and realise she's amazing too.'

'Everyone tells her so,' Kialessa admitted.

Kialessa looked over at Allastassia, breathing in deep. What they told her didn't matter; it was what she thought of herself that would define who she became. Loved, or hated, what mattered was what Allastassia thought of herself.

'She's such a natural,' Kialessa muttered.

Allastassia arched her back, but then didn't have the courage to try for the backflip yet, and straightened up.

'It's not talent,' the dwarven priestess Federach stated. 'She's been learning how to dance since she could walk, from some of the best instructors in all the Great Kingdom, I'll wager. Her parents have taken her on tour as they've discharged the king's business her whole life. She's *skilled*, that's all. If you really want to know what she's talented at, it's enchantment.'

Kialessa watched, waiting for Allastassia to try again.

'I hate to say this,' Federach said, 'but she really is the natural choice for lead role in the play.'

Aolith glared at her, then looked back at Allastassia. It was clear to Kialessa that the older girl knew some of the *real* reasons, and concerns, that the ringmaster had made Aolith the lead instead. 'She's good, it's true. And a little enchantment never goes astray in the performing arts. But this role called for one with just a touch more experience than her.'

'And the role of the carpenter's son did not?' Natasha said with a cunning grin.

'Look,' Aolith whispered, looking right at them. 'She's good, I already said. But she's too invested in this play. It's *her* play. If it doesn't go off perfectly, she'll be scarred for life! And let's face it, what play ever goes off *perfectly*. No. Too invested. She needs to calm down- '

And Aolith left it at that, her voice lingering. It was as if she'd really wanted to say, "Calm down, because she's going through her change right now, and the last thing we need is a stressed-out enchantress with a shattered chrysalis and enough power to hold lightning."

Allastassia huffed, breathed out, and flipped over backwards. She wobbled unsteadily on the beam, but stood.

Everyone clapped.

And amidst the noise the dwarf turned to Aolith and whispered, 'Well, let's hope our little enchantress doesn't hold that against you, eh?'

***

They all had handkerchiefs pressed to their noses.

Aolith looked terrible.

She was terribly, terribly sick. She'd retired to bed early that night, and by the next morning was covered with green spots.

'Trollsoath,' the head mistress muttered as soon as she saw her, slapping her handkerchief over her nose immediately. Everyone knew the smell alone was enough to bring about a similar illness in others. 'Call the priestess.'

Natasha pressed past Kialessa, her cervitaur hooves clicking on the floor as she went. Like most priests, she had little to fear from other's illnesses. She put her hand right on Aolith's forehead, and the ill girl groaned.

'Lumos will cause a stay of the infection,' Natasha said, 'but you will require rest.'

'How long?'

'Well...' Natasha thought out loud. It seemed to Kialessa that Natasha had been studying up on illnesses recently. She was a capable healer, especially good with bruises and sprains, which made her a popular choice in combat training. Just the other week she'd set and mended her first torn muscle,

　　　　By Dr Joseph Ireland "Dr Joe"

something Posk had given Marchan in training once more. Everyone was really impressed with her, and the high priestess at the Moon Falls had immediately graduated Natasha to adept status, the youngest in the kingdom so far.

It made Kialessa wish she had such talent with sickness and healing, but only Darrix showed any real potential among the younger students. Even so, he'd only helped with scratches, and sprains, though the priests of the Eternal were acknowledged to be particularly effective against demons and poisons, and he'd certainly earned the title "demonbane".

Aolith's miserable groan returned Kialessa from her thoughts. She looked terrible.

'She'll be out for a half season, at least,' Natasha told them.

'Poor Aolith!' everyone chorused.

'Wait a moment,' Patsi asked, 'what about the play? Who will take the lead role now?'

It was such a silly question, perhaps that was why no one bothered to answer.

They all turned to look at Allastassia.

And she just smiled, blinking back her tears for Aolith. A cute, pretty, innocent smile.

***

'It wasn't you, was it?' Kialessa asked her the first chance she got, on their way between morning classes.

'Whatever do you mean?' Allastassia said, seeming surprised.

'You… I mean… Aolith…'

Allastassia seemed aghast, then melted. She could tell there was no point pretending with her. 'No, I … at least, I don't think so. I have never done a curse like that one someone, ever. And I don't think I ever would.'

'But Trollsoath?' Kialessa asked. 'Not deadly, just enough to get her out of the play long enough.'

'What are you saying, Kia?' Allastassia said, voice rising. She lowered it once more. 'Sorry… I just, I don't know if I should even blame myself. Enchantments take time to master, Kialessa. I know we make it look easy, and can usually throw in a bit of variety for flair every time. But enchantments actually take *time* to create. My mother and I have found we need to meditate at least an hour every day to do it properly.'

'An hour?' Kialessa was bemused. When did Allastassia find an hour just to sit around thinking?

She seemed to know what Kialessa was wondering. 'You have to imagine each enchantment happening, as powerfully as possible. It's almost like I have to prepare my mind and body if I want to have any hope of actually using an enchantment at the right time. I know I'm talented, that I'm more attune to magic than most people. But that doesn't mean I can just do anything. I have never pictured Aolith… I mean, diseases… I've never even *imagined* anything like that before.'

'Yes, but you've never held lightning either.'

'Actually… I've been dreaming about it for years.'

'Really? I didn't know that.'

'Well… whatever… just, don't go stirring people up now, all right? I'm sure it wasn't me anyway, but if I get to be the lead role then that's fine with me. All I need to worry about is if Posk can open the curtains in time!' And turning on her heel, she stormed off.

Kialessa watched her as she went, not sure whether she had accidentally cursed Aolith or not. It didn't matter, Aolith certainly wasn't contesting Allastassia's claim on the lead role, and immediate healing of common illness was generally deemed unwise, considering it better for a person to overcome their sins and thus defeat the illness on their own. Aolith was going to sit this out… and Allastassia would take the lead.

     By Dr Joseph Ireland "Dr Joe"

Just because it's hard doesn't mean it's not worth doing.
Py, athletics tutor

That afternoon they had their first dress rehearsal, which meant, according to Flower, that they were to continue no matter what happened, from beginning to end. No mess-ups and no breaks when they messed up.

The curtains rose, Posk yanking on them so hard they hit the roof with an audible thump. The only other audible sound was Allastassia's sigh of exasperation.

Patsi was waiting on the stage, she stuttered as she spoke.

'Folk and fair ones from far and from fear,
Draw nearer and … listen, my tale to hear,
A story of hero's sword pointed and who,
And damsels distressed… oppressed, and who,
In bright night of darkness, their freedoms declare,
And demons and demons, and peril, and share,
A bright knight of wonder, the Carpenter's son…

… so listen up all, till the tale is done!'
Patsi cheered herself, but Allastassia groaned out loud.

The first scene went off without much of a hitch. Allastassia bounced around and sung a song about how happy she was and how nice it is to be a princess while adoring townsfolk listened in rapture. Everyone clapped, and she looked quite pleased when she was done.

Darrix was on next, and sang his little song about how pretty she was. Allastassia, the princess, then sung a song about how nice the carpenter's son was and how it would be nice to get to know him if he wasn't so shy enough to speak to her. It was a lovely scene, and everyone clapped once it was done.

Then the scene was supposed to move to the fiery pit where the demon lived. The lights went out, and Federach rushed on stage, but when the lights came back on again she looked quite out of place against the town background. Allastassia screamed at Posk, who was chasing grass flies by this time, and he rushed up to the ropes and pulled frantically, accidentally pulling up the castle scene again. Everyone panicked again and started shouting, and eventually Posk got it right but not before the play had lost momentum.

The demon then said its little rhyme, her deep dwarven voice doing the part of a "man" true justice.

'Each day in burning I am pained,
By wrath of gods most pure,
And though I suffer, it is clear,
A greater pain I must endure,'

'For love unanswered, it is known,
A greater pain there is none,
And I will die before I see,
A princess marry a carpenter's son.'

      By Dr Joseph Ireland "Dr Joe"

'For she is mine! I do declare,
From earth to hell below,
That she I'll wed, and death to all,
Who my love will not bestow…'

She spoke the rhyme perfectly, but then completely forgot her next line. She was supposed to be talking to a little demon about her terrible plans, but needed so much prompting from Allastassia, who had the whole play memorised, it looked silly.

'Yes,' Federach declared, 'I will…'

'… woo her,' Allastassia's course whisper echoed from the side of the stage.

'Yes! Woo her!' Federach proclaimed, 'And she will… will…'

'Be mine! Oh for goodness sake!' Allastassia huffed.

'Yes, woo her, for goodness sake!' Federach repeated.

'No, oh!' Allastassia mourned.

'No! Or, Yes! Woo her. And she will love me and redeem me from this pit of fire!'

'Pit of coals!' Allastassia corrected.

'Coals?!' Federach repeated indignantly as though she'd never read the script. 'What's so hot about coals? At least 'burning coals'.'

'Because it fits in with the rhymes later on!' Allastassia demanded. 'And how can you be bringing this up now, did you even *read* the script!'

'Well, the script doesn't make much sense to me,' Federach stated.

And so it continued for the rest of the scene, Allastassia gradually growing more and more frustrated as time went on.

Eventually, much to everyone's gratitude, the scene ended and the princess's father decides to hold a ball to check out the royal suitors. He informs the princess to see who she wanted, and she immediately mentions the carpenter's son. Well, the king wasn't too pleased by this, and told her in no uncertain terms she could not invite the commoners. Or, he would have, except it was the rude boy playing the king , and he delivered his lines with such a monotone it sounded like the king didn't care at all and was about to fall asleep at any moment. Allastassia scolded him, and he stormed off without finishing his lines.

The ballroom scene began, with Posk half rolling down the backdrop of the demon cave before he realised his mistake. The dancers came on anyway, and Allastassia and Darrix danced in from opposite ends of the stage. She looked glorious, and he a little uncertain, which suited his part actually. She twirled into his arms and he only just caught her in time. Suddenly Allastassia got up and stomped her feet.

Then, in spite of all the warnings not to stop the rehearsal, she held up the play while chastising the dancers. 'No, no! Dancers! Its step two three, step, step two three, not step three step! Watch, you're all doing it all wrong! Watch me. Do it like this.'

They tried their best to keep up, but she just had no idea how talented a dancer she was and they simply couldn't keep up. Finally she waved her hands and said unkindly, 'You'll never get it.'

So she twirled into Darrix's hands and everything was going just fine until a dancer moved closer than she expected, and they locked heals and both tripped over.

Allastassia was up in an instant, the air twingling dangerously around her as her hands lit with arcane lightning in her rage. The other student cringed on the ground, and everyone froze.

That was when Kialessa noticed Natasha. Always standing next to the stage with the rest of the choir, her hand was pressed to her dress, right where her holy symbol would be. Kialessa had known the paralysing numbness that would overcome Natasha's foes when she'd used that faith in combat training. Her eyes flicked towards the stage wings, where Kialessa now noticed Federach already had her hand by her sword hip – even if real weapons were forbidden outside combat training.

A terrible lump formed in Kialessa's throat, and she dreaded what might be about to happen.

'Allastassia?' Darrix asked her.

Suddenly all the tension disappeared. Allastassia dismissed her lightning and smiled encouraging at them all. 'Not to matter. Come on, let's keep going!' Her voice was light and happy, but nobody else said anything. The music started up again, and some dancers began to move, but a moment later the student ran from the stage, his dancing partner calling after him. Allastassia ignored it.

Kialessa couldn't sing after that, but she watched closely. The rest of the dance went well, and the music stopped to announce the arrival of the demon. Federach, predictably, missed her cue so it looked a bit poor. She was supposed to slay three people dramatically with her demon vision, to the horrified and synchronised screams of all present. But instead she just ran on and touched them on the shoulders proclaiming: 'You're dead, you're dead, you're dead.' And they all fell to the floor in a scattered heap while students squealed uncoordinatedly.

Allastassia was clearly angry, but tried her best not to look it.

The demon proclaimed its "undying love" for the princess, who denied it, and then it shrieked in rage. Except Federach's shriek was more like a groan. Then Federach declared,

'Peace forever will be denied,
From my love you cannot hide,
Each day a loved one will be slain,
Until my prisoner you remain.'

And Darrix boldly proclaimed;

'Touch her not, you fiend of hell!
Speak not of love, you cannot tell,
A prisoner of her you shall not make,
A prisoner you are, of your own mistake.'

'You cannot force a love so true,
But choose to love, and soon will you,
Find love again, but not through this;
To force a love and steal a kiss.'

Federach stood there a moment till she remembered to hiss.

'She will be mine, oh, you will see,
For this written, in destiny…'

So Darrix charged Federach who attempted to disarm him with a motion so clumsy he had to drop his sword deliberately, while Allastassia clicked her disdain.

And the rehearsal continued downhill from there.

*****

Allastassia buried her face in her hands. 'Why is it going all wrong?' she muttered.

For her part, Kialessa was just glad nobody was throwing lightning around.

'Oh, don't worry, old buddy,' Flower said with a grin that couldn't quite hide her tension. 'It's always like this on the first rehearsal. And the one just before performance night – chaos – trust me! It all works out on the night. Always!'

Kialessa could tell it was serious. Only the six of them were there. Allastassia had called a quick break, and pulled them aside to lay out her fears.

Posk, it seemed, was particularly concerned about Allastassia. He'd even gone so far as to bring her a pair of her shoes.

'I don't think you need to worry so much, Alli. You're stressing everybody out,' Flower promised.

'But they're hopeless!' she cried, while pushing aside the handful of ribbons Posk had now brought.

Darrix smiled, giving her his best friend one armed hug. 'Calm down, **princess**. You're not working with professionals. The audience will know it, you will see. They'll laugh along, and call it cute. Like Federach-'

'Oh! Allastassia groaned. 'She is the *worst!* I don't know what the ringmaster saw in her. I still think you'd make a better demon Kialessa.'

'No, **thank you**!' Kialessa asserted.

'And Patsi! Why is she ignoring her lines!'

'Actually, Allastassia,' Darrix tried to tell her, 'maybe Patsi is trying to tell you something. She's pretty good, when you aren't measuring things against perfection. Clever, very trusting, quick to improvise. I know she isn't taking it so seriously, but maybe that's because she's trying to tell you to calm down. We're only young.'

Posk held out a bouquet of flowers to her that he'd picked himself, roots and all. He smiled broadly.

Allastassia huffed, and pushing the flowers away seemed to agree with Darrix. 'All right. Fair enough. I can ease off. But at least there is one problem I know I can deal with right now. Piex: give Posk your wizardry headband.'

Special Training

Can you be generous to a friend in need? Then you have done a kindly deed. But can you be kind to an unworthy friend? Then you are a true friend, right to the end.
The Irrefutable Sage of Venterrin.

Piex looked up in pale fright. 'No!' he muttered in misery, as though he was fighting a battle he knew he'd already lost. 'I need my headband, it's so important to me!'

But Allastassia was not to be dissuaded. And when it came down to it, Piex was one of those people she always got her way with.

'Don't be selfish,' she said, perhaps a bit hypocritically. 'Posk needs it more than you, right now. You can use the old hat. Besides you're not casting any spells, so what's the problem?'

Piex didn't have words.

'Alli,' Darrix cautioned her.

'Besides,' Allastassia argued, 'we need Posk to do this or the play will just look stupid.'

     By Dr Joseph Ireland "Dr Joe"

'If he doesn't want to, he shouldn't have to,' Kialessa defended Piex.

'No, no, it's all right,' Piex suddenly agreed. 'I don't mind, just so long as he doesn't break it.

'Do we even have the wizard's permission-' Darrix began.

'Don't be such a stick-in-the mud,' Allastassia ordered him. 'Besides, he'll only use it in rehearsals. No one will know.' And with that she ripped off the hat on Posk's head and placed on the headband that Piex had already given her.

Posk dropped the flowerpot he was carrying. Kialessa wasn't sure why he was carrying a flowerpot, but it was probably another gift for Allastassia.

As soon as the headband went on, the change in Posk was much more noticeable this time. He stood up straight, like a normal human, not slouching so that his fists touched the ground as he usually did. He was actually quite tall, almost as tall as Darrix. Then he blinked twice.

'Allastassia.' Posk said, clean and calm. 'You… want … me… to lift…?' his voice was clear, but slow and halting.

Kialessa's mouth fell open in amazement; Posk was using sentences!

'Oh, this is going to be good!' Allastassia gleamed, and grabbing Posk by his huge half troll hand, ran back towards the rehearsal.

For rest of the evening, whenever they got the chance between practicing, all anyone could do was ask Posk questions.

'What's your favourite food?' Patsi drilled him.

'I enjoy… meat, with gravy,' he announced. It was no surprise.

'Who do you think is the greatest warrior of all time?' Federach asked.

Posk said nothing for a moment, and then cunningly replied, 'Tomin, the paladin.' They all agreed, but Kialessa suddenly got the thought that Tomin couldn't be Posk's favourite warrior; he clearly didn't like Posk at all. Perhaps Posk was just aiming for the answer that he knew would please others, which was a kind of unexpected clever she'd never though Posk was capable of.

'Which girl do you like the most?' Natasha teased.

Posk just smiled at Kialessa, but then looked long at Allastassia practicing her dance on the stage. She had already lost interest in the half troll gimmick.

'***Beautiful*** Allastassia,' he dreamily replied.

They exploded in laughter, but Posk didn't seem to mind. Allastassia stopped her dancing to see what was going on, and saw Posk staring right up at her.

She stormed off stage.

Posk smiled. 'She will… be back.' The laughing died down, but Posk still spoke. 'She will always … return to the stage,' he proclaimed.

No one laughed now. His obvious affection for Allastassia was almost… adult. He was being serious.

Kialessa didn't need to see to know Allastassia was listening. It seemed amazing to Kialessa that the curtains didn't burst into flames right there and then.

***

That evening no one dared bring up the issue of Posk with Allastassia. That he liked her was cute, almost comical. That she thought so very little of him made it no laughing matter. The one-time Patsi did ***think*** about teasing her Allastassia's hands sizzled with a touch of lightning on their own once more. No one dared bring it up again.

But Kialessa didn't have time to consider that now. It was evening, and the ringmaster had narrowed the group for "special training" down to just a handful. It was elite gymnastics training.

Kialessa watched in silent wonder.

The ringmaster arched her back so far Kialessa thought it might actually snap. Then she cartwheeled backwards on a single rope. She turned half again, did a one-armed handstand, and held it there.

Then she appeared to fall off, but never letting go of the rope she pulled herself back up again, did a double front flip, and landed on the rope once more.

Everyone cheered.

All five of them.

There was a thin human boy from the senior class, and a female gnome. The other girl was the daughter of an elven ambassador, and she was only staying for three years in Lenmer'el.

Then there was Kialessa, and she couldn't escape the feeling that the only reason she was here was because she had such good balance. And the only reason she had such good balance, was because she had a tail.

'We have so little time,' the ringmaster said as she stood without apparent effort on the rope. 'The training that the other students will receive is standard. But you four, I have seen I may expect even more. You will learn to catch your enemies' knives. You will learn to dance on a thread, and slip your way through the eye of a needle. There is magic in this world, and it serves wizard as well as enchanter. But neither seem to appreciate the magic of the circus!' she said, and from nowhere, breathed fire.

They clapped in awe.

'We train 'till midnight, every night. Let us begin.'

Dreamdancer & Shadow Weaver

*Have you ever noticed that wherever you are; that's where you are? This simple fact **fascinates** me.*
Humdug, dwarf scholar.

Kialessa stumbled toward the dormitory late at night once more. Circus training was **much** harder than battle training! For reasons of her own the ringmaster seemed to take extra delight in training Kialessa. She kept calling her talented, and special. It was nice, but it was very hard work.

She had to knock on the dormitory door to be let in, and it seemed the night watchman was happy to take all the time in the world to assist her. He looked bothered that it had all been for a tae'anaryn, or a student, there was no real way to tell.

She stretched out her aching arms, grateful that tomorrow

          By Dr Joseph Ireland "Dr Joe"

was Serrosday, praying she'd have the strength to wake up on time and get to the shrine again.

She tiptoed along the rows of silent, sleeping students, envious of their chance to rest. So she was surprised to find one of them standing, wide awake, in the moonlight.

It was Allastassia.

A bright beam from Lumos' waxing crescent flooded into the high western window of the girl's dormitory. Allastassia stood there, gently glowing with blue energy. Tiny specks of dust, glittering radiantly, slowly danced around her. Under her feet the wood glowed so brightly it looked to be made of silver.

'Allastassia?' Kialessa asked.

The enchantress said nothing.

A solemn fear settled on Kialessa. Was Allastassia really awake, or sleepwalking?

Or was this whole image a dream?

Kialessa approached her, the air softly twingling with the unshaped magic that flowed around her silent friend.

'Alli?' she said, and reached out to touch her.

Allastassia turned, and Kialessa gasped when she saw her face; her two eyes inhuman orbs of silver-blue. She spoke, saying something confusing, in a firm commanding voice. But it was all in a language Kialessa had never heard before.

Suddenly the room shifted and smeared, then disappeared altogether. Kialessa found herself standing with Allastassia on a platform of white metal, written over with circular runes of arcane mystery. They were in a clearing, in a forest of some kind. But the trees were strange to Kialessa, their trunks white.

Kialessa was terrified. Something was wrong. How was Allastassia doing this? Or was it her at all. 'Allastassia. Where have you taken me?' she said. 'We aren't supposed to be here.' She couldn't help but whisper, she didn't know what was out there, and the place felt sacred. She felt like they were being watched.

Allastassia lifted her arm, and a steel rod appeared in her

hand. She pointed it at Kialessa, and spoke again.

Kialessa didn't know what she wanted, but found she would have preferred Allastassia was holding lightning back in the safety of the king's college once more.

Allastassia waited and the scene shifted. They were in a huge cavern, with magnificent buildings made from blue-grey stone. They were very beautiful, but still so different to anything Kialessa had ever seen before. The enchantress pointed, and Kialessa looked to find a building. Before it was an impossibly large statue of an extremely beautiful woman, made entirely of silver. She was holding a book. Kialessa had the distinct impression that she had seen this woman before, she looked so familiar.

Yet the entire underground hall was completely, absolutely silent.

Despite her fear, she felt her curiosity tingling at the edge of her mind. 'Allastassia, where are we?'

She turned her head, a sudden mist surrounding them. The next moment they were standing on the water, in a massive and placid lake. Their feet left silent ripples that disturbed the otherwise perfectly flat surface.

It was nowhere that she knew, and she did not feel safe.

Allastassia spoke her strange language again.

Kialessa felt her eyes tearing up, 'Why are you doing this, Allastassia? Where are we?' Suddenly Kialessa had a sinking feeling she knew where they were. 'You brought me to the dream world, didn't you?'

Kialessa reached out for someone she knew often came here, and never had trouble getting back. Her almost brother, Kiel.

But one look on Allastassia's face told Kialessa she was wrong.

They weren't in the dream world, which left the very real chance that they were somewhere … actual.

Allastassia lowered the rod that she seemed to be offering Kialessa, and slowly looked up. Without knowing why, Kialessa looked up too.

There, hovering in the sky, was an orb, an impossibly massive ball. It was blue, and green, and covered in clouds. Kialessa had no idea what it was, but she sensed a definite, godlike power from the sphere. It was terrifying.

She screamed, 'Alli! Get us out of here, I want to leave here now!'

There was a loud thump, and Kialessa turned to see what it was. For a distinct moment she was profoundly disoriented, it was just another student climbing from their bed. It took Kialessa a moment to realise she was lying in her own bed. She was back in the dorm and everything was exactly the way it should be.

Allastassia had sent her back into the dormitory of the girls, and thrown her on to her bed.

Jumping up she ran to Allastassia's bed. Stumbling, almost falling, so desperate was she to see if Allastassia was all right. She was not in her bed.

'Kia, you all right?' another student asked.

Kialessa was about to burst out the entire story when she heard Allastassia's voice from the bathroom. Ignoring her still aching muscles Kialessa ran, only to find the auburn enchantress calmly chatting to two other students while brushing down her long, curling hair.

'Ooh, hey Kialessa. Sleep well? I know I did,' she said, not sparing more than a glance at her.

It had all seemed so real. Kialessa looked down at her hands. Then out at the moon that glinted dimly in the morning sky. There were so many unanswered questions. But one thing she was sure of from an entire year of experiencing strange things: That was no dream.

***

Kialessa waited. Allastassia denied the whole experience, and no one seemed to care if they believed her. In the end, Kialessa's head was hurting from wondering if it had even happened at all.

A day later it was lunch time, and for Kialessa that meant it was somewhere between thinking about the morning academics, and thinking about the afternoon manual arts. In a sense, it was time to not think at all.

She sat by the steps, Piex beside her, his nose buried in a book he'd probably read a dozen times before. Allastassia was sitting with some of her other friends, quite close this time, but Kialessa wasn't listening to what they were saying.

'What do you think, Kialessa?' Allastassia's voice suddenly brought her back to reality.

She was standing with Flower, and they were expecting some kind of answer.

'I'm sorry, what was that?' Kialessa had to ask them.

Flower answered, 'Allastassia just wanted to know what that cute castle guard's name is.'

'No I did not!' Allastassia grinned. 'You did!'

'You started it,' Flower shouted with a smile. 'Anyway, look. I was wondering if you'd mind sneaking over there and listening in to their conversation. Maybe see if you can get his name?'

Kialessa didn't know what to say. Why would Allastassia want a guard's name? And why did it matter if he was "cute" – whatever that meant; she was part tree, after all. And what was this about asking her to sneak around again, why did people always ask her to do that?

'I'm not going to sneak off. Why don't you just ask him?'

They giggled, 'We can't *ask* him, Kialessa.'

That made no sense at all. Did she like him, perhaps? Was it another silly game?

'Well I'm not going to sneak off and do it.'

'Oh,' Flower begged. 'You're just so good at it! Nobody

would even notice if you started to sneak off right here, Kialessa.'

'Actually,' Allastassia, told her, 'it's quite easy to tell when Kialessa is planning to slink off.'

'Really, I never can tell,' Darrix seemed to have joined the conversation.

'Truly? Haven't you noticed? She goes all dark around the edges, like she's weaving shadows or something,' Allastassia told them.

'Whatever do you mean?' Kialessa wondered out loud. She had no idea what the enchantress was talking about.

'Oh, that, yes. I've seen that,' Piex suddenly lifted his head out of his book.

'What?' Kialessa had to ask. This was all news to her. About this point Posk scurried past chasing a ball someone had thrown, panting with delight. They ignored him.

'Like when you cower in battle training against the senior students. I thought you'd know? You turn down the light around you and blend perfectly into darkness.'

Kialessa could not believe what she was hearing. 'I *what*?!"

'Oh, that!' Darrix agreed, 'Yes, didn't you know Kialessa? I figured you were aware or, if not, it was more important that you weren't consciously aware of it. We learn about that in sword fighting at times, to go beyond awareness and trust to instinct. But it's out in the open now so I suppose we might as well tell you: you have quite literally been wrapping yourself in shadows every time you've tried to hide.'

'What?! How did I not notice this!'

'I guess you were just distracted,' Piex offered.

She had hoped for something more intellectual, especially from him. "Not notice?" how does one not notice the way shadows act around them? 'Are you folks kidding me? You're kidding me, right?'

They all looked at her as if they didn't know what to say.

'Kialessa, you're a shadow weaver,' Allastassia announced.

It was a good thing she was sitting down. This was crazy talk.

'Look, I'll prove it,' Piex offered. He grabbed her hand, and held it just above the ground. Then he took his own, and placed it right next to hers. It was partway in the sunlight, and partway in the shadow of the steps.

'See? Notice how your shadow is deeper than mine? That's not possible to explain by the movement of light alone.'

It was, she could see it, but she still didn't feel it proved anything.

Allastassia knelt beside her. 'Shadow weavers are a form of enchantress, Kia. I don't think it'd be a surprise to any of us to see you use enchantments – most tae'anaryl can. Look at your shadow. Can you see it?'

'Yes.'

'Now, make it grow. Just imagine it stretching out, if you can, pull it up from the ground.'

That did sound crazy, 'How?'

'It's *easy*! So easy, maybe even too easy! You just have to want it to, to wish it. Almost, just… let it. That's how I do all my enchantments.'

'Really?' Kialessa asked her.

Allastassia looked a little concerned. 'All right, no, it's not all.' Allastassia sat down, drawing them all close. 'Listen, everyone… what I have to tell you I don't want you to tell anyone all right? It's an enchantress's secret.'

'I swear,' Piex promised.

'I agree,' Darrix said.

Flower's eyes glowed – not literally, she just looked really interested.

Allastassia nodded. 'I know I make it look easy, Kialessa, and sometimes it is, it really is. But we enchanters want everyone to think it's easy. That way, they don't realise what it takes. Sure, there's talent. But it's a little more than that. You need to spend an hour every morning, at least… imagining. Do you

 By Dr Joseph Ireland "Dr Joe"

understand? Really *vividly* imagine what you want to have happening. You know how I like to brush my hair every morning?'

Everyone did, 'Yeah, for like… an hour.' The realisation began to dawn on Kialessa when Allastassia was finding time to meditate each day.

Allastassia went on, 'And you know, like, how I hate being interrupted.'

Kialessa nodded. Very few things were more terrifying than Allastassia getting interrupted from her morning preening.

'It's because I'm focusing, enchantress style. I'm completely lost in my imagination at the time! What I do is I like to vividly, powerfully, imagine the kinds of magic I'd like to be able to do that day. If I skip a day the power isn't as great the next, and I really think if I never meditated I'd lose the magic all together, well, almost.'

'Really?' Piex almost gasped.

'Truly,' Allastassia replied.

'Then you *do* work on your magic!' he triumphed.

She shook her finger at him, 'But you can't tell anyone, remember!'

He looked sad, like it was a promise he really didn't want to keep. But she knew he would anyway. He may be a little foolish at times, but he did keep his promises exceptionally well.

'Thank you,' Allastassia continued. 'And if I know we're going to need a certain magic for the day, I focus on that enchantment. And I go over it again and again in my mind until I can see it happening all around me, like… inside me. Till my skin tingles with the power and I-'

'Hey,' Piex interrupted, 'that's what wizardry feels like.'

Allastassia looked confused, and maybe just a little incredulous, 'I thought you just used words and books.'

'We do, but it's to get the magic *inside*. You need to feel it before it happens.'

'Well, interesting,' Allastassia admitted.

Kialessa looked at her hand, and wondered what it could do. What she could do with the shadows.

'All you need to do,' Allastassia said, 'is picture what you want to have happen. If it's too much, you won't feel the magic in your soul. If it's too little, it is just boring, try wrapping yourself up in shadows.'

'Won't I look like a big black blob?' Kialessa wondered.

'Only if that's what you picture it like,' Allastassia said.

'When I see you hiding,' Darrix explained, 'you just blend right in. It's like there's no Kialessa anymore, just shadows. I know you're still there and I can see you when you move, but your form blends so perfectly into the shadows it's really hard to make it out. Sometimes the shadow isn't even really dark, you just… blend in. Try wrapping yourself in shadows and see how it feels.'

'You don't suppose,' Kialessa wondered, 'that shadow weaving is, you know, a little bit evil?'

'What?' Piex asked, then returned to his book while still speaking. 'Not at all, each element serves its role in Creation.'

'Besides,' Darrix said, 'there is no more evil in shadow than evil can hide within the light.' It sounded like scripture but Kialessa didn't know where she'd heard it from.

She decided to give it a go.

And nothing happened.

'Don't be discouraged,' Allastassia said. 'Enchantments take practice. Oh, I wonder if you can get off a good sleep enchantment? They're quite easy, well, quite easy for me. Most people are never far from sleep.'

'Oh, can you teach me to *see* magic!' Kialessa begged, looking at both Piex and the enchantress.

'Sure, but let's focus on shadow first, since you're naturally very good at it.' Allastassia told her. 'Besides, you've seen Piex do it dozens of times, I'm sure he can show you. Just don't listen to any of his words or they'll mess things up.'

Piex protested.

 By Dr Joseph Ireland "Dr Joe"

'Just listen to the magic tell you what it wants to be. You'll be an amazing enchantress one day Kialessa, I just know it!'

***

Shadow weaving, her first enchantment! Kialessa was very excited. All she needed was some time to practice and meditate alone.

And that, it seemed, was a magic she didn't have.

Over the next few days, she tried to get into the "zone" while she was brushing her hair, but everyone was so busy and distracting. She would have gladly gone for a walk but there was simply no time for that in the morning while everyone was preparing for study. Maybe she needed to get up just after the full moon like Darrix did so that he could pray, and then clean the horses, but there was no bringing herself to get by on so little sleep!

And as soon as the lessons started there were things to be learned. For the next two days everything seemed to rush on from one thing to the next, and she never found more than two moments to focus on her weaving. She thought she might have managed to get her shadow to move a little, but it was difficult to tell.

She was just beginning to think she might *never* have the time. It was during a very boring lesson on local lore and she was sitting in her usual seat at the back of the class, and her thoughts began to drift away. She was imagining what it might be like to be a real shadow, able to forge weapons of pure darkness to use against her enemies. To hide so perfectly in the night that no assassin would see her until it was far too late for them, to find the hidden monsters in the dark and reveal them.

Then a fellow student gave an alarmed little, 'Eek!'

Kialessa's mind snapped back to the present, and she found that every student within arm's reach was leaning, or in some cases standing up well away from her. Instead, all around her, shadows had grown up from every corner and under her chair, twisting around her in beautiful patterns of curling darkness. Shadows grew from her arms and hair, and as she waved her hand through them, they twisted about her fingers.

Then, because she didn't really want to get into trouble for not paying attention, or terrify any of the humans who hated her even more, she wished the shadows away. They disappeared like mist melting in the daylight.

She smiled, but the group looked back at her with wide eyed terror. Clearly, her friends didn't think there was anything innately evil in Kialessa's shadows, but these students did.

Then there were footsteps as Allastassia walked right up to her, and gave her a big, friendly hug right in front of them. 'Good,' she announced. 'You've been practicing what I taught you. Keep it up!' she said in a cheery voice, and walking back to her seat simply sat back down and looked ready to pay full attention to the lesson.

'Perhaps... you may practice your shadow weaving... in your own time?' the tutor suggested.

'Yes, sir. Sorry sir,' Kialessa whispered, hoping she wouldn't get slate duty again.

She didn't, but it would have been worth it.

***

Soon after she realised she could practice any time she wanted, whenever nothing much else was happening. And for her the best time was not when she was brushing her hair.

It was when she was dancing – during special training, or during lunchtime breaks. She seemed to have to keep moving to assist the magic to find her. It was, she thought, simply enchanting.

 By Dr Joseph Ireland "Dr Joe"

Improvisation & Fire

You will see, the greatest things in life aren't prepared for, they're lived.
Flower, the circus performer, 313 CY.

The next rehearsal for the play wasn't much of an improvement. People continued stalling things, and Allastassia didn't seem to want to go on until every previous step was perfect. It was beginning to really grind on everyone's nerves, when Flower suddenly stopped the rehearsal.

'Right!' she shouted in great command, and everyone stopped still and silent. 'Troupe meeting, NOW!'

People gathered around her, in a wide circle. So Flower began to dance. It was pretty, but simple. Then she sang,

'A tale so long, a tale so true!
A tale worth telling to all of you!
Reach up, reach out, give them your best,
Keep all the best and forget all the rest!
It doesn't need to be perfect, it only need be,
And that is the best kind of art to me.

Sing to the people, sing to the mothers,
Sing to the children, the sisters and brothers,
Don't worry so much that it isn't all right.
Because that's not what they'll remember tonight.'

She paused, a moment, thinking.

'They won't remember the dancing, or the prince's fine steel,
All they'll remember; is how you all made them all feel.
*It doesn't **need** to be perfect, it only need **be**,*
And that is the best kind of art for me.'

Everyone clapped, and Flower bowed.

'That was divine!' Patsi congratulated her.

'Where did you learn that!' Natasha asked.

Flower waited till everyone was listening again. 'I didn't learn that. I made it up as I went along.'

Allastassia gasped audibly, and even Federach looked impressed.

'Made it up?!' Piex whispered as though he didn't believe it.

'Yes, made it up! On the fly, on the wing!' Flower spread her arms with her enormous smile. 'Without preparation, without perfection. But that's ART, that's life itself! You're all losing the very spirit of this project. It's *imperfection*. You will see, the greatest things in life aren't prepared for, they're lived. You have to live this play anew every time you perform it or nobody will believe it.'

'It's supposed to be a certain way, director,' Federach argued.

'No it isn't. Chaos, random chance. These are your truest friends on the stage. How people see you react to what you didn't expect is what makes one a master artist, not consistency in every single act.'

　　　　By Dr Joseph Ireland "Dr Joe"

She paused before continuing her little lecture, 'It's all right to be wrong in the mess that is real life, and it's all right to make a mess in a play about life as well. You will see… every audience is different. Most of them have never seen the play before. And they will tell you, in how they cheer, and gasp, and even in their silence what kind of experience they need to have on the night. You need to learn to go with that, to trust your intuition *and* your experience. Perfect practice makes perfect, it is true, but when you're in the moment, when you're among their wishes and hopes and fears, simply be. Know when to… improvise.'

She let her words sink in.

'I don't know what you mean,' Patsi complained.

'Watch: no two performances will ever be the same anyway, so let each performance simply be what it is becoming. Make do with every accident and make it a part of the performance. Trust your instinct, be real with your audience, and for gosh sakes have some fun with this! Leave "perfection" to the wizards, this is art!'

The chorus members went away mumbling, but Allastassia called a restart to the practice and started from the beginning.

It was still a mess, but it was a gorgeous mess. Only Allastassia had any dependable talent at improvisation – when a stagehand knocked over a potted plant in the middle of her sentence she turned, looked at it, and while remaining completely in character said, 'What, is this kingdom falling down around us already!' Nobody could keep a straight face with a joke like that.

And to Kialessa, the rehearsals started going a little smoother from about that point on.

***

Fire is beautiful, Kialessa thought.

'These salts are expensive, and rare,' the ringmaster told her. 'And their potential for magic is not to be underestimated. But sometimes it's just worth it.' And with that, she threw the thin powder into the fire around Kialessa's hand.

And to her delight, the fire turned from bright orange to deep green.

She had been using the wizardry *finger fire* that Piex had taught her in Tobiuus's tower last season, and now Flower was trying to get her to use it as part of some act she was still putting together. They were still training late into the night, but at least she was used to it now. Kialessa found she was getting better at wizardry too, and never felt drained afterwards. And when she had the time, she still tried to sneak a peek at everything Piex was reading.

'I can't tell you how useful it is that you already know some magic, Kialessa.' Flower gushed. 'First shadow weaving, now I learn you can make your own fire! What fun we're going to have with this!'

Kialessa couldn't help but share in her squeal of delight. It was so easy to like this strange, enthusiastic, actor.

A man approached them. It was Chéri, Flower's father. 'Calm yourselves little ones, else how are you going to contain yourselves if I show you this!'

He pulled a ribbon from behind his back, and Flower squealed again as soon as she recognised it. The old man spun it around him in a very dainty fashion, puckering his lips in a wildly implausible imitation of a woman.

'Daddy, show!' Flower danced, seeming to forget how to speak.

Chéri twisted the ribbon and held the handle out in front of them. 'The hilt is hollow, filled with an oil that burns easily and draws readily. See how the ribbon has this main channel here? It allows the oil to fill the length of the ribbon. As soon as you set fire to it you get about four moments of solid flame. We never used it without gloves as it gets quite hot, and our last girl gave herself a nasty burn trying to be too clever with it. But as *this* is a girl that does not burn, as long as you keep it far away from the hay at the edge of the ring, I'm sure you'll be all right!'

Flower shoved the ribbon into Kialessa's hands. 'And you can ignite it on your own magic! Show us, Kialessa, make a dance for us?'

Kialessa found it was getting easier to be spontaneous in Flowers presence, and so spun around in a tuneless dance.

'Now, bring the fire!' Flower begged.

'*Ignis didgitis!*' she proclaimed, and to her delight the fire raced down the ribbon and filled the air around her.

Flower squealed, and leapt back, dancing with enthusiasm.

Kialessa swirled and moved in the flames, and they too seemed willing to move at her will, or if they did not, they could burn neither her nor her armour. It was the perfect dance for her, but it could only last four moments.

'That was magical!' Flower smiled, 'do a plié, oh, can you do a backflip? No one will be expecting that!'

Kialessa smiled, Flower had been trying to teach them all backflips but it was never as easy as she made it look. It would take more practice.

'I really wish-' Flower began, but stopped dead as a man's voice bellowed from the end of the circus tent.

It was one of the royal guards, speaking to the circus performers at the door.

'He's looking for you,' Flower said, looking worried.

Kialessa was surprised, she was used to having a very good sense of hearing, but it seemed Flower exceeded her at this as well.

Kialessa offered the ribbon back to Chéri, but he indicated she should keep it. Flower showed her how to roll it up while the soldier approached.

'Kialessa the tae'anaryn,' the man announced. He was tall, with a moustache, and looking to be in his late forties, which was as old as most healthy non-nobles' humans got in life.

She nodded; there was no possible way she could be anyone else, and wondered why he felt the need to announce it.

'High Captain Bon Shur'e requires your presence immediately.'

Flower gasped, and Kialessa felt a twinge of fear. Why would the king's highest-ranking bodyguard and general of the entire army be asking for her? Personally? Late at night after most other students were getting ready for bed? Was there trouble about? Was she in trouble again?

'Can I come?' Flower asked, seeming to see Kialessa's nervousness.

The guard looked dubious, but nodded. It was tradition to travel to formal meetings with a companion.

Flower grinned broadly, but Kialessa was still very nervous. Why would the captain be asking for her, at this hour?

　　　By Dr Joseph Ireland "Dr Joe"

To Faraway Places

A sword is only a curse. It cannot be used to heal, only harm, and in harming I pray you will use it only to protect. I am sorry to lay this burden on you.
Bon Shur'e, High captain of Lenmer'el.

Following the guard in silence through the city within the castle walls, he led them toward the keep itself, through the great hall that Kialessa had seen only once when she'd been the guest of honour for saving the king's life. The guard took them down an unnecessarily narrow, winding staircase to the dungeons underneath.

There, within a large room supported by numerous stone archways they found the captain. He looked to be relaxing at a heavy wooden table, filled with maps and military orders. The table itself held a detailed model of their country, with small models probably like toy soldiers dotted around the countryside. The guard stopped them before she could get a good look, and the captain moved to block their view.

'Dame Kialessa,' the captain smiled, with a small,

professional bow, 'and the acrobat. Where's that minotaur you're never without?'

'My manservant, Ugly, is tending the circus beasts at this hour I expect.'

'Quiet type, isn't he.'

'He … was rejected from his people as a child, and has taken an oath of silence.'

Kialessa tried not to look surprised. Why was this story always changing?

The captain shrugged as though it was not important. 'You trust her?' he said to Kialessa.

She nodded furiously, glad someone was here with her, but just a little sorry it wasn't someone like Darrix. He was much more at home among soldiers covered in metal suits. The captain seemed very much at ease, but Kialessa still didn't know why she was here.

He smiled, laying a hand on the hilt of one of the many axes he seemed to always need to carry. 'Calm yourself, little tae'anaryn. The king has another gift for you.'

She must have looked very surprised, for the captain laughed again. He motioned for the soldier to follow them, and another armoured page whose job it seemed to be to carry keys. He was a very fit looking page.

The captain spoke as they went along, through dark corridors she had never seen before. 'Word spreads quickly in a little town such as this, dame Kialessa. We understand you are a shadow weaver. The high priestess was greatly disappointed, she was sure you were a dreamwalker, but not to worry,' he laughed again.

After passing a locked gate the captain continued. 'The king has always expressed a certain measure of regret that you were armoured, but not armed, among his gifts to you. But none of us could agree what you should wield! Little matter, you are too young anyway. But since you have demonstrated the gift of shadow weaving we realised this might give us a unique

          By Dr Joseph Ireland "Dr Joe"

opportunity, and so it might be better for you to choose your own weapon.'

Moving through another iron grate the page unlocked, the captain choosing to fill their silence, 'Have you received the *Nocte Tenebrosi* yet? The wizard was instructed to let you have it. It's a book, you see. An old one too, quite a kingly price. I think we only have sections of the original from the library at Emerel. It describes a potential of shadow weavers to pass through the shadowrealm within an instant. Did you know this?'

She shook her head, while Flower listened in silence. The acrobat's feet made next to no sound as she followed quietly along.

The captain continued, 'Well, as we understand it if you take a familiar object or place, such as a chest or cupboard, and fill it with shadows, it not only becomes impossible for non-weavers to see within, but you are apparently able to take items from said cupboard from any point in the realm, or even on the world. Or so I'm told.'

Flower looked over at her with great excitement.

The captain laughed. 'I've sent an artisan to replace the lock on the chest at the foot of your bed, Kialessa. Oh, here's the key.' He waved to the page who handed her a small silver key. 'And had that new wizard, what's his name... Marchan do up a sealing enchantment for you. It needed to be a familiar object to you, Kialessa.'

'Thank you,' Kialessa said.

'Don't thank me, just doing my job,' he replied.

They had arrived at a huge metal door, embedded in the stonework with dwarven precision; there was not so much as a hair's breadth between the door and its way. 'But if you want to call a weapon to hand, my young enchantress, they tell me it takes a weapon already forged in magic. Rather than go to the expense of forging a new one, the king requires I give you one that sees little use. Do you know where we are?'

Kialessa shook her head.

'You say so little,' the captain appeared to complain, then smiled. 'Good. You will go far. This is the king's armoury. The most heavily defended trove of weapons in all the land. I doubt you will ever be here more than once.'

They waited in silence.

'Umm,' Flower asked.

The guard laughed.

'We have to wait till the hour. The door only opens once each night, to prevent theft. Go on, you can try it if you like.'

Kialessa didn't move. She was not about to test the magical defences of her king's trove.

But Flower shrugged, jumped up, and began hauling at the great wheel that stood in the centre of the door.

The captain looked amused, till the wheel gave a metallic screech and moved around a hand width. Then he looked decidedly nervous.

'It seems stuck!' Flower protested.

The captain reached out and hauled the handle all the way around, and the door popped slightly ajar.

'Thanks for that,' Flower said.

The captain looked worried.

'Five moments early, I make it,' the page said with a concerned look on his face. 'Perhaps it is the presence of the tae'anaryn?'

The captain looked at her accusingly. 'If so, then clearly the gods approve of her being here. Oh well, not to worry, let's go in!'

He smiled, but to Kialessa's eyes his face bore a very real worry. She had no doubt but that the king would know of Flower's ability to open magical doors before the hour.

The room within was large, but had a very low roof. The stones were cut so well that there appeared to be no seams between them. Within was lit with magical torches that gave no heat, but never went down. And within was an orderly array of fully laden weapon racks, cabinets and trophy stands.

      By Dr Joseph Ireland "Dr Joe"

There would have to be more than a hundred weapons in there. It was a trove indeed.

'Well, don't stand idly looking on. In, girl, and choose yourself a weapon!' The captain shoved them in.

'How?' Kialessa asked.

The captain laughed, 'Take any that capture your fancy, pray if you must. Just… make sure it's one you can handle.'

She looked among the rows and rows of weapons, all of them made for adult warriors. Axes, and swords, how she hated swords! Spears, far too large to be useful. Most glowed with clear magical powers. And most were just too large.

'What about these?' Flower asked. She was standing by a small, glass topped cabinet.

Within there were a curious selection of weapons, the page explaining each as she looked them over carefully. Six knives as a matching set, each with a different hilt of pearl. 'Traded from the sharkmen of the Bounteous Shallowsea, capable of cutting the hardened armour of even the blackfish.' A curved blade with a sandstone handle, 'A gift from a blithling king for training his son for a season. It can turn into sand and back again at will, it is told.' A black, straight, narrow, double edged blade with green runes down the side, 'A present from a dwarven lady, it imbues its strikes with the power of earth and acid.'

There were more, but Kialessa's attention was caught on that pretty green dagger.

The captain stopped the talking and instructed the page to unlock the cabinet. The old man took the blade from the soft felt, sheathing of its dark scabbard.

'You've an eye for quality,' the captain said. 'Amburg work, from the north, near the *Feuerdrache*. Even a scratch will leave a painful reminder.'

Kialessa smiled.

'This is not a blessing, young Tae'anaryn,' the captain said, brow furrowed and looking very serious. 'A sword is only a curse. It cannot be used to heal, only harm, and in harming I pray you will use it only to protect. I am sorry to lay this burden on you. '

Kialessa nodded.

But the captain grinned, 'You've chosen well, young one. Now, let us take you to see the wizard.'

***

It was a great relief to see that Piex was up, again, in a late-night study session with the wizard.

'Kialessa?' he said with disbelief as soon as he saw her, and Flower, approaching with the captain. The page and other attendants had left them, and she carried the short sword, or long dagger, depending on one's point of view, in both hands. It was, to be honest, a little large. But its narrow blade was unyielding, covered in glowing green runes that were simply enchanting.

She curtsied to Piex, as much in play, as to an honoured wizard's apprentice. Piex would have said more, but looked to his master for his cue.

The old wizard looked at the dagger in Kialessa's hands with respect and understanding. 'The Dwarven Lady's gift, a wise choice, and one I admit I did not foresee. But an excellent choice; the earth elements will help you stay grounded with the great power fate intends for you, and the acidic enhancements will sting at your enemies. Let me assure you, a simple scratch from this blade will dissuade many a foe. A wise choice, dame Kialessa.'

'Thank you, Gentle,' Kialessa bowed with all her respect.

The captain moved forward. 'Now is as good a time as any.'

The old elf sighed, 'I suppose.' He turned to rifle through a few drawers, till Piex pointed one out, and opening it, the aged wizard removed a dark vellum scroll closed by the king's seal, tied with a ribbon of pure shadows. It was clearly a magical scroll.

          By Dr Joseph Ireland "Dr Joe"

Piex grinned broadly at her.

Flower stood behind the door, seeming to hope nobody minded her being there, or if they did, that they would not notice her.

Taking a small thread of spun golden wire, no thicker than a strand of her own hair, the wizard broke the seal and perused the magical scroll. Muttering under his breath, the door swung shut on its own with a solid clunk.

'I take it I can count on your companionship in this journey?' the wizard muttered to no one in particular, it seemed.

'Of course!' the captain replied. 'But wouldn't the priestess be your person of choice?'

'You are adequately armed, as history has taught me. Besides, one of your… personal alignment… is going to attract far less attention than one such as she, in this journey.'

The captain laughed, 'Missing your meat shield of late, Cour De'Feur?' He spoke the wizard's full name.

The old elf looked up at him, and huffed. 'Quite.'

The captain grinned, and taking out his favourite axe anointed it with a vial of oil he had at his hip. It smelt of sandalwood and sage, and had a robust, safe scent.

Kialessa, Piex and Flower were silent, but Kialessa could feel her heart beating in her chest. If she had to guess, it seemed she was about to go on a journey, a journey to somewhere unique. With a wizard that could teleport right into the heart of their nation, it could be anywhere.

The wizard took a ring off his finger, and replaced it with one he took from a pouch at his hip. It had a purple amethyst engraved with a sacred symbol of the pantheon – the old symbol, not the new, messed up one the High King had tried to force on them last season. A symbol no one had used since, much to the chagrin of Darrix's father.

Lost in her thoughts Kialessa only now noticed the wizard gesturing to Piex, holding out the golden thread. 'You will hold this for me,' the wizard informed him.

And immediately Piex's smile disappeared. He would not be going on this journey, Kialessa realised.

'Oh don't fret so, young mage,' the wizard chided him. 'Have you no idea of the importance of this task! To whom else might I entrust the holding of the only reliable means we have of returning?'

Piex brightened a little. 'I am good to the task,' he promised. Then he went to a corner of the room and grabbed a handful of dust from a bowl. He threw it in the air, and glittering it fell into an ornate cylinder around him, glowing silver in the dim candlelight.

'Your boy knows his stuff,' the captain complimented the wizard.

'He is sufficient to every task thus far given him,' the wizard said in a gruff voice, but with a gentle gleam in his eye that betrayed just how much he respected his most talented apprentice.

'Ready?' the captain asked the wizard, axe still drawn.

The wizard fixed Kialessa with a serious stare. Kialessa had seen the old elf battle an archmage, and win. She knew just how much command he had of time, and matter, and energy. She was very glad he'd never turned her into a toad, or even seriously expressed the thought of doing so, though he probably could. She listened very, very carefully.

'You've a talent, Kialessa, an enchantress's talent. We are glad to have found it, because like all talents it can be used for great good, *great good…* or great evil. Shadow weaving, in particular, corrupts many a good soul. So I am ordered by our king to take you there myself, so that you can see you have little to fear and much to gain, and to see how you will choose to use your growing talents yourself. Are you ready?'

Her thoughts tumbled about in her mind, where were they going? Instead the only thing she could think to say was, 'Go? To where?'

The wizard smiled, and shook his head. He looked like he

might have said "to the shadowrealm, silly!" but instead elaborated; 'We are going to a place of great danger to those who are made of light, as we are, Kialessa Tavernskeep.'

She'd never been called that before, and wondered why he would have called her that.

But he was moving on before she had much time to consider such things. 'Clasp my hand firmly, child. And place your other hand in the captain's hand, but not his weapon arm. He'll be needing that. Don't let go. Remember that. In the shadowrealm, space is different than in the living realm – far more … malleable, more… susceptible to thoughts, or to fantasy. Be careful Kialessa – it is said that the shadowrealm is quite near both the realm of dreams, and the afterlife. Be careful what you wish for. But our goals are minimal tonight: take you there, see how you react, and gather some shadow weave if we can. Nothing more. Understand?'

'I understand,' she said sincerely, meaning every word of it.

The wizard nodded. Grasping her hand in his right hand, and testing the thread was secure to his belt, he nodded at Piex who nodded back.

The captain lifted his axe and showed a battle readiness that was truly unsettling.

Kialessa turned back to see Flower, nodding enthusiastically with such a large smile it put her at ease. This was just a simple trip, and little visit. How long could they spend in another realm anyway?

With a nod to the warrior, he began his magic. The scroll unrolled and levitated in the air. The wizard took his time, leisurely intoning the key words to activate the very complex and lengthy spell already written out for them on the vellum. Dark tendrils of light soaked from the scroll, floating about in the air as though influenced by some arcane breeze. Kialessa didn't say a word, holding her breath for fear of disrupting the wizard's focus, though that was probably impossible. Soon the softly dancing threads formed a dark circle, and beyond the room seemed even darker than before. No candle shed its light, and the edges of the materials there seemed to blend and merge into each other with wispy threads of shadowy material.

It was dark, but to Kialessa, inviting.

The wizard stopped, and with a nod from the captain, they stepped forward into the shadowrealm.

 By Dr Joseph Ireland "Dr Joe"

The Shadowrealm

All kindness you receive is a test; how will you show kindness to others. And every cruelty is a trial; will you rise above such to show kindness to those who deserve it the least? Of one thing I am certain – you will receive again every kindness and every cruelty you send away.

Jacinthia Stonehall, high priestess of Lenmer'el.

It was odd. Every step in the shadowrealm seemed to take them at least ten paces distance compared with the normal world. They passed through walls without effort, slid by the castle fortress without impediment. Wherever Kialessa looked, twilight darkness pervaded. Everything seemed to be made of shadow material, with only faded tinges of their real colours. The red pavement stones were a dim burgundy, the vibrant green of the plants a muted olive colour. But it was beautiful as well.

And silent – so wonderfully silent! Never had Kialessa enjoyed such peaceful absence of noise. Always there was noise;

the guards on duty, the whispers of fellow students, the laughter of guests at her parent's inn. But here, such blissful reverence pervaded, such absolute hush. It was just so… quiet!

She sighed at the alien beauty of it all, and the wizard stopped walking.

The captain turned to watch their rear flank, never letting go of her for a moment.

Kialessa watched the men. They were burning lights in the avid darkness. Both had glowing fire around them in what Kialessa assumed was their souls. She looked at her own hands, clasped in their two, two of the mightiest warriors in the entire kingdom. The wizard's light was a deep indigo, a vibrant purple tinge all around it. The captain's a solid brown, the only vivid green tinges at its edges. Her light was a lively, flickering red, with touches of gold along the edges.

The captain's axe drew her attention. It blasted a blinding, uncomfortable white. Its edges, unusually in this place, were solid and unyielding. It looked even more dangerous here than in the real world.

'This will do,' the wizard said. 'Now, young dame, can you tell me what you see?'

Kialessa looked out at the world. They were in the courtyard before the castle keep. It stood tall, shadow grey flickers reaching up into the unending sky. Along the wall of the castle, dark motes of light rose into the air, seeming to her dark fairies charged with protecting the place. Each and every person, the guards on duty, were each clearly visible to her eyes. But they looked like flaming fires – red, and green, and blue. It was as if she were seeing their actual souls, and not only the shadowy echo of their physical forms.

It was impossible to describe. But she had to try. 'I see… everything! The men on the walls, how they burn with light! And the castle, it seems forged of shadow itself. It buries deep into the ground, like roots of a great tree… it feels so… safe here.'

The captain gave a course laugh, but even that felt muted. 'I suspected as much. Lucky little demon,' he said.

She didn't like being called that, but said nothing.

'Oh, are you troubled by those words?' the captain said, not even looking down at her. 'Perhaps I am rude because I am nervous. You see, half soul – I see nothing. I never have in this place, barely shadows and memories. Oh, no, I take it back. I do see something this time. Your eyes are glowing red, dame Kialessa. I must say, that's a very unnerving thing.'

Kialessa blinked. She wondered if she'd made her eyes glow again this time. Usually they only flared up on their own when she was angry, or upset. Maybe they always glowed, but could only be seen during the day on rare occasions? But no one had told her that her eyes glowed at night, so perhaps not.

But then again perhaps this was what her eyes were for. 'You really… you really see nothing, Honoured Bon Shur'e?' she spoke his formal name carefully.

He looked down at her, as though trying to make out her features. 'Apart from your glowing red eyes, almost nothing. I certainly have never seen men as fire, or castles with roots.'

'Nor I,' the wizard confessed. 'Not outside my visions and dreams, that is.'

Kialessa was still astonished. 'But… it's so beautiful.'

The captain huffed, as though he wanted to agree, but simply could not.

'And what of the shadows?' the wizard asked. 'How do they seem to your tae'anaryn eyes?'

'They're everywhere,' Kialessa said, wanting to reach out, but finding the captain clutching her hand even tighter in the thought. She relaxed. 'They curve outside of every edge, they float above every object. They … make up… everything here, and seem to be made by it.'

'Does there seem to be an excess of it anywhere?' the wizard asked.

'Everywhere,' Kialessa truthfully replied.

'Good. Then in a moment you can let go of the captain's

hand. Reach out, and gather some shadow, if you'd like. Put it in this magical bag here. We'll take it back to the castle, to my study. It can be useful for many great things, Kialessa, magic of great value.'

Her heart sank. So this was it, they wanted her to farm for them? Gathering something they could not see, and probably even touch?

But even in that thought her sense of duty took hold. They had just spent thousands on bringing her here. They spent who knew how much training her at the college. Perhaps she owed it to them? Perhaps she could repay her king's kindness with a talent that only she possessed?

If a handful of shadow was the only expense in her journey here, then it would be well worth the opportunity to see this beautiful place.

'All right,' she said.

Cautiously the captain released her hand, gripping his weapon with both of his own. He looked very nervous, but kept his eyes fixed on her.

Kialessa reached down, feeling the grass at her feet. To her surprise, she could feel **through** the grass, her hand passing right through it. There, she felt a few cotton-like strands of shadow. They were frail, and wispy, yet gathered in her hand as she bent down. She noticed the few threads on her clothes and in her hair – each of the travellers bore a few strands on their journey here.

But even if she'd gathered it all, it would only be such a small amount, she doubted others would be able to hold it, let alone appreciate it. And it felt so light and fragile, as though a single beam of sunlight would evaporate it in the real world, or maybe even here during the day.

Looking around, she noticed a great bundle of threads along the castle keep wall, packed behind the well.

'I see some shadow threads, over by the wall. Come,' she asked, pulling on the wizard's hand.

The captain was already holding the wizard's shoulder. She

          By Dr Joseph Ireland "Dr Joe"

pulled them over, and they walked unsteadily, with great caution.

It was, to be honest, a little frustrating.

With one hand, though she really needed two, she gathered a great armful of the threads. They were dark, and still flowed about on their own. Yet they held a substantiality as though they were solid, and real. It felt to her hands as though this material could easily be shaped, by any wish as though in the dream realm and she wondered what marvellous things could be made of the shadowrealm threads.

She piled it into her arms, but it was falling out. The wizard was holding on too tight, and kept her from moving well. She needed two hands for this job.

'If you release me, I could far easier gather the threads,' Kialessa confessed.

The wizard shook his nervous head, and the captain spoke, 'We won't be doing that, Kialessa. We can't afford to lose you. You are too valuable to our King. Too… valued by our King,' he corrected himself.

Kialessa nodded, more to herself, and satisfied herself with what she could gather. The wizard held out the bag, and she piled all she could in there. It was slipping out and falling at his feet, melting into the flow of all the shadows already there. It seemed odd; he refused to look at it as though completely blind.

'You really cannot see in here, can you?' Kialessa asked.

'Not much at all, though it begs the question: how well do you see in the usual nighttime, Kialessa.'

'As well as the next child, I suppose,' Kialessa said, but then felt the untruth in it. All her life, no human loved the darkness as she. They hid from it. They lit candles all the night. No one saw her in the darkness. She had learned she could walk right by the castle guards in the night if she made no noise, and they rarely even looked her way.

'When the clouds cover Lumos' face,' Kialessa asked, talking of the moon, 'and night covers the land, can you see the forest?'

The captain laughed. 'None can, oh! But can you!'

'Can't... everyone...?'

Now the wizard laughed. 'No, Kialessa. When nighttime rules, and the war of Serros and Waglah rises,' he said, speaking of thick clouds that bring rain, 'none can see the forest from the castle walls. Not even my elven eyes can piece such darkness. Have we found another talent for you, young dame?'

Kialessa was shocked. *No one?*

That explained a lot. It explained why her father never let her outdoors after dark. It explained why they all kept away from the shadows. It explained why they all walked so slowly in the darkness, arms outstretched, faces worried.

Very much the way the captain and the wizard were walking right now.

'I can see in the darkness, and you cannot,' the realisation struck her.

The captain nodded.

'And like most great truths, you must keep this to yourself. But I suspect we will have need of your talents when next the night watch is startled by the moving of the forest at night.'

Kialessa knew what he meant, 'It's usually bats.'

He laughed again. 'We thought as much.'

The wizard looked a little bothered, holding up the bag as though his own personal reasons for bringing her here were more important, and being overlooked.

Holding her hand, perhaps so that she could not get away, he knelt down to look her in the eyes. He seemed to know where they were, and in their light, she could visibly see his spirit. It went in and through him, wisping out of him in shadow-lights of living colours. It felt like ... stories... but she could not read them yet.

'Kialessa. It is said that those who can shadow weave can enter and leave this place at will. That they can travel great distances in a thought, and pass by normal wards and guards. Look to the castle Kialessa, what do you see?'

'It's very beautiful. It looks strong in this place.'

'That is good. Now look for the keep.'

The keep was the innermost building of the castle, and the strongest. It was where the king lived, and ruled.

And it was completely missing. 'I do not understand. It isn't even in here. I see the passageways leading up to it, and I see them leading from it. But there is not even a dark place where it should be. The entire realm bends together as though the keep never existed here.'

'Ah, ha!' the captain gleamed in triumph. 'Looks like the enchantress Greens'holm did her job right then!'

'We never had any reason to doubt her,' the wizard said, looking annoyed at the captain even though they probably couldn't see each other at all. The captain did seem fairly careless about who heard him. She imagined such information was usually a secret, such as who had the knowledge and power to conceal or remove an entire castle keep from the shadowrealm entirely.

Kialessa had no idea how that might be accomplished.

Suddenly there was a motion to her left.

Kialessa jumped up, and grabbed the captain's hand again.

He straightened, and tightened the grip on his weapon. 'What is it, tae'anaryn?' he said.

She looked out in the shadows.

It was cat, and after a moment she realised she recognised it. It was one of the stray cats that hid around the city within the castle walls, and that were permitted in the name of keeping away the mice and rats. It was black, with white patches on it paws so that they looked like socks.

But what seemed most amazing to Kialessa was that it was clearly here, it was in the shadowrealm. It had the same realness about it like the captain and wizard did, with less shadow and more light glowing from it.

The cat was *in* the shadowrealm.

'It's a cat,' Kialessa told them.

'Be off with you!' the captain told it, holding up his burning axe. 'This place is not permitted you, shadow being!'

Well, Kialessa did not think it was a shadow at all, but it fled with impressive speed. It was a pity; she was almost tempted to pat it.

The wizard composed himself, and prepared to lecture again. 'Space, as we mentioned, behaves differently here. When you learn to enter this realm at will, and you will, you can use it to travel great distances. When you learn to protect yourself here, and you already seem more equipped to do so than we can provide, you will travel with great speed and in great safety. Does that sound interesting to you, Kialessa?'

'Oh yes!' she admitted, thinking it would also be the perfect place to hide and rest in the actual silence. But the two warriors seemed very nervous here, prepared to even draw weapons against a cat. Perhaps it wasn't such a good idea. But then again, if the shadowrealm really was anything like the dream realm it was only as dangerous as one believed it to be. And to Kialessa this place was a corner of paradise.

'Good, good,' the wizard said. 'Now, I'm unwilling to allow you any free range in our first excursion here, and you must not travel beyond the castle walls. First, you need to know how to get back. Now this is very important Kialessa, I need you to listen!'

She was listening, but had begun to look away at the serene beauty of the sleeping, shadow world. She fixed the wizard with her gaze so he knew she was paying attention.

'Good. Now look here, see this thread here?'

Kialessa looked carefully at the golden thread. She saw it now, trailing back to towards the wizard's study. Looking again, she saw Piex and Flower carefully watching the portal. They looked as though they could see nothing, but to Kialessa they were bright as day. What was even more impressive, she knew, was that she was looking through several stone walls to view them.

'This may be your only guide back to the portal we created at study. This alone –'

Despite better training, Kialessa interrupted the wizard. 'What do you mean? I can see Piex and Flower from here.'

The captain scoffed, his hand on the wizard's shoulder still, and the wizard looked quite surprised.

'How is it that you can see them?' he asked, and she wondered how once again he did not seem to know the answer already. 'Are we not in the courtyard, by the well?'

'We are,' Kialessa explained. 'But the shadows here… I can see through shadows, and everything is made of shadows here. Shadows, and lights. Living things have lights. I can see all the people sleeping. But not the throne room or the Keep, it's as though it isn't even here.'

'That's still a serious breach in security,' the captain muttered.

It seemed to Kialessa that there were far too many breaches in this castle. For a kingdom built with magic there was too much they did not seem to know about. Perhaps having a shadow weaver on staff might actually be of great benefit to them.

At that thought of hope, Kialessa both saw and felt the light inside her glow warmer and brighter. She was … useful! If she was smiling broadly, none of the others here would know.

'Do you think you could make your way back to them?' the wizard asked.

'With ease,' Kialessa confessed.

'Oh, that's good, but I'm still unwilling to put that to the test-' the wizard began.

'Wait a moment,' Kialessa interrupted again. Something was wrong.

She was looking hard at Piex now, the image seeming to grow in her vision.

It was Flower.

They were staring hard into the shadow portal. They seemed

to be talking. Piex was shaking his head.

Flower leant over, seeming to want to get a better look into the portal. And as she accidentally rested her head inside the silver field of dust that surrounded the apprentice mage, it vanished. All the dust suddenly fell to the floor.

Piex looked like he cried out in dismay.

Flower covered her lips, and looked horrified.

And as Kialessa watched, the golden thread in Piex's hand fell slack. The golden string of light joining them to the real world faded, and then disappeared.

'What just happened,' the wizard said, the edge of fear in his voice.

'I don't understand. Flower, the circle around Piex, I'm sure it was just an accident!' Kialessa promised them.

'She broke the circle,' the captain said, his voice grim.

'That could not have dispelled it,' the wizard said. 'Nor have severed the thread. Are you sure there's not more that we should know about your young circus friend there, Kialessa?'

At that instant, she realised they probably already had their suspicions about the child personally blessed by the Star King. Kialessa then wondered if she should too. Was there something that Flower was not telling them? Or were there things she did not even know herself? Like Kialessa, who had lived all her life around humans and didn't even realise they could not see in the dark.

'It would seem,' the wizard began, 'that we now have no choice but to trust you to guide us back, dame Kialessa.'

She nodded, but then remembered that they could not see her. 'I can,' she promised. 'And I will.'

Without pause she took their hands, they held on to her gently, but with great determination. As though their lives depended on one whose bones both men could easily break.

They began to walk, each step a dozen in the waking world. Again, they passed through stone and wood as though in a dream. Within only a few breaths, the light from the portal began to be a visible reflection on both her guides. She saw the relief on their faces.

'I see them!' Flower shouted, but in this realm her voice was shadowy and indistinct, as though said from a great distance.

Piex was staring with all his might, but the look of relief on his worried face as they began to step through was priceless.

'I'm so sorry, I'm so sorry!' Flower begged. Her eyes were filled with tears.

'That's all right!' Kialessa told her, without any real authority. But it seemed she was, in a way, entirely in charge of the events of this night.

Flower sprang up, and hugged her. To Kialessa's surprise the portal began to waver in Flower's presence, or was it perhaps because the spell was ending since they'd left the shadowrealm? With a firm hand the wizard pushed the two of them to the far end of the room.

Neither adult seemed to know what to say, but the portal stood firm.

Flower hugged her again; she was quite strong because she was an acrobat and dancer. 'What's that stuff?' she asked, looking over Kia's shoulder.

The shadow material still wafted in the wizard's bag, like newly harvested cotton in a gentle breeze.

'Master!' Piex exclaimed, 'you have harvested shadow weave!'

'Yes, but only enough for some minor testing. We-'

His voice cut short. Flower was reaching out as though to feel the strange, gossamer material. In an instant it melted before her outstretched hand, dripping in black puddles on the floor and quickly evaporating.

'What did you do, child?' the captain almost roared.

Flower pressed herself to the far wall, covering her mouth as her eyes filled with tears. 'I'm so sorry, I didn't mean to!'

The wizard tried to salvage what he could from inside the sack, but it was useless. 'No, no, no!' he mourned.

Flower began to weep, and Kialessa tried to comfort her. She put her head on Kialessa's chest. 'Oh, this is always happening to me!' Flower wept. 'Always. I'm so sorry! This is all my fault.'

'Now, child,' the captain began as though he would disagree, but held his silence.

'An evening's harvest, wasted!' the wizard said with regret. And within that regret, Kialessa felt she could hear the touch of threat. There was something very important about gathering shadow weave this evening. Was it a promise he'd made, a promise to their King?'

'No, it won't be,' Kialessa stated.

The captain figured out what she was planning before she'd even moved. She saw him tense up in battle readiness. He would grab her before she had a chance to move.

'Let me borrow your axe,' she pleaded.

He laughed, 'Unlikely you could even hold it, let alone wield it. I will come with you back into the shadowrealm.'

'We haven't time,' the wizard disagreed.

She nodded, and stepped towards the portal, but she knew he would only slow her down. He reached out to grab her hand, but at the last instant she snatched her hand away and dove for the portal.

He was fast, inhumanly fast.

But she was made to dwell in shadows, and he could not see in here. As soon as she hit the shadowrealm she whisked about as fast as a wish. Within a breath she had gathered a huge armful of shadow weave. Dodging the old captain, who stood calling for her at the portal, she shoved the material back into the normal world.

Laughing, and before he had a chance to catch a hold of her again, she jumped away. It took less than an instant; she was at the castle moat, then gathering at the castle parapets. It seemed where people travelled less the threads grew the thickest.

Soon she was running bodily into the tiny thickets, and they would catch hold of her. Again and again she poured armfuls of the shadow weave through the portal, far more than the single sack could hold.

Thankfully, the captain relaxed. He stood guard by the portal, his brightly glowing anointed axe a great comfort, and his indomitable courage at guarding her while being entirely blind, an inspiration. Her laugher must have become contagious, for he began to smile.

Flower was hiding well outside the room, and Piex and the wizard took to shoving pillows full of the material into any space they could.

Eventually, Kialessa began to feel that the people in the castle were becoming aware that something was happening. Their spirits were beginning to brighten, as those who were awake already did. She was making too much noise in the realm of silence and shadow.

One last time she swept into the silent realm, running faster than fire, gathering the last of the wispy threads from every corner and crevice of the city within the walls. She left nothing of the shadow weave, of which she could tell.

And as she last visited the fountain at the upper end of the king's court, she caught a fleeting glimpse of two, miniscule individuals with insect like wings floating on little leaves in the water. The young man held a small fairy woman, who trembled in his arms. They wore stitched leaves for clothing, lively green even in the place of shadows, their spirits bright and alive, his deep blue and hers a glistening yellow. Glancing around, looking for all they were worth.

She'd finally seem them, the fairies in the fountain.

And they had not seen her.

With a giggle and a grin, Kialessa ran back towards the light at the edge of the wizard's study.

 By Dr Joseph Ireland "Dr Joe"

Confessions

'Even the worst man on earth can find himself surrounded by friends. And the best man on earth is going to make enemies that hate him. You just need to know you're doing what's right, because someone will love you for it, someone else is going to hate you for it.'

Queen Aolith, 313 CY. Cited in 'the year in jail' by the tae'anaryn.

'That was fun,' Kialessa confessed. 'Oh, that was so much fun!'

Flower walked beside her in the midnight hours, walking Kialessa back to the girl's dormitory. 'I overhead the wizard say you gathered over five thousand coins worth of the shadow weave, Kialessa. That's a lifetime's wage! Surely it will be worth ten times that once they use it to make something useful. You have a profitable future ahead of yourself, if you're keen on it.'

'Oh, I just love the shadowrealm,' Kialessa admitted to her. It had been thrilling, much better than gold.

'So, you're an enchantress too,' Flower wondered out loud. 'I wonder when you'll go through your chrysalis?'

Kialessa stopped walking. 'Chrysalis?!'

Flower laughed, her voice still soft in night, 'Yeah, you know, like Allastassia. I wonder if you'll all be, "None of you ever listen to me"!' She giggled then, and not very kindly.

It left Kialessa to wonder. 'You don't seem very impressed with her.'

Flower sighed, and looked down. 'She's… not the easiest person to like, sometimes, Kialessa. Not like you.'

Kialessa liked to hear that. 'Thank you, Flower. But what do you mean?' She was a little troubled by Flower's admission of how she felt about Allastassia.

'I, oh,' Flower muttered. 'Don't get me wrong, she's an amazing person, and she cares, she really does. But … it's always got to be her way. Always. I've known her since she was four and it's always been in her shadow. Not that I mind, she's kinda fun to watch at times. But … don't tell her I said this, she *never* listens to *anybody*!'

It made Kialessa wonder what Allastassia had done to earn Flower's ire like this. It was late at night, and Flower had had an upsetting night. Yet why all this sudden back-stabbing?

Or was it justified? It wasn't exactly… untrue. Allastassia did have a way of getting her own way. Was Flower just trying to protect her from the powerful enchantress's whimsy?

But Allastassia wasn't all bad, either. She was good at heart, Kialessa was sure of that. There was a certain… kindness? Allastassia had a genuine desire to make the world a better place. It couldn't be been easy to be the daughter of the most powerful enchantress in the land. So much was expected of her. It was a lot to expect of a thirteen year old with more power than she knew what to do with.

But then again, sometimes, Allastassia was really only for Allastassia.

'You're not saying anything,' Flower said.

Kialessa huffed. This was too serious and personal a conversation after a night of magic. 'I just… I remember that the priestess taught that we should live as though all our words were written down, and that any of them may be read out before all the people one day. I don't know what to say about Allastassia. She is my friend, and… she has a lot to learn too, I suppose.'

'Ooh, the diplomatic answer!' Flower gave her a hug. 'That's why I like you Kialessa.'

She couldn't not smile. 'Thank you, Flower. You seem as nice a person as I've ever met.'

She smiled back, and they walked on a moment in silence. It seemed as good a moment as any to ask her own questions. 'Flower,' Kialessa asked, 'how did you know all about me when we first met, on the hill?'

'And chasing that stupid trumpet chicken!'

'That's the day, yes.'

Flower grinned to herself. 'Well, the circus gets invited everywhere. Last year we were in Emerel and heard rumours of the tae'anaryn girl who did not burn, who saved the king of this far away land with his own sword. And I thought to myself, "This must be a very special girl. That's a very brave thing to do." And look, here we are!'

Kialessa was shocked, 'What do you mean, they know about me in Emerel?'

Flower laughed and hit her arm. 'What do you mean, "What do you mean", of course we've heard about you! You don't get to save a king without getting into the news.'

Kialessa was still surprised, and a little worried. How did people in a country she'd never visited already know about her, and what she'd done? And even about what she looked like? People she'd never met, and might never even see, might already know her. It was more than she could imagine.

'And on our way here, we cancelled the first visit due to the little "rebellion". But when we heard about the boy who tied himself to a pole I was not surprised to hear the whispers about the tae'anaryn girl who stood by him. Some people were remarkably scandalised about that, but we circus folk are a little more open minded. I knew you were just helping a friend.'

Kialessa almost chocked on her surprise. 'You all know about that too?!'

'Not **all**, no. I suppose… Mother likes us to know what's happening. It's very important to know what's happening so that we know which folks will need a circus, people recovering from a rebellion, for instance.'

'It wasn't a rebellion,' Kialessa argued.

'Sure. Anyway, she likes to keep tabs on who's who, and what's going on, and of course who the rising talent in the kingdom will be. So I guess our visit here really was with a double purpose. I suppose it always is.' And here Flower looked at Kialessa very deliberately, as though there was something much more that she was trying to say.

Kialessa sighed to try and clear her head. They knew her in Emerel? Who else had heard about her? She didn't know what to think, it was hard enough finding acceptance and freedom to learn and live in her own city, let alone other countries. Would they learn to welcome her, as people had here? She could only hope so.

And what was this about talent? Why were Flower and the circus folk on the lookout for new talent? Surely it wasn't just for new performers, but then again, maybe it was?

'You don't say much,' Flower admitted. 'I guess that's another reason to like you.'

Kialessa huffed. She would say much more if her thoughts would only turn into words, like Flowers did so easily. Or Allastassia's.

By now they'd reached the dormitory. The old lady glared at them – she looked so tired. It occurred to Kialessa that perhaps she only slept once all the youth were in bed? But she was always the first to rise. Perhaps she never slept at all? It would

 By Dr Joseph Ireland "Dr Joe"

explain the unexpected mood swings.

The old lady held up a lantern to help them see, and in the next instant Allastassia was there in the lantern's light. 'You're up so late, Kialessa! And what are you doing here with Flower?'

Before Kialessa had a chance to answer, the circus girl stuttered with anger. 'Why's it always got to be about *you*, Allastassia!'

'I was just asking!' the enchantress replied, while the old lady hissed them to silence.

The two girls ignored her.

'What, can't Kialessa and I go out on our own without your express permission?' Flower whispered angrily.

'It's not like that!' Allastassia hissed.

'It's *exactly* like that!' Flowers voice raised.

'Enough!' the old lady stopped them. 'Daughters, it's late. You're tired, and probably hungry. Flower, go to bed. Allastassia and Kialessa, in. Now.'

With angry stares the two girls parted, and Kialessa was left to walk in alone. She was too tired to think about her friends fighting all of a sudden, but it still upset her. She really just wanted to go to bed.

Allastassia threw herself on her bed loudly. Then she put the pillow over her face and muffled a tired scream. Then she kicked and punched the mattress in a way Kialessa had only ever seen little children do.

Kialessa sighed. There was still work to do.

She opened the chest at the end of her bed, using the key the captain had given her. The new lock was strong, and the entire chest hissed gently when opened as though the air within was squished down and unable to get out. She held out her new dagger, carefully holding the sheath to the blade.

'Allastassia, look,' Kialessa said.

She muttered, 'Go away.'

'Allastassia, look!' Kialessa dared risk offending the old lady once more.

The blond curls popped up from under their pillow.

Kialessa held out her knife.

Allastassia looked puzzled, then curious. Then looking around to check the old lady was nowhere near, she crept over.

'What is that?' she asked.

'A gift from our King,' Kialessa explained. She drew the sheath down just a little way, the green runes glowing brightly in the dim night light.

Allastassia gasped.

'Acid powers. Dwarven make,' Kialessa whispered, sure the old lady would notice by now.

'Why?' Allastassia asked.

'Special training. We went to the shadowrealm tonight.' Here she pulled out some of the gossamer threads of shadow weave she'd saved. They flowed from her sash, and then she emptied them into the chest. It blanketed the dark interior with complete blackness, covering her father's whip that usually waited there, and the other pouch with her coins she had nowhere else to keep. They were completely invisible within; it was comforting to see – to human eyes at least.

Kialessa rested the dagger in the darkness.

'Ooh,' Allastassia muttered.

Sharp footfalls sounded as the old lady approached.

Allastassia flew to her bed and did an impressive job of looking asleep right away.

Kialessa fumbled with her key, then realised she had no real reason to hurry. Carefully she shut the chest tight, and placed the key in the hidden folds of her magical sash where she'd successfully hidden her shadow threads. She said her evening prayer about as fast as she could, and began to climb into bed.

The old lady was there in a moment, lifting her up and almost shoving her in. 'What am I going to do with you, dame Kialessa,' she said, now with the touch of uncertainty and kindness in her voice.

'Thank you, kind gentle,' Kialessa whispered. She wanted to

rest her hand on the kind old servant's face, but it was clear this person did not like to be touched.

The old lady smiled, and then grew serious. 'Now go to sleep, we can't have you burning out for lack of rest tomorrow. The steward will have my hide!' and with an angry glare, she strode away.

It would be past midnight, Kialessa knew. In one evening she'd been given a truly lethal weapon whose only role was to harm, travelled to another realm whose beauty no one else would ever know, defied the greatest warrior in the kingdom to gather threads no one else could find… and watched two of her best friends in the whole world pick a fight with each other.

It was a lot to think about, which might have been why she found herself pressing away the tears that edged to the corners of tired eyes.

Liber de Nocte Tenebroşi

Kindness breeds kindness, and the greatest deeds are made of such simple things. Never forget what a simple kindness it is to just be there for a friend, and include them in your life.
Lady Greens'holm, 319 CY.

The boys were lined up along one wall and the girls on the other. It was always that way before they went into class. But the tutor was late, and that always left space for trouble. Despite herself, Kialessa found herself wishing for the quiet of another realm. It had been a late night last night.

'What are you yawning for, **half soul**!' the rude boy said to her, loud enough for everyone to hear above their whispers. She hadn't even realised she was yawning again.

'Hey!' Allastassia almost shouted, 'leave off the young dame, boy! You could not even begin to imagine where she has been!'

He scowled, and a friend whispered to him, and the boys snickered. Kialessa ignored it. That rude boy, whatever his name was again, was simply not worth her time.

     By Dr Joseph Ireland "Dr Joe"

Just then Darrix ran up. He looked tired too, and his pants were scuffed from his morning labours of prayer and cleaning the horse stables. The rich scent of grass and hay came along with him.

'You've got to take a bath more often!' The rude boy told him.

'I'm sorry Appleson, but when was the last time you rode a horse?' Darrix teased with a grin.

The rude boy tried to shove him and missed. Darrix just laughed and shoved him in the arm. The rude boy and his buddied shoved back, and an instant later all four of them where shoving and throwing mock punches while everyone else looked on.

'Why are boys always wrestling?' Flower asked. Her minotaur friend Ugly was never with her in classes.

'I guess they just have smaller brains,' Allastassia replied.

'They do realise Darrix could break their arms if he wanted to?' Kialessa wondered, secretly hoping he might, just on accident.

'Naw, Darrix is too smart for that,' Allastassia said with a confident nod. She was probably right.

Piex took advantage of the distraction to break the rules and walk over to the girl's side, holding out a rolled-up scroll of expensive paper, not parchment. It was tied with a red ribbon, and marked with his own personal wizard mark.

'I made this for you,' he said.

'Thank you,' Kialessa replied, and thinking it wise to accept a present from a wizard, opened it. It was a magical spell, complete with complex runes, unpronounceable words, and strange symbols that could only mean advanced maths.

'It'll take you some time to scribe your own copy, but maybe you can simply use your enchantress talents to claim the magic on your own? I don't know. But it's the *mage eye* spell, Kialessa. Once you understand this scroll, you will have eyes that can see magic.'

Kialessa was almost ready to jump for joy. 'Thank you, Piex, oh, this is so wonderful!' She tried to hug him, but he didn't seem very comfortable about that.

'Here, let me help,' he took the paper.

He began to try to explain it to her, Flower and Allastassia listening on as the boy's shoving started to get in the way. It really was the wrong time for advanced maths and primal words of creation, but even then, Piex made no sense to her. It was as if he started at the most complex ideas possible and assumed she'd somehow catch up. It would take a long time to learn, but as he rambled she promised herself to look at it often, and to understand it one day.

Tutor footfalls sounded from the next hall and the tussling stopped. Kialessa quickly tucked the scroll away. It would belong in the chest at the foot of her bed, hidden away, till she could study it properly.

Counting them off, the tutor let them in. When he came to Kialessa, he bowed. It was odd how most of the adults were doing that now, but that's how it was.

Then he stopped her. 'Ah, young dame, that reminds me, 19 out of 20 for your last test on the people of Nomer'el. Second best in the class, very good!'

'Why… thank you, Gentle!' Kialessa was amazed. She'd only just begun to stop failing tests, and now to get second best in class!? Normally everyone was trying to find fault in her. It was very good news indeed!

'Everything spelt incorrectly, of course.' The tutor added, 'But I gave you points for trying. It'll set you up for today's surprise test. Good job, dame Kialessa!'

Aaand there it was, she thought.

Still, second best. There were no guesses who received top marks. Kialessa entered the room and there Piex stood, waiting, in front of the entire class. It meant only one thing.

'Why do we need a surprise test today!' muttered Patsi.

No one liked surprise tests, except perhaps Piex. It was his job to mark the tests, which he would do simply by looking at a slate for a moment or two. By then he'd memorised the entire page and was able to tell exactly where all the mistakes were.

Kialessa sighed, and got out her slate.

They were just about to begin, the tutor even clearing his throat, when there was a very official knock on the classroom door.

Everyone turned to see a young man with the official tabard of the kingdom on his shirt. It was an official messenger from the city, perhaps even from the king himself.

The tutor moved and opened the door.

The messenger strode in and held out a large bundle to the tutor, covered in dark cloth. 'High Lord Cour De'Feur bids give the tae'anaryn this tome, and begs your kind assistance in helping to read it.'

'I, um, hmmm,' the tutor seemed stuck in though. 'Well, all right. Put it on my desk I suppose.'

The messenger thumped the package down, and called Kialessa over. She wasn't sure if official messengers outranked tutors while on college grounds, but she came over as quick as she could. It seemed her life was full of gifts right now, but none were quite as public as this.

With a small flourish the messenger threw back the covering, and it revealed a clearly very magical tome – a book. It was dark, with shadow weave blending into every nearby shadow. A dark moon symbol made of some kind of pale stone adorned its surface, and it was tied with two black ribbons, one clasped with a silver lock, the other with a series of rings.

Everyone stood up to get a better look.

The messenger then handed her a sealed letter. 'Rite of ownership passes to the tae'anaryn Kialessa of the inn. Enjoy.' He spoke as though he saw such things of magic every moment of every day, but still enjoyed the attention the moment brought. With a grin, and a very formal bow, he walked out.

She tried to curtsey, but the entire class rushed up as soon as he left to see the book. None of them dared touch it.

'What is it?' some asked.

'Why does she get a book?' the rude boy complained.

'Stand back, stand back!' The tutor insisted. Students jumped back, and the old man stepped forward to examine the book. Without daring to lay a finger on it he waved Piex forward.

Piex hummed to himself and without touching it, held out his hand for the note Kialessa was holding. She gave it to him, but he didn't take it, giving her a "don't be silly," look.

She realised what he was thinking, and broke the seal on the note herself. Giving it a quick glance, for no words made immediate sense to her but her own name, she let him read it.

He looked impressed. 'A gift just arrived from Emerel, courtesy of the wizard to thank you for your assistance the other night. It is the book of the *Nocte Tenebrosi*, the "shadowed night". Written in ancient Aurem, I think you'll find it quite tricky to read Kialessa. May I read it to you, young dame?' he asked, bowing his head.

'Ahh, yes!' she replied. While it was wizard business, she thought he was being rather formal. Perhaps there was some actual danger here? Or maybe he just liked the attention?

He thanked her again, and taking a deep breath, reached out his hand. Suddenly the magic around him sprang to life, and Kialessa stepped back. Nobody else seemed to notice, except Allastassia, who was too focused on the book to be impressed. Flower was standing well away the whole time. Piex seemed to be struggling to concentrate. Then he spoke, *'Apertus'*. The threads unwound themselves, the rings spun about and unlinked, and the first page slowly turned itself open.

'Fascinating,' Piex said.

'Well?' the tutor demanded after Piex remained silent.

'It is safe to read, written in an ancient dialect of the common language. It was written by a sage long ago on his research into the shadowrealm. I think Kialessa will find it very interesting.'

'I think we'd all find it interesting!' Allastassia told them.

Everyone agreed.

The tutor did not look pleased.

But as they looked at the dark, mysterious tome on his desk, shadow weave gently wafting towards her and then disappearing into near shadow, curiosity seemed to win the tutor over as well. 'Very well, a few readings will suffice, I suppose. Not every day you get a wizard to read from the pages of an actual enchanted tome, no?' he sounded very excited.

'Indeed,' Piex sounded very dry. He turned a few more pages, reading each in a moment. 'The wizard mentioned you read the section on shadow calling, Kialessa. Let us begin there.'

Piex made them all wait the twenty breaths it took him to read the entire section, and then he recited it from memory, translating as he went. It seemed the author sage had learned, after much time and through great effort, to call objects to hand through the shadowrealm. He kept them in a personal chest, covered with shadow weave, and had even learned to cloak himself in the shadow weave whenever he wanted. All the equations where there, and several diagrams. They seemed to help, but Kialessa wasn't sure how she would use them.

Just as it seemed some of the students were losing interest there was another knock at the classroom door.

The tutor opened it.

Outside stood a page, one of the castle boys who did not attend the college. He was only a year to two older than Darrix. 'The king has asked to see dame Kialessa,' he told her.

Everyone looked at her.

'It's your day,' Allastassia said with a sad smile.

Kialessa was up almost before he'd finished speaking. The tutor said nothing, for he had no authority once the king had spoken.

Piex wrapped up the book and looked like he planned to read it all himself, which was probably wise.

On intuition Kialessa remembered she should bring

someone. It was her right to, the king had said so himself. As she looked at the class, people stared back, their faces a mix of envy and gratitude. Most of them feared the king mightily, but Kialessa knew he was a good man. As for envy, many would love the chance to speak to him, ask him for favours. He'd told her before very few were truly sincere, which was one reason why he enjoyed the company of children.

'I can't believe she gets to skip the test,' Patsi muttered to someone.

It made her smile. All right, maybe some of them were jealous because she got out of a test more than got to see the king pretty much whenever she wanted.

Flower looked worried, Darrix grinned broadly. Posk was trying very hard to get his ruler to balance on the edge of his desk, and Piex was correcting the tutors' spelling mistakes on the test.

And Allastassia looked sad. So without hesitation Kialessa called her over. For a moment, the enchantress hesitated. It was strange, and just a little unlike her. Allastassia never missed a chance to talk to new or famous people, Kialessa had observed. Now she hesitated.

But only for a moment. Without looking back she hurried out the door. They followed the page as fast as they could, and he was a fleet young boy. It was never wise to keep a king waiting.

They found the king in the inner keep, in the chambers above the throne room, but beneath the bedrooms. Kialessa enjoyed visiting the Keep. It was always warm, and decorated with great care and expense. It was where they often talked.

The king was sitting in a sturdy wooden chair she'd not seen before. To his left the queen held his hand, and to his right, the priestess. Before him the high priest of Mya stood, in his sturdy leather apron an assortment of metal tools – including drills and plyers of curious shapes. He was gazing intently in the king's mouth as he held it wide agape. Kialessa knew him to be a travelling priest, and had never met him in person before.

'Ahh, your little tae'anaryn is here, my love,' the queen informed her husband.

'Oh good, we can get started now,' the priest informed them.

The king muttered something incomprehensible and held out his other hand as the high priestess Jacinthia stood back.

Without waiting Kialessa rushed to grab his hand, afraid something was wrong.

But the gentle king smiled down at her. 'Oh don't worry, Kialessa, it's just a sore tooth.'

Kialessa gasped, sore teeth were very bad news. Most had to be torn out, for few had the virtue or luck for them to heal.

'It will not be a problem,' the priest of Mya informed them. 'My goddess has stayed the infection, but it will provide a site for new infections or unclean spirits unless we drill the tooth and plug it with this amalgam of quicksilver I have prepared.'

Kialessa felt sick hearing that.

'Don't worry child,' the priestess informed her. 'By my prayers he will feel no pain, none at all.'

'That may be so!' The king said in a loud voice. 'But I find the whole experience so very … unpleasant. Kialessa, will you hold my hand for me?'

'Gladly,' she smiled.

The operation was brief, but still most of it too much for her to watch. Allastassia, however, craned her neck as far as she could to see it all from where she was standing. No doubt she would have loved to have gotten her lens in there as well.

The old priest stuck a large drill with a small drill bit right into the tooth and drilled it out, then washed it with some clear coloured wine. Next he pressed into it a small dab of glistening silver metal, and with a prayer, turned it as hard as stone. After a moment or two of drilling to make sure the fit was right, he gave the king some bitter herbs to chew.. 'The healing is sufficient, my king. You will be fine for dinner tonight, but I recommend you take the afternoon off.'

'Already planned,' the queen assured him.

The king did not look so pleased, he liked running the kingdom. 'Thank you, my dear,' he said anyway. 'And thank you, Kialessa. You did an excellent job!'

Kialessa shivered and had trouble meeting his gaze. It was lucky she'd only had to hold his hand; it was quite a queasy experience for her! Most people didn't get to keep their teeth, only a handful could afford the expense of enchanted health care even in a magical world.

The king was trying to pay the priest, who refused payment for his services. So he offered him a small gift, which he also refused. It wasn't until the king agreed to make a donation to the shine to Mya at the docks that the priest smiled at them all and turned to leave.

'You'll not be staying for the evening feast?' The priestess Jacinthia asked the priest.

'A certain merchant begs me bless his new gem mine, and the stars are in alignment only tonight,' he replied, and without further ceremony, as was the way of the priests of the Earth Mother, walked straight out, his gentle footfalls making no sound as they fell against the polished stones of the castle floor.

The king smiled, and the priestess helped him rise. He brushed her aside and straightened his red tunic, waving away the soldier who offered him his cloak.

'You'll take it easy, won't you?' the queen asked him.

'Yes, yes, of course, of course,' he said, but grinned at Kialessa and Allastassia with a wink.

Taking their hands, he walked them out and down the stairs to the private garden at the north side. If the fairies were there now, Kialessa had no eyes to see them. The garden was just as pretty in the day, as though someone brought flowers there even in winter, so that blooms coloured the beds all year around. It was small, but perhaps, the prettiest garden in the whole world.

The king sat on a bench, seeming just a little tired. He sat them on either side. Allastassia took a handkerchief and laid it down before she sat, as a lady might. She said bolt upright, hands clasped politely in her lap. Kialessa just bumped down as soon as the king did, knowing he would speak first.

'So, my young prodigies, how goes your studies?'

Allastassia was the first to answer, 'Excellent, my liege,' she said with a polite voice.

'All right, I s'pose,' Kialessa said, kicking the grass at her feet.

Allastassia gave an almost silent gasp, and tried to catch her gaze. But Kialessa ignored her.

'Academics are hard,' Kialessa confessed, not looking at anyone when she spoke. A part of her knew this would annoy the overly polite Allastassia, but the king preferred honesty, and sincerity. 'I can't see why we have to know numbers the long way. The times-tables I mean. "Ones four is four". It's so much harder to remember that way.'

'What do you mean?' The king asked.

She showed him. 'I like to use my fingers – to count on them like this, four, eight, twelve. Much faster, and so much easier to remember!'

The king nodded, 'Well, I do like your way.' He neither agreed, nor disagreed.

'I liked doing the history of Nomer'el last week too,' she admitted. 'But I wish they would tell us more about dragons.'

'You do like dragons, don't you, Kialessa!' The king laughed.

'Yup,' she agreed.

'Well,' he said, putting her under his arm. 'Not everyone has had the chance to ride one, have they!' He booped her on the nose, and then she had to scratch it. 'Perhaps you will write a book one day, and tell us about your experiences. I think intelligent young minds like yours would enjoy hearing your story.'

'You think?'

'I am sure!' he said, but grew a touch serious. 'Still, our

weather might depend on dragons, and a great many other natural things. But our society, our civilisation, tends to depend on people, does it not?'

They both agreed.

'So what of some of the people you have met? What do you think about the circus folks, girls?'

Allastassia looked suspicious, and looked at Kialessa. Kialessa couldn't hide her annoyance; it was not like they were spying on the circus folks for him. He just wanted to know if everyone was happy, and how he could help.

'They are … wonderful,' Kialessa thought. 'They're teaching us to act, and dance. And have you heard, I'm in their special class for advanced learning. It's *exhausting!*'

They laughed, and the king continued, 'And that little one you were with yesterday, the dancer, what was her name?'

'Flower?' Allastassia offered.

'That's right, Flower. I remember now. Blessed of the Star King?'

'Indeed,' they agreed.

'I wonder what her powers are?'

Kialessa shrugged, 'She doesn't know either. She is flexible, but that might be a circus thing. She has a dimensional pocket inside the back of her throat, that's weird.'

'Agreed,' the king said. 'Is that all? A curious gift from a good king.'

That's what I thought, Kialessa pondered a moment. 'And there's something weird going on with the magic around her. I don't know, sometimes it's like it doesn't work just right. She doesn't know either.'

'Interesting,' the king admitted. 'You will let me know if you find out?' he almost begged.

'Of course!' Kialessa agreed, gently hoping Flower wouldn't mind. But King Dunnkan was a good king; surely he would be kind with that information. Besides, what secrets could be hidden from the king anyway? He would find out eventually, and all the better to hear from her.

'And how is the play progressing?' the king asked Allastassia.

'Oh, simply wonderfully,' Allastassia lied. But it wasn't all untrue, Kialessa had to suppose. Allastassia talked a moment about the progress, putting a very positive spin on it. Her biggest concern seemed to be about getting Posk to do his job properly, which really was a lost cause if perfection was the aim.

'And are you enjoying the play?' he asked them.

Kialessa shrugged, snuggled under his arm, not sure what to say. It was a good project, but it was testing a powerful young enchantress's patience to the limit. People were starting to miss battle training, in comparison. But it did seem fun to learn to sing and dance instead.

Apparently the king was still waiting for an answer, and squeezed her in his one armed hug. 'Won't you show me something you've been learning, Kialessa? Something to take my mind off this dull ache in my mouth here.'

She jumped up. 'I love the dancing!' she admitted. Picking up a stick, she used it as a pretend ribbon, turning around.

The king applauded.

Then she got an idea. Concentrating, she tried to pull shadow weave onto the ribbon using only her mind, pulling it directly from the shadowrealm. Nothing happened.

But someone seemed to guess what she was trying to do, and with a wave of her hand, Allastassia made magical threads tie themselves from nothing onto the end of her finger, forming a long, beautiful ribbon.

Kialessa laughed, and turning the ribbon in her hands tried for a backwards cartwheel as she'd learned a week or three ago. It went off perfectly.

'Marvellous, simply magical!' the king clapped.

'Keep dancing, Kialessa,' Allastassia whispered, almost begged.

6 Kialessa dances

As Kialessa spun around the garden the reeds in the pond seemed to hum a tune. Then they actually *did* hum a tune as Allastassia weaved magic into the air. Deep thuds of resounding bass echoed through the soil, and a hundred crickets strummed in perfect tune. The melody was uplifting, the music inspiring. It was a perfect tune for her to dance to, one she'd never heard before.

'Lumière de la Lune?' the king asked Allastassia, speaking elven, possibly naming the tune.

Allastassia simply nodded, concentrating hard.

Suddenly a million butterflies sprang into existence and danced around Kialessa. She felt like she could fly, giddy with

　　　　By Dr Joseph Ireland "Dr Joe"

enthusiasm and enthralled by magic. She danced like she had never danced before, with all her might. Music flowed around and within her, obeying her, and guiding her. The ribbon flowed at her whim, spinning at her command. It grew, and grew. And as Kialessa sensed the song was coming to an end, she wove it around her. As she leapt high into the air, Allastassia seemed to grasp her intent, levitating her up high just like they'd used so many times in battle training. Turning a double back flip with ease, Kialessa floated back towards the ground.

The king clapped, standing to applaud them. 'All my troubles are well paid to see and hear such beauty this day, young maids! I count myself the most blessed king in all the land to have two such kind and faithful subjects as yourselves! Well done, well done!' he praised them, and hugged them both despite Allastassia's discomfort.

With a sigh, he continued. 'But we have tarried too long in this magical garden, methinks. I have enjoyed your company, children, but I *must* be getting back to work.'

'But the queen insisted you rest!' Allastassia argued.

'And rest I will, as I see fit! There's just too much for me to do to be sitting too long, children. I don't much enjoy the taxes, but there are some judgements that have waited too long. You have touched my heart, young gentles, and I am feeling inspired.'

He breathed in deep, and bending down, hugged them both again. Allastassia patted his back softly, but Kialessa buried her face in his bead the way she liked to, and didn't let go till he did.

He laughed a rich, hearty laugh, and indicated it was time to leave. They had not even left the garden before the steward was standing by his king, a roll of parchments in his hands. Kialessa wondered how close the part-fey councillor must have been to have arrived just as the king decided it was time to work again, or had he been the cause of it? In the end, Kialessa reasoned, it did not matter.

Kialessa wanted to run back to their class, but Allastassia

seemed in no hurry. Kialessa slowed down, and was surprised to see that tears rimmed the blond enchantress's eyes. 'Allastassia, are you all right!' Kialessa asked with concern.

Allastassia wiped her eyes. 'Yes, yes.'

'I though you would be happy to see the king!' Kialessa replied, troubled that something had, once more, upset her good friend.

'Oh, Kialessa!' Allastassia said, and bursting into tears hugged her so fiercely it almost hurt. She was a strong girl!

But it still took her a moment to stop crying, and to say something coherent. 'Oh, Kialessa. Thank you, thank you so much! Today, I made music for our king!'

Kialessa wasn't sure why that was quite worth bursting into tears for, till it occurred to her that Allastassia's reputation with the king can't have been doing very well of late. Allastassia had almost levelled the college hall, and she had possibly cursed one of her own classmates. Her powers were growing, and it was getting harder and harder to control them. And instead of mild herbs and quiet conversation, she was staying up late dancing and shouting at everyone. Things were not going so well for Allastassia right now, so the chance to do something right for the person in change might just possibly mean very much to her, very much indeed.

So without another question Kialessa hugged her back until she let go.

Then, grabbing Kialessa's hand, they ran back to class together.

   By Dr Joseph Ireland "Dr Joe"

Ever Training

Uplift! Reach up! Ever believe! And if you can't bring yourself to believe, at least stand up tall. You will find your faith, in a little while, if you believe.

Tomin, during his sermon at Lenmer'el, 313 CY.

There was a small click, and before she had time to panic in her already terrified heart, the catapult lifted her up and threw her high into the air.

Kialessa was beginning to hate the circus.

She felt the now familiar sensation as it seemed her stomach lifted into her throat. Luckily, she didn't throw up this time.

But she was still hurtling through the air, and that had to be dealt with. At the far end of her flight, the other four students waited, grinning artificially. It was their job to catch her, just as she had been trying to catch each of them in turn since the hour their training had begun tonight.

And it was a busy night. Everyone was out practicing for tomorrow's performance, something about the military show.

Kialessa and the other students weren't invited, of course, but their unyielding trainer had told them that they need to learn to focus in distraction. So the air roared as the fire jugglers practiced, and the safety net moved almost continuously as the high wire performers practiced falling onto it. Men juggled knives of flashing light, while the minotaur in a clown outfit rode a hardened barrel with surprising aplomb. Chéri cracked a whip repeatedly in his direction, less for the threat and more to give the massive creature something to concentrate on rather than the riot of motion and noise around it. And all around clowns, with unusual sincerity and intensity, practiced everything from singing in harmony to falling onto their faces.

And despite it all, Kialessa managed to strike her pose mid-air. It was the second most important thing about being shot from a catapult. The first thing was to remember to smile.

Always. "Never let the audience know your distress, and whatever happens they'll always believe you meant it. Break a leg, they'll just clap if you do!" Flower promised them.

Kialessa was slowly getting less sore with each passing day. Yet with only Serrosday to recover she'd slept through most of it and missed the morning services last week. But she didn't want to complain. Training was hard, but it was worth it.

After all, Kialessa found, once she was up in the air she actually really loved it. Like riding a dragon – the only problem was trying to not hit the ground.

And so, as she ended the peak of her flight, she begun to fold her body back out into a plank position so that her class mates could catch her. Their faces would be grim with concentration underneath their false smiles, she'd seen them that way every time, she probably even looked like that when it was her turn to catch them. Flower was there too. It had been her job to teach them how to form the human net that would stop Kialessa from hitting the floor – hopefully. The first time they'd dropped Flower, but she'd stood up, smiled, and got right back on the catapult. They hadn't dropped anyone else since then.

    By Dr Joseph Ireland "Dr Joe"

And that was when Kialessa saw, walking in from the far pavilion, her four best friends.

She almost squealed with delight, the thrill of the fall mixing unnaturally with the joy of seeing her friends till she lost all concentration. She found herself falling towards the outstretched arms, and remembered too late to straighten out.

Much too straight. With the arms held taunt Kialessa accidentally arched her back, and rolled forward right off. They shouted and tried to catch her, but she went through their hands, her arms flailing wildly, and spinning completely around at least twice ended up face first on the floor.

It hurt.

She heard everyone running up to her, but struggling to her feet she turned to look at her fellow trainees. They looked chagrined, and Flower looked horrified.

Kialessa stood tall, despite her burning hands and the ringing in her skull, and smiled.

For a moment they stood there.

Then Flower clapped, and they gathered around to congratulate her.

Faster than should have been possible, Allastassia was by her side. She looked terrible worried as well. The other three were running up, but even Darrix slowed when it seemed she was all right.

'Are you all right?' Flower asked.

'Sure!' Kialessa lied. She felt her knees bleeding for sure, but refused to look just in case. And her wrist really hurt. She turned it, and it felt quite sprained.

Without pause Allastassia brought out the enchanted handkerchief her mother had given her. She started to clean Kialessa's knees, the pain disappearing immediately, the dust falling away. It wasn't much use in combat training, but Allastassia used it several times a day and it never got any dirtier.

Darrix arrived then, and almost without thinking she held

out her wrist to him. He was getting better at healing every day, now that he was a paladin, or at least a squire to one. Not every student had the faith to heal, and only Natasha seemed to be able to knit bones in a single prayer. But as Darrix's hand clasped around her wrist she allowed the pain to drift away, through him, to the deity he served. She turned her wrist and was glad to see it felt as good as ever.

'Thank you,' she said, looking upwards as Darrix had instructed her. He never let anyone thank him personally for this rare gift he had that few others shared, and turned away as though embarrassed.

'Champion smiling,' Flower congratulated her.

It made Kialessa smile again.

'You alright?' Piex asked.

She nodded, she thought he didn't ask because he couldn't tell, he was showing that he cared.

'Good,' Flower announced. 'Up again Kialessa, you can do it again.'

Kialessa's shoulders slumped. Kialessa had known pain, but not like this. Nothing had prepared her for the intense physical training the circus was determined to inflict on them. She was sure it was worse than even the soldiers received. They would run, and jump, and hold unnatural positions for hours. And naturally, because she had a tail, the ringleader insisted she learn to hang from it. She couldn't seem to get it yet, but that didn't stop the practice. She was honestly hurting in places she didn't know even had muscles, and which no one here could relate to.

Yet hardest of all, it had to be done with a smile. A perfect, natural smile, any momentary distraction and *crack*, the ring leader let loose her whip. Under that motivation Kialessa had learnt to juggle, then to juggle knives. They'd been shown how to do a backflip, then how to do it on a narrow beam. Finally, they were expected to do it on a rope. Only Flower managed it, every time. Everyone else fell off, whacking their head or elbow or back on the barely softened earth.

     By Dr Joseph Ireland "Dr Joe"

And if they didn't stand up, immediately, grinning broadly.
Crack!
Smile. Never stop smiling…
'Sure,' Kialessa finally said with the least faked smile she could manage.
The other four "elite" began to wind down the hated machine.
Posk ran up to it and watched with avid fascination.
'Wait a moment Kialessa,' Allastassia said, concern evident in her voice. 'Are you sure you're all right?'
Kialessa turned, and nodded, 'Sure!' she promised. But even she noticed how hard it was to look in her friend's eyes.
Allastassia walked up, and put a sympathetic hand on her forearm, 'Are you sure? Maybe you folks should call it a night. We have play rehearsal tomorrow.'
Kialessa couldn't help the trembling in her tired, terrified legs. She looked at Allastassia's kind eyes, and found her burgundy lips stated to tremble too. The golden haired enchantress gave her a big, welcomed hug. It seemed to be filled with strength and courage – and maybe just a touch of magic. She felt Darrix pat her shoulder, and Piex even almost patted her hand with unfamiliar discomfort, but his eyes were filled with worry.
'It's just that you hit the ground so hard, Kia,' Piex muttered.
Kialessa nodded, 'I'll be fine,' she confessed, and truly believed it.
'Are you enjoying special training?' Darrix asked.
'I prefer ribbon dancing to flight by catapult,' she admitted, and everyone laughed.
They helped her into the catapult bucket again. Kialessa smiled. Looking up at the room as the bucket slowly lowered, she noticed the trapeze artists had wandered into her flight path.
'Not yet guys,' she told them.
They were still winding it down anyway, heaving away at the great crank that bent the shaft. They weren't supposed to

crank it fully, since they were only students.

There was a deep grunt from below, and the bucket gave a sudden lurch downwards. Kialessa looked down to see that apparently Posk had gotten bored waiting for things to happen, was working the crank single handed.

'Slow down, boy!' Flower complained, 'You've gone too far, now we have to reset it!'

Kialessa was just about to get out, just about to prepare to stand up, when Posk's unquenchable curiosity struck again. With an innocent, puzzled expression he reached out and hit the release button. Everyone went flinging away from the dangerous siege engine – but none more so than she herself. It seemed Posk's intervention, rather than sending her further along, sent her flying directly upwards.

With a scream, a trapeze artist desperately tried to dodge her uncontrollable ascent, and collided with the other artist she was supposed to catch. Their combined weight immediately overcame one of the strong ropes that held them, and they plummeted towards the floor. At the last instant one of them grabbed the safety net, and combined with the remaining ropes strength wrapped them up tightly in the net like a cocoon. Their unexpected movement, combined with the cracking of the whip, somehow upset the minotaur who fell to the floor, smashing the barrel of oil the fire breathers were practicing with. The ball of fire lit the room beautifully from one end to the other – including the safety net, the roof, and the hay bales they used to define the edge of the ring.

People screamed and chaos ensued. Of course, at the peak of her ascent up into the air Kialessa had a beautiful view of it all. But looking down at the floor she realised she would probably be paying a visit to Natasha today, once the fall broke both her legs. She felt her tail spin, trying to keep her upright – she was not going to fall on her face again. But somehow in the seeming silence of freefall, she didn't feel any fear at all. Her stomach stayed right where it was supposed to and for just a moment Kialessa thought how nice it would be if she could never touch that ground at all, and simply fly away.

And an instant later her world was wrapped up in a sheet of Piex's golden chains. They spun her in the air, and she screamed.

A moment later she looked out, taking a moment to realise the chains held her upside down, with only her left arm free. Everyone was running to and fro in the chaos. Allastassia began to summon water from the air, and Flower was trying to distract a frantic minotaur, while Posk ran around with buckets of water.

Darrix walked up to Kialessa, he looked really worried.

She grinned, 'I think it might be time to call it a night, after all.'

He laughed.

She smiled back, and booped him on the nose.

Existential

'Life… is beautiful. But… why?'
Posk.

Everything was going along, and people were really trying, if not for Allastassia, then for their own glory. Allastassia spoke often, inspiring and directing them. She really was getting amazing at making things happen. They were going to put on a play that would rival the circus! Everything was going along just the way she wanted.

Everything… except that **one thing**.

Posk still wasn't living up to her expectations. He was trying, that was really clear. He was really giving it his best go. But he kept on getting the backdrops mixed up.

Which meant, in Allastassia's world, that he needed another headband…

She didn't dare ask this time. She made her wishes known to everyone that Posk needed a better wizardry band. Then she just took to sighing every time the wizard was in view, and making sure he saw it. And, once or twice, she let little tears run down her face when she knew he'd be looking.

It only took her three days.

They were in an assembly, listening to the tutor read the roll. The tutors were all there, even the wizard which was unusual. But there was some award to give to some students for something, and it was his job to oversee it.

And Allastassia sat there, eyeing his headband. Tiny tears running silently down her face.

Suddenly the wizard shouted, 'Oh, fine! Here, take this blasted headband you wet blanket!'

Allastassia gasped in joy and surprise.

'Don't say I didn't warn you. This was won by me from a battle with an archmage. I doubt it will truly help you with pulling a curtain.'

Allastassia bowed the most gracious bow Kialessa had ever seen.

'No harm or ill will come of this, I promise,' she said.

He looked at her grimly, and said nothing as though he already regretted his decision.

***

It was afternoon, during one of the fevered evening rehearsals that were scheduled all that week, for there was only two weeks to go before the play was to be performed. Allastassia walked right up to Posk, ripped of Piex's headband, and laid down the delicate silver circlet. 'Try messing things up with this on, smelly!'

Posk said nothing.

Nobody moved.

Posk just sat there, thinking, for the rest of the evening. They couldn't even get him to lift the curtains, and it took two clumsy boys to try and take his place. But nobody dared take the headband off, after all the trouble she'd gone to get it.

It was late at night, after almost all the other students had left, when Posk finally spoke, and when he did it was to ask a question. 'I have… hands,' he stated. 'Why do I have hands?'

Kialessa looked at him in surprise.

Darrix gathered around with his two friends.

'And why are they *my* hands?' Posk asked them. 'And see, my hands do what I tell them to. But why are they *hands*?'

One of Darrix's friends laughed, but the laughter quickly died when no one joined him. Posk was being very sincere.

'And … my voice.' Posk continued, 'I am making noises, with my voice, and it carries my thoughts, and you hear my thoughts. How do you do that? How does this happen?'

'It is pretty amazing, I suppose,' Piex said.

'I like the night,' he stated, suddenly seeming to feel the need to change the topic. 'But why must there be night? Is there a reason? I suppose the night creatures must feed, and the earth must cool down. But what is "night"?'

'I can't answer those questions,' Darrix admitted.

Posk smiled weakly. 'I never knew I had so many questions. My head hurts, and I am sad,' he confessed. 'Life… is beautiful, but… *why*?'

***

It was no better the next day. Whatever anyone attempted to teach, at all, was met with a barrage of questions from Posk. His questions did not stop, but they were the kinds of questions that didn't have any fixed answers.

"Why is air?", "Where do thoughts go when they are forgotten?", "Why are the tutors in charge of us?", "At what point did I learn I was alive?"

They were in their academics class, trying to learn about Lenmer'el's brief yet amazing history. The tutor was just telling them about king Peyter's untimely death at only fifty years old, when Posk suddenly blurted out, 'Hold a moment, how do you know this?'

 By Dr Joseph Ireland "Dr Joe"

'It was written down,' the tutor patiently replied.

'By whom?' Posk demanded.

'One who was there, I suppose. A chief scribe perhaps? The wizard is old enough to have been there, perhaps –'

'Yes, but *you* weren't there,' Posk pointed out. 'How do you know? I mean, how do you know that you know?'

The tutor stuttered for a moment, when suddenly someone shouted from the back of the class, 'Posk, will you stop asking *stupid questions nobody can answer!*' the rude boy shouted.

The room fell deathly silent.

Slowly, Posk turned to face the boy.

Nobody made a sound.

Posk stood to his full height, and took two paces toward him.

The rude boy broke out in sweat, 'Ahh, tutor?' he pled.

Nobody moved.

Posk walked right up to the rude boy's desk, staring down at him. Kialessa didn't know what was going to happen next, but she didn't bother moving. It was unkind, she knew, but a part of her really hoped Posk would snap his desk in half and punch him right in the face.

Finally, Posk spoke, 'I *pity* you. You have a wonderful gift; a mind that can ask great questions. Yet you do *not*. Every day you waste your life doing what you've always done, thinking… as you've always thought. You like to think yourself a great man because of your skill with a sword, but I tell you that you are weak: you have never risen to the challenge of creating a purpose for your own *existence*. How quickly you tear others down, always insulting. Are you so shallow, so fickle, that the only joy you know; is in destroying beauty you do not understand…?'

Little tears glistened in the rude boy's eyes. It was clear Posk's words had cut him to the core.

And the truth in those words would be a far more powerful motivation for change than having someone push the rude boy to the floor and throw a desk upon him. For just an instant, Kialessa felt a twinge of pity for the small boy.

Posk walked back to his seat, and sat out the rest of the class in silence.

***

The evening at rehearsal it was no better. Everyone was practicing, doing their best to get their parts, yet Posk couldn't find peace with any of it. Why was the carpenter's son a better choice than the demon? Why did the princess have a choice of suitors when others do not? Why did she insist on wearing a dress when it was clear she was trying to dance? His questions went on, and on, and on.

He did, however, get the curtain calls spot on. He debated the wisdom of holding the ball in a castle though, and thought the fields were the much more sensible location for dancing.

He was, after all, half troll.

In the end, the evening grew late, and Allastassia seemed content to end the rehearsal early. Kialessa had a headache from listening to all of Posk's questions. Most people did. They walked away, their tired footsteps expressing their heart's weariness.

Posk, however, remained.

He waited until everyone had left, except the six of them. He marched right onto the stage where Allastassia was coaching Darrix in their dance.

'Allastassia,' Posk announced. 'You are the most beautiful young woman I have ever seen, and I am in love with you.'

She stopped.

Everything stopped. Even the night seemed to hold its breath.

Kialessa edged toward the stage, and looked around. Allastassia had inadvertently hidden halfway behind Darrix, who looked concerned, and just a little amused. He had pulled

     By Dr Joseph Ireland "Dr Joe"

himself up to his full height. Piex was sitting, reading. If he had any idea of what was going on, he gave no indication. Flower was fixing the chairs with a screwdriver, but it hit the floor and she sat, eyes wide, seeming paralysed.

Allastassia stood up, and still holding Darrix's hand moved in front of him to stand directly in front of Posk. 'Posk, you're really sweet. But I'm afraid you're just not my kind of guy.'

Posk looked puzzled, then frustrated. 'Oh, and who is? This armoured dancer?'

That bothered Darrix, but he did not move. Allastassia put her hand on his chest just to make sure he wasn't going to start a fight, but that was ridiculous. Darrix would never *start* a fight.

'If you must know,' Allastassia said, 'yes. He is. But that doesn't matter. You're a great guy Posk. Funny, and strong. Unexpectedly … philosophical. I just know you're going to make some girl the happiest person in the whole world one day. Some… nice… half troll… somewhere.'

Kialessa thought that was a good line. Allastassia had plenty of practice turning down guys; she was approached on average twice a week.

But, Kialessa knew, she probably would only say yes to Darrix, yet he never asked.

Posk threw his hands up in frustration. 'Why? Is my love not strong enough? Or pure?'

'Love?' Allastassia laughed. 'You're so sweet Posk! And so young, do you really know what love is? Am I not the first you have ever said you loved? This is a child's affection. You don't know me well enough to say that you love me.'

That stopped him. For the first time that evening, Posk had no questions. 'But… I have never felt like this before,' he replied.

'And, trust me, you will again one day. I am not your true love, not at all Posk. Oh, you're just so sweet. But sorry: No.'

'But… this just doesn't make any sense…'

'I know,' she said, and laid a daring hand on his arm. 'But it will. I'm not your type Posk, you'll see one day.'

'Why?' he shouted and stood away so she could see he meant no harm. He was just upset. 'Is it because you are a princess, and I am only a half troll.'

'It's nothing like that,' she said blushing.

'Then what is it?' Posk begged.

'I just ***don't want you***,' she told him, flat out.

He stepped backwards, as though she'd hit him. He looked like he was having trouble breathing. His arm muscles bulged, and Darrix tensed.

Posk sighed, looking out at the stars and gathering moon. 'This just doesn't make any sense,' he said, and left the night to end in silence.

***

It was around midnight that Kialessa, still concerned about Posk, broke a curfew nobody seemed to care if she kept and went out to look for him.

She found him sitting exactly where she'd left him, on the stage, looking up at the stars.

He heard her approach, but did not move. For a while longer he just sat there, till with tired legs she came to sit by him as well.

He sighed. It was clear that he had been crying. 'Why do we feel love if it can hurt so much? What point is there of feeling love, if the person you love cannot feel love for you in return? How will I survive?'

'Posk. It's not... you're just too young. You're nine, ten years old, why are you even talking about love?' Kialessa asked him.

'But we trolls age a lot faster than humans. I am fourteen in human years. That must count for something.'

Kialessa pondered.

Posk sighed, 'No, no. I understand. She is my *love unreturned.* I understand there is nothing I can do about this. But it does not seem fair, and yet it still is. And it still hurts.'

'Posk.'

 By Dr Joseph Ireland "Dr Joe"

'Never mind,' he told her, and turned away.

Kialessa caught a movement from behind her, and there, from the back of the stage, stood Allastassia. Like a ghost, completely see-through.

Or a dream.

Allastassia huffed, and looked annoyed, then angry.

Then finally, her gaze softened into pity.

She walked up then, and put a gentle hand on Posk's shoulder. He didn't seem to notice.

For a moment longer he sat looking far away, far into the darkened night where a silent moon watched their conversation.

And so they just sat there, on the edge of the stage, till the moon was quite full and the silent stars slowly dimmed in the night sky.

Presenting Problems

*'You will do well to consider honouring those the king chooses
to honour, for you will prosper no faster way.'*
Lord Tar Greens'holm, Allastassia's father.

Kialessa sat, not daring to touch the most expensive piece of furniture she'd ever been sat next to, at least as far as she was aware. The harpsichord was worth as much as a magical sword; rare ivory inlaid with gold, the coral fittings painted sky blue and white. What was it, ten thousand gold coins in value? Twelve? Somewhere between being introduced to it and told to sit down, she'd forgotten that part.

With that much wealth she could probably buy her entire hometown, peasants and all. She'd treat them well too. But there was no getting this massive musical instrument out the narrow doorways, which begged the question of how they'd gotten it in there in the first place. Perhaps they'd removed the entire window, or simply built the mansion around it? It was quite possible.

　　　　By Dr Joseph Ireland "Dr Joe"

Kialessa heard whispers in the next room. Allastassia was talking to her father again.

'... the tae'anaryn...' she heard Allastassia whisper.

Why hadn't she used her name?

Kialessa had learned, from sneaking around so much this year, that if she sat perfectly still, and silent in her own heart, she could hear very well, really, *really* well.

'What have you to be nervous about?' Her father's voice was deep and confident, the kind it was natural to believe. He was tall, a rare male part dryad, and a long time noble in the court of Lenmer'el. 'You are the most powerful rising enchantress in this kingdom, and one day entire armies will be at your command. You will never go hungry for your great wealth, and princes will be lining up to see you. What have you to fear?'

'I'm not, I'm not nervous,' Allastassia protested. 'She's just...'

'A tae'anaryn?' her father finished.

'No,' Allastassia said in an unconvincing voice, 'She's just so … provincial. Simple. Everything's right or wrong with her, just like Darrix.'

'Oh,' her father mocked in false sympathy, 'having difficulty mingling with the commoners again, are you, Allastassia?'

It sounded like she play-hit him.

He laughed. 'You will do well to consider honouring those the king chooses to honour, for you will prosper no faster way.'

'I know that, daddy,' she protested.

It made Kialessa's heart sink. Then she became extremely angry. So that was all she was to Allastassia, not a friend, just another way to impress the people she liked, just another way to get what she wanted for herself?

The room was silent, and then she saw her own reflection in the polished gold of the music stand.

But then again, at least Allastassia was *someone* who was willing to try, even if it was for her own reasons.

And then, Kialessa found herself thinking, weren't all friendships a bit of give and take? Darrix liked her for who she was, but she was still grateful that he stood up for her in front of the less mature boys. Piex taught her to read. Posk didn't do anything, apart from help them win in training.

Or did he? Maybe he helped her feel needed and important? He was always deferring to her, and didn't care in the least that she was a tae'anaryn, or even very uneducated one. She was his friend who gave him the confidence to turn up at the college, and the whole world was a better place for it.

So maybe it didn't matter all that much that Kialessa was Allastassia's "make over" project. That Allastassia really only needed her to keep the other students at bay during combat training with her keen bow and sharp senses.

She began to wonder if it really was wise to waste time being offended, and instead choose to see how her own life was bettered because she was one of Allastassia's "projects". Allastassia was a way to meet people she would never know otherwise. Allastassia taught her the things no one else knew, about faraway places, and nobility and history. Allastassia knew all sorts of things no one was supposed to know about who knew who, and what they thought of each other. Allastassia had taught her how to weave shadows, and then made it alright to do so in front of everyone who feared her.

And despite her mistakes, Kialessa was convinced that Allastassia was still a very good person at heart.

But it was probably a good idea not to tell Allastassia everything, Kialessa reasoned. Perhaps it was her thieving mother's own paranoia – she never trusted anyone. Allastassia was a good friend, but maybe not a best friend, a sort of challenging friend. A very best frenemy?

The door to the room popped open, and Kialessa gave a start. She hadn't realised she'd stopped listening, and wished she'd heard the rest of the conversation.

Allastassia was smiling, looking welcoming even if it was, to

　　　By Dr Joseph Ireland "Dr Joe"

Kialessa's eyes, a tad forced.

But Kialessa jumped up, and gave her enchantress a big, meaningful hug.

'Did you enjoy the drawing room?' Allastassia said with a more elven accent than usual.

'Divine!' Kialessa gushed in a way she hoped Allastassia would approve.

She kept smiling, but didn't seem to be able to think of a reply.

It took the wind right out of Kialessa's sails. 'Oh, Allastassia. I don't belong in a room like this! I could not even dare touch anything for fear of getting dirt on it!'

That cheered Allastassia up. 'Oh don't be silly Kialessa. You do belong here; this is your world now. You will one day be the greatest defender of the king in the whole entire kingdom, with lands and servants of your own. You have to learn to recognise value!'

Kialessa wondered if Allastassia was meaning property, or people.

Then she wondered if it wasn't a good point, actually.

'Come, listen to this,' Allastassia said, and then sat down and began to play a lilting tune of dancing melodies. It was so skilled, Kialessa had to stand back and wasn't sure if it was magical or not.

Allastassia reached back, grabbed her hand, and made her sit down next to her. The enchantress's fingers moved with such speed it was impossible to keep up. Somehow she even found the will to talk at the same time. 'Quality instruments, built by masters, carry magic well. See, my mother brings me here to practice. Do you like this Kialessa?'

She nodded.

'You'll like this even more.' Suddenly a tambourine began to beat out a tune to the harpsichord, lifting up from its special stand behind them. Two flutes lifted up on their own, and the air moved through them as they opened and closed their valves.

Allastassia began to glow with magic.

It was one of the happiest tunes Kialessa had ever heard.

Then Allastassia stood up, but the harpsichord kept playing along. She was closing her eyes to concentrate.

And then Allastassia sung. It was a tune to Spring, accompanied by half a dozen musical instruments and sung by one of the most talented people Kialessa had ever known. She had no idea how long it went, but it was not long enough. Allastassia stopped, and Kialessa stood up to applaud.

Allastassia seemed pleased, and just a little tired, 'You're very lucky, Kialessa, my mother tells me I must save my best performances for rare occasions. Did you like that? I wanted you to hear my music. We never have time for music at the college, I only get to practice here in the evenings on Planasday, but if I had my way, I'd do nothing else. What do we need arithmetic and spelling for?'

Kialessa did not know what to say. It seemed like the kind of thing Allastassia said when she was expecting everyone to agree with her. But Kialessa did not agree with everything Allastassia had said. But she could agree with some of it.

'That is the best music I've ever heard. I wish you would sing for us more often, you have the best voice I've ever heard.'

Allastassia actually blushed, 'Oh, thank you Kialessa. You're not so bad yourself.'

'Pah,' she replied. Now she knew Allastassia was lying. 'I could not sing to open a flower.'

'I bet I could teach you how! Oh, that's an easy one; mother taught me when I was a toddler! Would you like to learn?'

Kialessa hadn't expected that reply, though she probably should have in the present company.

Allastassia took the time to fill in the silence, 'Why don't you teach me one of your skills, Kialessa? I would love to learn about your world.'

Kialessa looked at her – she seemed so very sincere. But Kialessa doubted Allastassia, with her perfect dress and flawless skin, actually wanted to learn how to cook meat by hand, or draw water from a well. Or how to lie between the shadows and rafters so that no circus master would see her. Allastassia never went crawling around. Never.

But then again... maybe learning about Kialessa's world would do Allastassia the world of good.

Kialessa looked down, and noticed the little plate of treats. 'How would you like to learn how to make cheese?' Kialessa asked.

Allastassia seemed surprised, then looked like she'd just regretted her own word. 'All right... then...' she agreed.

It was the happiest mess Kialessa had ever made. Poor Allastassia tried to get the milk churning, but was so delicate about it Kialessa had to take over. It didn't matter about the splashes, but Allastassia cringed. When she took to kneading the curds, the enchantress actually tried to make a house servant do it for her, which Kialessa wouldn't allow. After they'd kneaded the other ingredients into it, she packed it into shape and set it in the larder.

Allastassia look confused, 'When do we get to eat it.'

'At the end of season, though I think after autumn would be much better.'

'End of autumn, you've got to be joking!'

Kialessa laughed. 'Good cheese takes time, and you have to have the patience of Lumos for the very best results. Well done!' Kialessa complemented her, and meant it.

But Allastassia seemed sad.

'You all right?' Kialessa asked.

Allastassia grabbed her hand and they ran outside. There, Allastassia took her to a walled garden. It was gorgeous, beyond words. Every shrub and grass were in flower, hanging in broad baskets and trellises shading the area. Water like dew dripped down, watering the mosses that blanketed the ground and kept the place cool. A trickling brooklet ran the entire length, regaining height in three separate fountains. The dappled light reflected from the blooms, dousing the area with mystical hews of pale lavender, sky blue, and rose petal pink. It was a beautiful, enchanted place.

'Father brings me here, when we need to "talk",' Allastassia laughed.

Kialessa was enjoying the magic of the place too much to speak.

Allastassia sat down, and Kialessa joined her.

'I have a confession to make,' Allastassia said. 'This play is killing me!'

Kialessa gasped.

Allastassia giggled, 'No, not literally! I'm just… it's so… phew! So much more than I ever imagined!'

Kialessa nodded, and held her friend's hand.

Allastassia's eyes ran with tears. 'Federach is insufferable, and Appleson virtually a mute! The dancers still can't go *en pointe*, and I simply cannot prevail upon Marchan to use his fireworks for the intermission! What am I to do?'

Kialessa looked at her. Surrounded by beauty and wealth, all she wanted was a play to go off perfectly.

As perfect as her own little world.

Kialessa sighed, but spoke her own thoughts, 'You've taken on too much, Allastassia. You expect us to be perfect, but we're just kids. And we're not professionals like the circus folk. I've seen them practice, they… it's like their lives depended on it.'

'It's how they earn their living,' Allastassia said dryly. 'Their lives do depend on it.'

That sounded harsh, but Kialessa didn't get distracted from the point she was trying to make, 'And ours don't! No one in the entire play, except yourself intends to continue on as a full-time enchantress or performer.'

Allastassia sat back, as though she'd never thought about that.

Kialessa sighed, she hoped she did not sound too harsh. 'You make the entire play look wonderful, you know. You taught everyone how to dance, and sing in harmony. You virtually rewrote the entire play from scratch –'

'Pah, those circus folk had no idea.'

Kialessa just grinned, and shook her head. 'And that's why, I really think, you'd do yourself a huge favour and give up the play…' she could tell from Allastassia's glare that was not an option, '…or, at least, go easy on yourself, and others. Stop trying to *force* things all the time. Just, relax.'

Allastassia sighed. 'I prayed to know wisdom, and promised I'd listen if you had the answer … Mild herbs, ewe!' she sighed again. 'But I guess… I guess… well, you're right, you know. We're not professionals. It's not like mine or anyone else's future is going to rest on the result of one stupid play. And even if it did, I can still give *my* best. Maybe I would be a little less stressed if I didn't worry so much about what others were bringing to the play. Just… take what I can get and make the most out of it… but stop trying to make everyone care about the play just as much as I do.'

Kialessa couldn't help but sigh with relief. It was as if a stifling pressure had been taken off her chest.

'Thanks for listening, Kialessa,' Allastassia smiled. 'You are a good friend.'

It made Kialessa grin. 'And you are a good friend too.'

Allastassia started singing to herself. She sounded happy. They sung together and Allastassia taught her a few new songs, even the one which was supposed to open flowers. They even managed to get it to work for Kialessa, but only on the blooms that were about to open anyway. Still, it was another kind of magic all to her own, and Kialessa was very proud of herself that day, and glad she had a friend in Allastassia.

It wasn't until the day was done, and she bid them all goodnight as their carriage dropped her back at the college for the night, that Kialessa's heart felt a dark, grey misgiving in Allastassia's last words;

'Have a good night, Kia, we'll get back to getting everything perfect next rehearsal,' and Allastassia laughed, the cold edge of empty humour in her idle jest.

 By Dr Joseph Ireland "Dr Joe"

Dreamtime

Change will come, change is inevitable; you will change, your friends will change. The whole earth might be turned upside down! But don't get lost in change, and forget who you really are inside. Your inner self, your unchanging worth; your power to make the world a better place no matter what happens to you, or it, or me. These things must never change.

Doreth, cindersmith (priestess of hearth and community), to Allastassia 313 CY.

The time for the play grew closer, and with it, Allastassia's levels of stress and fear. Kialessa was worried about her. On the outside she seemed to have everything under control, even though it was clearly a very stressful time for her. But Kialessa still wanted to make sure. Allastassia was dreaming about holding lightning, and doing it. She had blown up the college hall and possibly cursed someone to make sure she got the lead role. She had taken Kialessa to another world, and still nobody would believe her.

I wonder what else she dreams about? Kialessa found herself wondering almost constantly.

And she knew someone who could answer that question.

That night, and praying she'd find a way, Kialessa was delighted when she realised she was dreaming once more. She didn't know how long she'd been asleep, but she finally became aware that she was dreaming. And that meant she could remember what she'd come to the dream realm for; Kiel.

She wanted to find her almost adopted brother. She remembered what he'd taught her about finding things in dreams. About just reaching out, and expecting them to be there, and they would.

So she shut her eyes. The whole of creation seemed to pause for a moment, filled with power and expectation. *Kiel,* she thought, *how nice it is to see you.*

And she opened her eyes, in her dreams.

She saw him then, but she was very surprised to see him talking to someone. He looked confident, as he always did in dreams. But he held back from this woman, as though they'd only just met.

The background was dark, as if they were some place Kialessa could not see. The woman he was talking to was strange, as if she had two forms, and Kialessa could not place which was real. She was, at the same time, a tall and noble elf, dressed like a queen. But she was also a twisted and hunchbacked crone, with ugly warts and gnarled skin. Kialessa was, for a moment, repulsed.

Kiel suddenly turned, and saw her, 'Oh, hey Kia! How are you doing?'

'Fine. Look, there's something we need to do.'

He looked serious. 'A task? And you're dream walking now, aren't you? Must be important.'

The woman he had been talking with had already vanished from Kialessa's sight, and mind.

'It is. You remember Allastassia, the dryad enchantress? We

 By Dr Joseph Ireland "Dr Joe"

need to check up on her.'

'Sure, lead on,' he offered her the way, a path forming.

All right, Kialessa thought, *Allastassia, so nice to-*

Thunder stopped Kialessa in her thoughts. When she opened her eyes again she saw the castle of Lenmer'el, as though she was watching from the far hills. Above it a mountain, made of swirling white and grey clouds, fumed. Lights within flickered almost constantly, as though lightning danced in is depths.

'Oh, Kia,' Kiel mourned. 'Why have you brought me here? I've been avoiding this place for weeks.'

'What is it?' Kialessa asked.

'I've been too afraid to find out,' Kiel replied.

Yet Kialessa knew she would find Allastassia under that cloud, or inside it.

'Come on,' she insisted, and grabbed his hand.

He made a magic carpet out of thin air, and they rode toward the glowing storm.

Then he turned them invisible. Even the air seemed to pass right though them.

'That's so clever,' she told him.

He didn't reply, but looked steadily onwards. She could tell he was using all his skill at dream walking to not think of anything bad happening to them while they rode toward a storm. That was the way with the dreamrealm; it sent you whatever you imagined, good or bad, almost right away.

As they drew rapidly nearer to the storm they saw shapes moving in the air, long and snakelike. They seemed to be fighting back the storm, pushing apart the frantic storm clouds with their powerful wings. They rode around it in a counterclockwise direction, but it was a battle they looked to be losing.

'Can't we just dream it away?' Kialessa asked.

'I tried,' Kiel told her. 'We're not dreaming that, someone else is. Either that or everyone you know is refusing to admit something in the real world, and dumping all their fear here, in the dream world. It's making a real mess of things in Lenmer'el. I don't know how anyone sleeps.'

'We don't seem to be having trouble,' Kialessa told him, but then she thought. Were they? Were they really sleeping as well as they usually did? Or was there some discontent at the edge of their consciousness that everyone felt, but nobody named?

They flew under the cloud now, as fast as thought.

The castle was deserted.

'Every dream spirit has fled this terrible place,' Kiel informed her.

Just then a huge bolt of pure white lightning exploded from the king's keep, the most powerful and best defended of all the structures in the castle.

Immediately Kialessa knew where to find Allastassia. 'Oh, poor girl,' she muttered.

Kiel frowned.

By the time they arrived, Allastassia was holding court in the dream realm. She had the royal crown on her head, and the rod of the king in her hand. And before her, on the floor, knelt the king's highest advisors – the captain, the high priestess, the wizard and the steward. Thunder rumbled around them, and from the bright light that poured in from the windows Kialessa wondered if they were inside a bolt of lightning.

Kiel set the carpet down near the door. 'We should leave,' he whispered, nervous, but not afraid.

Allastassia turned to face them, eyes glowing with white fire. She looked terrifying, and regal. But she just sat there, on the king's throne, regarded them with silent eyes.

'Allastassia, what are you doing?' Kialessa wondered.

The enchantress said nothing.

'Allastassia. You need help.'

'Kneel,' Allastassia demanded, and a strange compulsion came over Kialessa.

Kiel stood in front of her. 'This isn't going to work the way

 By Dr Joseph Ireland "Dr Joe"

you hope it will, Kia. The best thing you can do would be to get out of here.'

'Kiel, don't worry, it's just-'

Suddenly Allastassia stood and shouted, 'Kneel!'

Kialessa felt her body fall forwards, and turned it into a roll. Before she had time to adjust, she saw Kiel pull a golden shield from the air and turn it against Allastassia's will. The command exploded against it in a halo of violent blue sparks.

'We need to esc-' Kiel tried to say.

Allastassia pulled the shield from his grasp, but another one appeared immediately in its place. Then she swept her hands forward, and the entire throne room collapsed against them. Kiel became a whirlwind, and protected them both.

'Run!' he shouted, and pulled out a golden sword and charged Allastassia in a single enormous leap.

She was about to sweep him away, when the enchantress found her arms chained to the ground. But just as his sword was about to strike, she vanished into the earth.

'Kiel, what are you doing?' Kialessa shouted, afraid if he hurt her here, he would hurt her in the waking world.

'Forcing her to wake up, and remember the dream,' Kiel explained, showing her the golden blade. She realised the sword was composed more of a single wish than actual metal. 'You should leave here, this isn't your kind of fight, Kia! I-'

He had stepped forward, only to find his foot sink into the stone like water. He was trapped up to his ankle.

'Run,' he tried to tell her, and he slashed at the stone. It chipped, but did not shatter. The sword disappeared, and he reached up and jumped as if he was trying to fly. For a moment he did, managing at least twenty paces right up into the air. But the stone stuck to his foot and became a pillar, wrapping up and around his knee.

It dragged him back, smashing him into the ground, burying him up to his waist.

Sweat broke out on his face, and his breathing became

ragged.

Kialessa ran up to grab his hands, but he refused her help, trying to push her away, screaming at her to run. He began smashing the stone with balls of fire, then a spear of ice. He smashed down on it with fists of pure iron.

And slowly, but surely, he was sinking.

'Allastassia, stop!' Kialessa shrieked. 'Kiel, just wake up.'

He looked up at her, stone gathering around his chin.

'Kiel, you can beat this!'

'She's too... powerful...' he muttered, and disappeared beneath the stone.

Kialessa screamed.

And from somewhere, a young enchantress laughed.

Kialessa spun around, and Allastassia was standing there, floating above the ground. Her clothes fluttered in the arcane breeze, and she glowed as if she was on fire. Her eyes and hands shone out with a brilliant, terrifying light.

'Allastassia, what are you doing!' Kialessa shrieked. 'You need to stop this, you need to-'

'Kneel,' Allastassia softly demanded. Kialessa felt her body beginning to obey. She fought with all her will, but quickly discovered the more she knelt, the more her soul surrendered to the enchantress's powerful will. She tried to roll, but found herself on one knee. She knew with dread certainty if her she ever bowed her head, her soul would die, and become a mindless minion to the amoral enchantress before her.

'Allastassia...' Kialessa begged, summoning the last of her will just to speak, 'please...'

Suddenly, in the very moment Kialessa was about to abandon herself to the enchantress's desire, the ground exploded out from under her. There was a man, made of pure gold. It... kind of looked like Kiel. He reached out and struck the ground, waves of golden light shooting in all directions. The light threw Allastassia away, and Kialessa found she was master of her own form again.

      By Dr Joseph Ireland "Dr Joe"

The giant man turned then, and with surreal slowness managed to pick Kialessa up where she had fallen. He seemed to say, *I tried to tell you this was too much for you.* Then, with a gentle breath, he sent her hurtling back into the waking world.

When Kialessa woke up, she found herself screaming. It was some time around midnight, and all the other girls in the dormitory were there. They leapt back from her and in the next instant Kialessa saw why – she was burning with golden fire, though it didn't damage the blankets or her wool rug in any way.

'Are you all right?' Natasha shouted.

'Allastassia! Where is Allastassia!' Kialessa screamed.

'Here!' Federach shouted from the other end of the dormitory.

The old head mistress was coming into the room now, holding a lantern and a golden symbol of the pantheon against the darkness.

'Oh look,' the dwarf continued, 'she's still asleep. How is she able to sleep with that scream-'

Kialessa ran to her bed, the fire dying around her. 'Allastassia, wake up!' Kialessa screamed, a little too loudly. Everyone covered their ears. She did not know what trouble Kiel was in, or how long she had before it was too late for at least one of them.

'What?' Allastassia said in a groggy voice. 'Oh, it's you. What are you shouting about, it's late,' she said, and rolled over.

'Allastassia, don't go back to sleep!' Kialessa screamed. She didn't dare think about what might happen if the enchantress fell asleep again, and went right on battling her brother in the dream realm. She grabbed her blankets and tore them away.

Allastassia woke up immediately then, and looked out angrily, 'What is it?!' she demanded.

'Yes, little tae'anaryn,' the head mistress scowled. 'What is it? There are no signs of trouble, why make them? Have you been dream walking this night?' She laughed, since it was supposed to be a joke. Dream walking was a very rare, and mystical, talent.

Kialessa turned to face her, saying nothing.

She held the lantern up to Kialessa's face. When she spoke, it was clear and demanding. 'Allastassia, get up. Federach, Natasha, get these two to the high priestess immediately. The rest of you, **back to bed this instant!**'

Everyone ran.

***

The four girls were escorted by two silent castle night guards, their bright armour and steel swords a strange comfort.

'So, what businesses compels four young maidens to see the priestess at this late hour?' one asked.

They did not answer.

'Bad dreams again?' the other snickered.

Something about that must have bothered Allastassia, who probably didn't want to be kept from her bed any longer than she needed to be, especially to cross words with witless castle night guards. 'Yes,' she replied, sparks dancing between her fingers.

They took one look and shut up, no further questions.

The high priestess, when serving the king, lived in a small room buried underneath the shine to the Eternal. They knocked firmly on the door, and waited a while before knocking again.

Soon the high priestess could be heard arising, and came to the door. She opened it, without holding out a light, and stared at them. 'Oh… dear…' was all she said.

Then she invited them in, began stoking a fire, and warming a kettle. After a few moments of simple conversation to wake herself up, she asked, 'Pray, tell the rest of the story that brings you here tonight.'

The dream tumbled from Kialessa as fast as she could get it out.

　　　　By Dr Joseph Ireland "Dr Joe"

For a moment everyone was silent.

Then Allastassia laughed, and the other girls with her, 'Do you really think-' she began.

Suddenly the high priestess brought down her walking stick, and it made a thunderous crack as it struck the stones, 'Enough!' she shouted.

Kialessa couldn't help but cringe, and found the others doing so as well.

When the priestess spoke, her voice was changed, as one with authority, like a queen in her own right, 'Enough, **enchantress**. You may think to weave your magics around the minds of those you play with, but do **not** think to deceive me as well.'

The thunder rumbled around the castle, and Kialessa wondered if the noise hadn't woken everyone up.

'I… I'm sorry,' Allastassia begged. 'I didn't realise.'

The high priestess didn't soften, not one bit. Her voice continued, words of judgement and condemnation, 'You did not realise? Do not lie to yourself, or me. To make a wish, and fill it with the power of your enchantments? You want everyone to believe that you are all right so badly you were willing to addle their minds to do it? That is dishonest, Allastassia. And it is wrong.'

Allastassia wept, and Natasha put her arm around her.

The high priestess softened. 'I'm sorry; I may have overreacted just now. Young girl, do you realise your laughter just then held a powerful enchantment?'

'I didn't… I didn't… I…' Allastassia claimed, but her defence crumbled under the high priestess's glare. 'I'm so sorry. I just so wanted everything to be all right. When I heard about that dream, about what my imagination was doing to this kingdom… it just seemed so wrong. I just didn't want it to be true.'

Tears flowed freely from her eyes, and Kialessa's as well. They held hands.

The priestess sighed. 'The head mistress was wise to send you here tonight,' she concluded. 'It seems we may have more work to do here than I expected. Mild herbs, no more meat. And those meditations your mother taught you about, have you been practicing them?'

One look at Allastassia's face told them all that she had not.

The priestess shook her head. 'I have much to be concerned about at this time,' she muttered. 'Prophecies, and seeking wisdom on behalf of the king. Every hour is taken up with service. I cannot be asked to hold your hand as well, young dryad.'

Allastassia nodded. 'Mild herbs. No meat. I almost don't eat any anyway. And I promise to get back into practice. I hope… I really hope it was just a bad dream.'

'That is the purpose of the dreamrealm,' the priestess said. 'To heal the waking world. If you do your part, young woman, I am sure you will be all right. The changes you must undergo at this time do not need any extra temptation to go awry, do they? Take *better care* of yourself!'

'I will, I promise.'

The high priestess nodded, and waited. 'And Allastassia, as much as this seems important to you, I want you to give up that play.'

Kialessa gasped, she couldn't help it.

Allastassia seemed chagrined. 'I know, good priestess. I know. But… I'm all right, I think. This has been a good, um, wake up call. Yes, I have been stressing far too much.'

The priestess looked grim, 'You have no intention of quitting, do you?'

Allastassia sighed, but did not meet the priestess's stern gaze. 'Everyone's going to love this play, you'll see. I know it can't be perfect, but they're going to love it.'

'It, or you?' Federach demanded to know.

Allastassia gave her a disarming smile, 'The play, silly. But everyone knows how much the director has put into it.'

No one spoke for a moment.

'Go,' the priestess finally said. 'There is no wisdom in keeping you up any further.'

They stood up to leave, but the high priestess added as an afterthought, 'Young Kialessa,' she said with a smile, 'I was unaware that you were a dreamwalker as well.'

'I'm not,' Kialessa confessed.

The high priestesses' smile vanished. 'Then how is it that this is accomplished?'

Kialessa felt very sure it was not time to tell them about her brother's talent, not just yet. 'I have… a friend.'

'I don't suppose… no… But tell me, is this person trustworthy? Have you met them in person, in the waking world?'

'Yes!' Kialessa said emphatically.

'Good, that is good then. But Kialessa, it's better that we don't know who your guide is in this thing. Dreams… are careful business, especially when enchantresses are concerned, well, in any world full of magic I suppose.'

Kialessa nodded, and left the high priestess standing there in her darkened room, holding her delicate clay cup. She seemed for all the world at peace.

And as soon as they shut the door, Kialessa heard her shuffling quickly into the other room, riffling through a draw for her jewellery, or weapons. The other girls didn't seem to notice, but Kialessa knew one thing.

The priestess was anything but at peace.

And that meant here was hidden news to find.

The News

If you do not realise it yet, let me make it most clear:
Your lives are in grave danger, as is the king's.
Lady Jacinthia, high priestess, 313 CY.

Kialessa found trailing the high priestess was much harder than any of the castle guards. She kept turning back, as though some part of her knew she was being followed. Kialessa left the other students before they'd even returned to the dormitory. She knew she'd get in serious trouble for that, but with luck, they would not care again.

Oh Eternal, Kialessa prayed, *I promise to only do good with the things I find out here. But if it's not your will, I will leave.*

She watched the high priestess scurry to the room where the steward usually stayed, organising a kingdom. She fumbled for her keys, looking around.

Looking like she had a secret to keep.

And that, Kialessa found, was very exciting.

And exciting was a good thing.

 By Dr Joseph Ireland "Dr Joe"

So she decided to keep going.

Kialessa watched as the priestess shut and locked the gate, so she had to climb up it and squeeze through the gap between the bar and the roof. It was a tight fit, but she was very small.

She dashed after the high priestess. Sure enough, she made her way to the steward's office. Looking around again she knocked on the door once, and it immediately opened. Light flowed out, revealing the silhouette of the steward.

Kialessa heard him say something, and wished for all the world she had an extra pair of ears she could send places and hear with. Then she noticed the sound of their voices was coming from another place as well. High up, between the corridor that led away and the windows of the steward's office someone had left a small, stained-glass window open.

And muffled sound flowed out from there.

Thanking her luck, or her grace, she scurried up the wall. She pressed against the pillar. It was made stone, and she had to reach uncomfortably to not press herself against the actual glass. She'd learned to stay out of the light when dodging lazy castle guards and made her way up to the window. It was as if all the other windows were magically made proof to sound, but when left open, the noise was quite clear.

She tried to make out their voices, unsure if she'd heard the first few sentences clearly.

'… keeping us up this late at night,' the steward muttered.

'Not until the captain arrives, Lord Grudon,' she replied.

'I can only assume,' the wizard's voice joined in, 'that your cause is truly urgent, to keep a wizard up like this. Wizards need their sleep.'

'I know, De'Feur,' the priestess apologised.

The door swung open, and solid footsteps that clinked with metal armour and weapons approached. It had to be the captain.

'Jacinthia,' he muttered, voice soft in the night, 'was that you only a few moments ago?'

'It was,' the high priestess apologised.

'What was?' the wizard asked.

'De'Feur,' the steward protested, yawning, 'I told you; you've got to unweave that sleeping blanket your mother made. Wizards may need their sleep, but no kingdom is threatened at the convenience of its wizards.'

The captain laughed.

'Well,' the steward insisted, probably talking to the priestess. 'What is the trouble?'

'First, our Tae'anaryn has a dreamguide.'

'Really?' the steward asked, seeming surprised. 'First she holds the rod of the king without harm, then weaves shadow without effort, now she dream walks as well?'

'I did not say dream walk,' the priestess reminded him. 'But a guide.'

'Well that's good, for her,' the captain offered. 'Isn't it?'

The priestess was silent a moment, 'It wasn't so good for you, was it Bon Shur'e.'

He coughed.

'At least it explains a few points from the recent mess with the wisp demon,' the wizard muttered.

'We'll need to contact the walker of the weeds. I'm sure she'll be only too happy to check out the situation for us once more… at her usual price,' the steward said.

'This does not bode well,' the priestess muttered. 'Things are moving too quickly. To have contacted a dreamguide so young? The portents spoke of danger this season. Yet it is this very concern that may have just blessed us the most tonight.'

'What do you mean?' the wizard asked.

'She dreamwalked into a dream her enchantress friend was having.'

They all seemed to get very interested at this point. The priestess continued, 'Her guide was able to protect her, but the dream was deeply troubling. It seems our enchantress seeks nothing but the throne of Lenmer'el itself, and the obeisance of us all.'

        By Dr Joseph Ireland "Dr Joe"

There was an uncomfortable silence.

The steward asked, 'You don't think this is serious, do you? It was just a dream.'

'You know better than anyone not to underestimate the revelations of dreams, Grudon,' the priestess chided him.

The wizard interrupted, 'I do not doubt the authority or skill of the priestess in interpreting dreams, steward. It is her place to do so, need I remind you?'

'And need I remind you,' the steward argued, 'that is has always been my place to talk some sense into the rest of you? To remind you not to panic over unnecessary things? To keep balance between searching for stolen children and gathering the late spring harvests?'

'Funny to hear you preaching about the need to not clutch at shadows!' the captain laughed.

The wizard stifled a chuckle.

The priestess continued, 'The tae'anaryn's visit to the dreamworld revealed a cyst that stretched far out beyond the castle walls, centred on the throne room.'

'Impossible,' the wizard muttered. 'There's simply no way she could accomplish this alone.'

'That *large*?' the steward agreed.

'It was difficult to tell, from the report. I must seek confirmation myself. But it seems the dream dragons are having a hard time holding it back.'

'Now that is serious. You sure?'

'I am convinced,' the priestess continued. 'And, deliberately or not, the enchantress tried to enspell everyone to disregard the tae'anaryn's report.'

The captain whistled. 'So, that was you then,' he muttered, probably referring to the priestess's thunderous denial of Allastassia's accidental enchantment with her walking stick.

'Indeed.'

'Well,' Grudon, the steward, muttered, 'it looks like you've got your work cut on, sister priestess. I assure you, we all have too many tasks to tend to at this time, what with the council of the king's coming up in Emerel next year and all.'

'It was not my intent to burden you without extra cause,' the priestess said, firmly. 'I have her under constant watch, do not fear. But did you not hear my report? She seeks your obeisance; she seeks the throne of the king.'

'Surely you don't think-' the steward began.

'Of course I do,' the high priestess reprimanded him. 'This girl is different. She is powerful, far more than her mother, and we have all witnessed what she is capable of when moved. Already this child has conquered a portion of the dreamrealm larger than this city, without apparent help or effort! Her every wish is a danger to us now. She must be careful; we must all be careful. Her life is changing, and if she ever desires results more than she desires peace… well, heavens help us all. If you do not realise it yet, let me make it most clear: Your lives are in grave danger, as is the king's.'

***

Allastassia wouldn't stop crying. 'I'm so sorry,' she begged. 'I just wanted you all to love this play.'

The ringmaster held her hand up, straight away. They were in the dormitory the next morning. 'I know, *l'ange*. Be that, as it may, I have come into contact with some terrible news I am not permitted to share at this time. I am sorry children, but it seems we will have to cut short our stay here in your beautiful city. I pray you will forgive me, but we will be leaving tomorrow morn.'

'But what about the last two weeks of performances?'

'Well, they didn't sell as nearly as we had expected,' Flower answered for her. Her eyes were red as though she had been crying all night, and her voice was tense. She looked like she did not want to be here. 'We will refund everything. But I wanted to tell you first, there will be no play this year.'

　　　By Dr Joseph Ireland "Dr Joe"

Everyone was silent.

Even Allastassia, though she was clearly devastated. Thankfully, this time, her emotions didn't seem to be affecting anyone else, at least no more than usual.

'I don't understand,' Allastassia said, looking over at Kialessa.

She wondered if this was all her fault, and wondered if Allastassia was thinking the same thing. Little tears flowed down her face once more.

'Don't cry, girl-ling,' Federach said, patting her on the shoulder. 'Maybe it's for the best.'

'Best?' Patsi asked. 'It's not for the best, not at all! You know how much work we put into that play, and now we're never going to get to do it. I don't think I can live with that!'

The room was silent, but Kialessa got the distinct feeling everyone agreed with her. It had been a long project, to abandon it only a week before the great day, even with all its faults.

It didn't seem fair.

But then again… with what was going on where no one could see. Kialessa felt she knew exactly why the clever ringmaster was leaving.

'I suppose,' Allastassia tried to bargain, 'we could try?'

Natasha held up her hands, 'Now, you junior students do what you want. You'd better hope the tutors agree! But, you know, if things haven't worked out so well so far… well, maybe you should get out while you still can?'

Aolith spoke, 'And leave a project undone? No, there is little honour in this.'

Many agreed.

'Then we finish this play anyway?' Patsi asked, her face brimming with excitement.

'I think we should at least try,' another agreed.

'Very well. But I don't think I should have the lead role anymore,' Allastassia promised them.

'But, who will play the role of the princess?' Patsi asked.

No one answered.

And a little feeling stuck itself in Kialessa's heart. Who could be the princess? Who had watched the entire play, and knew the lines, and could dance well enough?

'I can,' Kialessa admitted.

Allastassia beamed from ear to ear, and leaping up, hugged her.

'I was so hoping you'd offer,' she sighed.

And as they embraced, it was all too easy for Kialessa to push away the image of the pale girl that was backing herself away into the corner – Flower, eyes wide and hands trembling.

     By Dr Joseph Ireland "Dr Joe"

When The Show Must Not Go On

'Allastassia, stop!'
Darrix, 313 CY

There was a small furore when citizens learned the circus would not be staying the full time, but before the sun was full in the sky they were already packed.

They were leaving at the end of the day.

Flower and Allastassia locked arms and shared tears once more.

'Are you sure there is nothing we can do to convince you?' Allastassia begged.

She looked over at the ringmaster, 'No, but thank you. The circus life is a random one, with many beginnings and endings, and a life of adventure. Emerel will be glad to see us early, and we will spend our earnings making good our fortunes along the way. I cannot say how sorry we are that we... miscalculated how much time we had here. Please, please accept our apology.'

'I'll miss you, even more this time!' Allastassia cried. 'Oh, how I'll miss your voice in the chorus. You won't even get to see the play you worked so hard to make!'

They both seemed so upset, but to Kialessa Flower was beginning to sound almost a little too apologetic.

They hugged, as Flower looked over at Kialessa. 'My mother wants to talk to you, Kia.'

'What about?' Allastassia asked.

'Oh, training things, I expect,' Flower wiped away a tear. 'She feels so bad that we have to leave!'

'Where is she?' Kialessa asked, finding it hard to keep out of all the sadness right now.

'I'll take you,' she said, and with another hug watched as Allastassia fled away.

Kialessa took a step, but then Flower held out her hand to Posk. She spoke, her voice forceful, and not the least bit sad all of a sudden, 'But not with you.'

'Oh,' he said, and looking a little upset, he glowered suspiciously and stalked off on all fours, he was wearing Piex's headband all the time now, much to everyone's gratitude.

Kialessa wondered how Flower could be all demanding all of a sudden, was the sadness just an act?

A moment later they found the ringmaster in the main tent, dismissing some other helpers, 'Ah, the little tae'anaryn!' she gushed. 'How sorry I will be to miss you!'

Kialessa looked up at her, wondering what she wanted.

The ringmaster grew serious, she sat down so they could see eye to eye. 'I should warn you, little one. It's not safe to stay here. You should leave with us.'

'Leave?' Kialessa said out loud, she couldn't believe what the ringmaster was saying.

'Yes, come with us! I've seen your talents, and I know you have other talents still hidden. You could have a good life with us. Come, join the circus, abandon this foolish college and all their books. They will teach you nothing about the real world!'

Kialessa could say nothing.

        By Dr Joseph Ireland "Dr Joe"

'I see you are impressed, no? This is a good life, and one that is far freer than what you will find in stone walls.'

'Well,' Kialessa finally found her voice, searching for words Allastassia might say; positive, and inoffensive. 'I'm touched by your invitation. But this is my place… no… I want to stay here, for now.'

The woman smiled, 'That, I think I can respect.' She turned to look at Flower with a kind of **told you so** look.

The little girl looked visibly disappointed, and could not meet Kialessa's gaze.

Then the older woman's face grew serious, 'But I must warn you… I think you should reconsider this offer. Trust me when I tell you it really is in your best interests…'

Kialessa frowned, was that a threat?

'Don't look at me like that, little one!' the woman insisted. 'I don't mean to offend. I just want what's best for you.'

Kialessa smiled, not sure what to say. 'No, thank you. You have been very kind, and taught me things I never knew. But my place is here. This is where I need to be, at least for now.'

The older woman nodded, and for just a moment Kialessa might have caught the glint of a silver tear in her eye. Did she really care that much?

It was nice to be cared about.

'Well then,' the woman smiled, clearing her throat. 'Off with you, child! No point standing around when there is a world to entertain! Off with you then, horns!'

Kialessa couldn't believe she'd guessed her mother's old insult, but with a crooked smile, ran back to Posk.

***

Allastassia was shouting again. Things were not going the way she thought they should. And the more she shouted, the more people seemed to be unable to do things the way she wanted. And despite all the practice and lack of existential ennui, Posk still missed his cue at least once.

It was the night before the opening night. Kialessa thought she was doing a great job at being the princess, and Darrix was really fun to dance with. But she couldn't shake the feeling that nothing she did could meet the enchantress's expectations, or measure up to her enormous skills. They made her wear a bonnet the whole time, and she couldn't use her tail to dance which made things a lot harder. In her heart Kialessa couldn't believe that anyone would really learn to see her as a princess.

Suddenly there was a shriek from the stage. Patsi had missed her line, and Allastassia scolded her so fiercely she stepped backwards. There was a sickening crunch of fragile scenery and Patsi disappeared, leaving a Patsi sized hole in the entire scene. People scurried around to help pick her up. But no-one said anything to Allastassia.

The enchantress just looked blank. Then, without saying a word to anyone, she slowly began to walk away. Everyone fell completely silent as she did; no one dared to say a word over Patsi's soft crying.

A moment later, Allastassia walked right out into the forest and kept on walking.

'Do you think we should go after her?' Piex asked.

'Not this time,' Darrix replied. 'Not yet.'

Kialessa watched, torn between loyalties to two friends. In the end, her concern for Allastassia won out. Kialessa ran.

She found Allastassia a moment later, standing in a small clearing, looking from the dark forest towards the dimming daylight of the rehearsal grounds. Her face was strewn with tears. Dark scintillations of magic floated around her, and it felt to Kialessa as though a wicked presence held her back with its hand. Allastassia didn't even seem to notice she was there.

'I would give **anything** to see my play performed properly,' the distraught enchantress mourned out loud.

Kialessa's breath caught in her throat. **What** did Allastassia just wish for? Did she have any idea what she had just said?

        By Dr Joseph Ireland "Dr Joe"

Kialessa didn't have time to announce her presence before Allastassia turned from the light and began to walk into the dark forest. Magic flowed in her every footstep, and Kialessa had to run to keep up while the enchantress walked in a slow, leisurely pace. She called after her, but Allastassia acted like she couldn't even hear. They were moving into the deep woods, where they were told never to go.

The trees begun to bend more and more over the forest path, becoming increasingly unfriendly with every step. They seemed to speak in cruel voices as the wind rushed between them, and the sky darkened.

'Allastassia, stop!' Kialessa begged. 'We should not be here! You must not be here! '

But the enchantress did not stop, or could not; it was as if some evil power was driving her on in answer to her careless wish: *I would give* **anything** *to see my play performed properly…*

Kialessa begun to form wish of her own, *Eternal, please help me to reach my friend, and know how to save her!*

She ran, but no power she possessed could help her catch up with Allastassia. The forest was dark, and she began again to fear as she had the day the drake almost ate her. She could see no way of finding the enchantress now.

And what was Kialessa's surprise when she almost ran straight into Flower. She was standing in the twilight, dressed for travel, sitting atop her massive minotaur friend. Her expression was concerned, and she back flipped down and spoke before Kialessa had the chance to say anything.

'I'm so sorry!' she apologised.

Ugly grunted and sat down. He looked as though he'd travelled a long way.

Kialessa didn't know what to say. Was Flower trying to stop her? 'What are you doing here Flower? What happened to the circus?'

'Oh!' she waved dismissively. 'Mother is going to *kill* me when she finds out. I'm amazed they haven't found out already.

I ran away from the circus to find you, and it looks like I only just found you in time.'

'Time for what?' Kialessa asked. What was Flower going on about? She grabbed her hand anyway and made her run with her after Allastassia. For some reason having a friend seemed to make the journey much easier, though Ugly appeared to be having a hard time getting his horns though all the branches.

Flower continued. 'Before tonight, I never told you, and I'm sorry. But I can feel magic. I can make it slip around me, fold it up and … do things with it.'

'You're an enchantress?' Kialessa stopped.

'No, well, yes… maybe. Look, Kialessa. I came to get you out of here.' She stopped walking, and Ugly grunted and sat back down. 'You don't want to know what I've felt being gathered from the dream world around Allastassia. She's… going to do something terrible, I just know it. She's so ambitious; she needs to feel other people love her. It's not about the play any more Kia… she's going to enspell the entire kingdom, and she's prepared to die for that power.'

'What? You knew?! Why didn't you stop her!'

'I tried! I really tried. I talked to her; we talked to the priestess, and the steward. But things just kept… going downhill. Mother decided we just had to get out of there before things got bad. Haven't you noticed? The birds... and the faeries have been fleeing the place in droves. I don't know what Alli's trying to do over a stupid play but …'

'But we have to stop her,' Kialessa finished.

'She's too powerful,' Flower shouted. 'Maybe the king has some authority but by the time he calls it down it'll already be too late. I… we… ran away.' Tears fell from the edge of her eyes. 'We have to go now Kialessa. I care about you. You're different, and people never understand people like us. We belong away … we're only safe among our own kind.'

Kialessa was stunned. She didn't know what to do. Those were the kindest words, but exactly what lengths was Flower willing to go to in order to stop her helping Allastassia? She could only guess… but if she had to guess… Flower would not stop her.

'I can't,' Kialessa told her. 'I have to help my friend, or at least, to help my people.'

The young acrobat wrung her hands together, her face wrinkled in worry and fear. She looked at Ugly, and he just shrugged. Kialessa could only imagine what the last few days had been like for them. How had they survived alone in the wilderness all that time, and then known exactly where to find her just when she was needed the most?

'All right,' Flower said. 'All right. Perhaps it is time to be brave… but I want you to know something.'

'Yes?' Kialessa asked, dragging her on again.

Flower pulled her hand back. 'If we go after her, we will get caught up in her fate. The things she is doing, the result of her actions… we cannot be spared from them. So I hope you know what you're doing. I already told you, I'm just no match for her and she knows it.'

Kialessa nodded.

Flower waited.

Kialessa held out her hand, 'We can do this. I know we can't fix this but, perhaps, we can get through to her and then maybe she can fix herself.'

'I sure hope so.'

'Come on,' Kialessa said.

Ugly groaned and stood up again.

'Which way did she go?' Kialessa asked.

'Oh, I don't need to see her.' Flower cringed. 'The magic is like a light… in that space next to my imagination. It's all dark and twisted this way. *Oh*, I don't like it; it feels so wrong on my skin! So, yeah, that's pretty much where she's gone, I guarantee it.'

'I guess the Star King gave you a little more magic than your parents realise,' Kialessa said.

'You have no idea,' Flower gave a mischievous grin behind her frightened eyes.

They ran. Kialessa tried to dodge through the brambles and nettles which seemed to reach out and grab her every time she tried. She dodged and ran as fast as she could, but soon traded out her normal clothes for her work clothes. It seemed to help.

But it didn't help her keep up with Flower. All the magic in the world seemed to be slipping right past her, almost all of it. Sometimes a thorn would cut her leggings or pull at her hair, but she moved among the forest with unnatural grace. It was as if she was pushing aside not trees or hedges, but the very essence of the magic itself. She was jogging ahead at a normal hasted pace.

Finally they stumbled through the brambles into a clearing. There they found Allastassia, talking to a man. He was sitting calmly on a stone in front of her. He was holding out to her a little golden ring, with a bright yellow stone inside. It was a curious site, calm and clean – very out of place in the danger of the late afternoon.

'Oh no!' Flower whispered, and reaching out, touched Kialessa's arm.

There was a gentle rushing sensation, as if Kialessa was catching a hold of the other-magic around Flower. Then Kialessa saw beyond the illusion. It was not a man at all. He had goat horns on his head, and he was like an animal from the waist down. It was a satyr.

'Allastassia, d-' Kialessa begun, when suddenly someone grabbed her and Flower from behind, clamping their hands over their mouths.

'You again!' a cruel voice laughed. 'You're worth more trouble than I can imagine – your father would be so proud.'

Fear rushed through every fibre of Kialessa's body. She knew who owned that voice, the snide laughter in every word.

Uninvited Guests

'Then trust me when I say that thing is not for you. That man is not who he appears to be, and he is trying to deceive you.'
Flower, 313 CY.

'Dog,' Kialessa said, and at the sound of that name, the hand loosened. Kialessa took the chance to slip out of his grasp and whirl around to face him. Flower stood back, looking very worried, yet ready to fight for her life. Ugly was still a way off trying to make his way through the bushes, and hadn't even noticed trouble yet.

It was the cruel man; Jerik, the intruder, assassin of kings, the man who could turn into a dog and had tried to kill her earlier this year; till a tree had paid with its life to save her. But she'd hunted him, and eventually found him. The curse she'd laid on him last season prevented him from entering the castle, but clearly it didn't stop him from being right here, and endangering anyone he wanted – including them.

'The king would like to have a few words with you,' she

said, trying to sound brave.

'I'm sure he would!' the assassin smirked, leaning casually on a tree. 'But I doubt he ever will. Not after this quirky plan unfolds. Look, girls, just let the little enchantress take my gift, and we'll be done here!' He spoke calmly, as though they had all the time in the world.

'What is that ring?' Flower asked.

He didn't answer at first, 'You're from the circus, as I remember. You take after your mother I see; courageous, and with the nose thing going on. You really shouldn't have gotten involved in this.'

'Conversational, aren't you,' Flower said dryly.

The assassin bowed, but was still out of arms reach. 'The ring is a gift, if you must know. A gift for King Dunnkan, but your enchantress doesn't know that. She thinks it's just for her. But my … employer… has need of your King's throne, and after the fire and the wisp demon failed to put him aside, well, we've had to take more *creative measures*, haven't we, young Dame Kialessa Tavernskeep?' He smirked at her.

What she wouldn't have given to wipe that smirk away. But she knew there were other problems. Kialessa turned to face Allastassia through the underbrush, who was still talking to the satyr as though she couldn't hear them, though they were only a few dozen paces away. Desperately she wanted to dash into that clearing and tear away the satyr's mask, but she knew from experience that Dog's knife was less than a thought away.

'What are you going to do with her?' Kialessa demanded, well aware the fear was evident in her voice now.

'And why should I tell you?' Jerik teased, but Kialessa glowered at him with her fierce eyes.

He smiled calmly, and continued on like he was actually trying to be her friend. He stepped away, making it hard for her to see both him, and Allastassia. 'A budding enchantress has much untapped power. Were it to be unleashed in a single act, it could level the entire castle, especially from one as talented as your friend there.'

Flower gasped, 'You... you're trying to *shatter her Chrysalis!*'

The assassin just smirked.

'Allastassia, stop!' Kialessa shouted, but Allastassia did not even blink.

'You cannot break the magic of this place,' he explained, still sociable. 'Though I am a little surprised you made it this far. Please, little one, don't let this trouble you. Change is necessary, and change is coming. You can ride it, or die fighting it. It's your choice.'

'Then I die fighting!' Kialessa shouted, and managed a running backflip off a nearby tree in an attempt to kick out at his throat, hoping it would give her the time she needed to stop her friend.

Faster than she could think, he twisted his arm and knocked her away.

Just like she knew he would.

But there was a little plan, a secret advantage Kialessa had that, hopefully, Dog would not have figured out yet. With desperate prayers she reached into the shadowrealm. It was easy this time, now that the need was sincere. She reached out, not with her hands, but with her tail. Even as she spun in the air she wrapped the end of her tail around the hilt of her long dagger. Flicking it as she spun, the scabbard flew off, and the unsheathed blade lashed out.

It should have hit him right in the face. It should have struck him right in the temple. It would have ended endless weeks of fear, and frustration. But Dog was fast; inhumanly fast. He seemed to blur at the last instant as he noticed his danger with senses far beyond what was humanly possible. The dagger barely left a scratch on his other cheek.

Yet the hours of pain and training had paid off and she'd landed on her feet.

'Ouch!' he said, sounding more annoyed than frightened.

'Why are you trying to harm the king?' she demanded to know, again.

Closing his eyes, he muttered what seemed a brief prayer in a language she did not know, reaching down to rub dirt between his fingers. Instantly the wound stopped spreading, though a narrow, faint scar now adorned the other side of his face.

'Clever,' he complimented her. 'But we both have secrets. Like I, for example, *really* want to know how you managed to eavesdrop on my conversation with my master.'

Kialessa said nothing, her heart suddenly reaching out in fear to Kiel. She moved the long dagger to her right hand, but still felt wildly outclassed by the master assassin. In her heart, Kialessa felt her only hope was to get through to Allastassia, or at least, to give Flower enough time to.

Dog stepped closer, and she shifted her stance to cover the enchanted acrobat. He grinned, and stepping back gave them space. 'I want to know how you managed to dream walk right into the hidden chamber! Ahh, the dreamrealm, so *difficult* to control! I suspect my master will want to do something about that one day, being the *motivated* individual he is.' Dog muttered to himself, like talking to an old acquaintance, not a sworn enemy. Kialessa couldn't understand his confidence, what was he trying to tell her? Or was he simply talking so that she would make the mistake of trusting him?

He continued, 'You used the dreamrealm to get in, but we couldn't catch you then. We set traps. We posted guards, and yet you haven't been back. I'm beginning to think that you aren't the dreamwalker at all. Such a rare talent, yet you don't have the markings. So who is it, child? Any likelihood that you'll tell me who brought you in there?' and his eyes darted towards Flower. She was studying Allastassia with unbroken intensity, and Kialessa hoped she was up to something.

Kialessa stood, silent. She hoped he didn't find a way to force the secret of her dream walking step-brother from her.

'I didn't think so,' he said. 'Like I said, we both have secrets.'

 By Dr Joseph Ireland "Dr Joe"

He sighed, sounding just a little tired. 'Just when *are* you going to realise I have no desire to harm you?'

Kialessa was confused, no desire to harm her? Was he not trying to assassinate her king? Was he not trying to make a disaster at the hand of one of her best friends? Did he not once try to eat her alive with his pack of enspelled dogs?

Suddenly his eyes narrowed.

'Allastassia, no!' Flower shouted.

Kialessa spun around.

Allastassia's hand was slowly inching toward the simple golden ring. That was when Kialessa recognised it, by feeling if not by sight. It was a feeling she'd once shared in a powerful wizard's castle that'd she'd almost destroyed by creating an open spell.

That's what the ring was. It was an opening. To magic.

Endless power.

Zero responsibility.

And that was when Flower somehow managed to tear though the magical barrier that was keeping them back, and plunged almost headlong into the clearing.

Dog looked genuinely surprised at that.

Desperately Kialessa tried to place herself between them, but he hadn't even moved. She left him alone and tried to push her way through the trees to her friend. But they did not give way, and it was as if the air was somehow gently pushing her back, holding off her beating fists, and keeping out her shrill cries.

'Allastassia, stop!' Flower begged her.

Allastassia turned, and looked confused, 'Flower? I thought you left. This really must be a dream then.'

'No!' Flower shouted. She looked like she was about to run up to her, but the satyr reached for his knife and drew it out partway in a clear threat that Allastassia would not see. Flower stayed, but raised her hands as if begging. 'No! It's me Allastassia. This isn't a dream and you *know* that! Stop this, we both know what you're trying to create, don't use anything as an excuse to do what you're planning to do.'

Allastassia looked confused, 'I always knew there was more to you Flower. The magic is always brighter around you. You are a good friend.'

'Then trust me when I say that thing is not for you. That man is not who he appears to be, and he is trying to *deceive* you!'

He drew his knife a hairs breadth further, and Kialessa had the distinct impression that if Allastassia did not take the ring, he would kill her.

'You're not really here,' Allastassia repeated. 'And this doesn't really matter. I can want anything I like in this place, and there's nobody who can stop me.'

'Allastassia, no!' Flower cried.

'You'll see,' Allastassia said, her eyes already glowing with dire magic. 'You'll all see. It's a very beautiful play. And it's going to be done perfectly. Then everyone will love it.'

Flower took a step forward and shouted, 'Allastassia, stop being so **arrogant!**'

Kialessa screamed, she shouted, but nothing she did seemed to get through to the enchantress driven mad for power.

Slowly Allastassia slid off the ruby ring the king had given her half a year ago, and allowed it to fall to the ground unwanted. With an outstretched finger, she allowed the satyr to replace it with the golden ring.

The assassin had already disappeared.

Kialessa screamed, using her special voice, the one that made people cringe. The one she used to call Posk.

Allastassia looked about then, as though she'd heard a voice from far away, but she did not see Kialessa. Only the evil satyr saw her, and gave her a cunning grin.

Without so much as a hesitation, Allastassia popped the citrine ring on.

As soon as it was on, the Satyr raced away into the forest as though for its very life. A mighty wind tore through the clearing

     By Dr Joseph Ireland "Dr Joe"

and Allastassia begun to levitate off the ground, her hair whipping around her.

Suddenly the magic preventing Kialessa from entering was swept away, and she fell to the ground beside a trembling Flower. There was a bestial huff, and Kialessa turned to see that Ugly stood tall behind them, glaring at the enchantress.

Allastassia turned to face them now, her voice sounding deep and powerful as though it was no longer her own. 'You're too late,' she said, 'and it doesn't matter.' She began to change, taking on the appearance she'd had in the dream when she'd seated herself on the king's throne.

'What are you doing?' Kialessa begged.

'Please don't stand in my way,' the enchantress whispered, and the trees shook. For a moment she just stood there, in the air, looking sorry. But then the sorrow passed and was replaced by all her frustration and lust for power. 'I have *work* to do!' Allastassia shouted, and in a shatter of glimmered light, disappeared.

Kialessa ran.

She knew Allastassia would be going to the castle, and when she got there, there would be trouble far worse than any the dream world could image. But she knew she'd never get there in time.

Suddenly a voice she did not recognise spoke from behind her. It was deep, and powerful. 'Here, let me be of service,' Ugly said.

And that was when the massive minotaur, a lithe acrobat adorning his neck and horns, scooped her up onto his back and charged. Trees splintered at his reckless flight, an unstoppable behemoth of raw muscles and unbreakable determination.

It hurt, but Ugly was *fast*.

7 Racing the Minotaur

 By Dr Joseph Ireland "Dr Joe"

From the Heart

Because it doesn't matter how many friends you have, or how powerful you are, or how beautiful you are – if you do not accept yourself it will never be enough. Think about what you're doing… whose attention do you feel you need so badly? If you do this you cannot go back – is this how you want to be remembered?
Allastassia Greens'holm. 317 CY.

By the time they arrived back at the city it was obvious that something was very wrong. Dark black clouds, tinged with blue, covered the western horizon. Birds, and all manner of forest creatures, fled the unnatural storm that was bearing down on the castle and the outdoor theatre grounds next to it.

Students were milling about, looking at the magical storm.

'Run!' Kialessa screamed.

But she was already too late. A powerful voice spoke inside their hearts and minds. 'No. Stop. I'm going to show you how to do the play now. And everything is going to be perfect, and you're all going to *love* it.'

Kialessa watched with surreal horror as life and colour drained from everyone's faces. It was as if they'd lost their own souls. Ugly even stumbled, and crashed to the ground fast asleep. Everyone began wandering toward the stage. But it was not only students, it was everyone, all the people from the town. Allastassia held them in her thrall.

Flower held on to Ugly, trying to push away the magic. For a moment it worked, but she could not keep it up against the broken power Allastassia held.

Clouds thundered as dark blue lightning danced in their midst. The clouds began to swirl around the castle, reaching toward it. Within moments the clouds covered the stage, and the entire town. Everyone was there; unarmed guards, commoners and wives, even Pringol the money changer.

Everyone.

Kialessa watched helplessly as they formed perfect lines of exact rows, arranged by height. And when they did not quite fit, the ground rose or sunk to make sure they did. Everyone would have a wonderful view of the stage; if they only weren't soulless zombies.

Suddenly a bolt of blue lightning struck the ground. Kialessa ran over to see, and was shocked to find Piex had fallen over, Darrix leaning over to help him. Neither seemed trapped in Allastassia's spell.

Flower ran to them, 'What happened?!'

'Piex was trying to break the spell on the tutors!' Darrix shouted as the wind began to pick up, looking a bit surprised to see Flower, but not making an issue of it right now.

Kialessa looked down. Piex was badly hurt by the lightning, but it wasn't fatal. He'd been struck by lightning before, if not in combat practice, then by his own many mistakes in wizard training.

'That's not going to work,' Kialessa told him. 'She has an open spell.'

Piex nodded in an, *I kind of knew that already,* way. 'It was worth a shot. What happened, how did this start?'

'It was the assassin, the intruder.'

'Him again!' Darrix shouted in anger.

Kialessa reach out to help Piex sit as best she could. His wounds were charred where Allastassia had struck him with lightning. Darrix reached out, praying for him, and his wounds closed in an instant.

'He gave Allastassia a ring,' Flower explained. 'It's some kind of… portal… it makes a gaping hole in the magic of the world. I think its power might be limitless, and I would not be surprised if it is cursed somehow.'

Kialessa continued, 'He's trying to shatter her chrysalis!'

Darrix looked horrified. 'Alli…' he whispered, 'Allastassia is doing all this?'

A magical trumpet blast blew, almost deafening them.

The play was starting.

'We have to stop her!!' Darrix shouted. 'We don't know what's going to happen! We've got to get to Allastassia. Even she can't control this much power, it will burn her up, if not the entire kingdom!'

'We know!' Flower screamed back.

Kialessa jumped up with them and ran towards the stage. She saw Allastassia, glowing with dark blue light, and silhouetted by lightning.

But the moment she tried to jump on the stage she felt two impossibly strong hands grab her from behind. Kialessa struggled in their grip, but found the blacksmith and his wife hauling her off the stage. They carried her with inhuman strength back to the front row of the audience, and made her kneel.

Darrix was struggling against his own captors, and it took three of them. But they eventually held him fast. 'Allastassia, stop! You don't know what you're doing!'

Don't I? Allastassia's voice thundered in their minds. *DON'T I! I am going to put on a play today, and you are going to enjoy my little play. And it is going to be a perfect play. The kind of play that everyone one wants to see again and again. The kind of play that everyone should see again and again…*

Then the play began, and citizens made their way on stage, controlled entirely by magic. It was as if Allastassia had chosen them for the parts ages ago. Their mouths moved, but no sound came out. The entire play was narrated by Allastassia's ambrosial voice.

The actors performed their parts perfectly, and when that was not good enough for Allastassia, she made them do it again. And again. But nobody seemed to mind. It was clear she was erasing their memories of any parts she didn't like.

So the play was not perfect, not at all. It stopped, and started. They spoke in strange rhymes that were not at all pleasant. Even the demon was just as solid and obedient as all the lifeless actors, but the play finally seemed to be measuring up to Allastassia's unobtainable expectations.

'Kialessa, look!' Flower whispered, around intermission time when everyone clapped in unison and otherwise didn't move a muscle.

Kialessa turned to where Darrix was pointing.

The clouds. They had surrounded the castle of Lenmer'el. But they didn't yet seem to be able to cover it all. They'd formed a ring around the entire massive structure, a single beam of blue sky shining down upon it from above.

'What is she doing?' Darrix asked.

Kialessa had a dreadful feeling as she suddenly realised what was going on, and what the assassin's plan had been all along. No doubt he'd known about the dreams as well.

'You heard her!' Kialessa whispered. 'Everyone needs to see this play. Everyone! And that includes-'

'The king,' Darrix finished for her.

'And he is only safe within the castle from the assassin's cursing. Once the king gets out here, with no guards to defend him...' Piex left the sentence unfinished, still greatly hurt.

'It will be an easy task to destroy the king, and the nation,' Darrix replied, struggling against those that held him so well.

'What about the king's most trusted advisors?' Kialessa asked. As if in answer, a bright circle of white light radiated from the highest tower, momentarily scattering the darkening clouds. For a brief time they turned a natural grey, then Allastassia's magic reasserted itself.

'They're doing all they can,' Darrix informed her. 'But her magic is breaking the protections on the very castle. Once they reach the king, he'll become like the rest of these people... helpless.'

As if to validate his words, armoured guards, ones that usually patrolled the outer wall of the castle, had already began to make their way down to the performance field, fully armed. They came and stood among the unblinking audience.

'So why aren't we like everyone else?' Flower wondered.

Piex coughed, 'I am guessing she feels more for us than those others. She wants us to appreciate her as ourselves. We are not just a mindless audience to her.'

Darrix thought, 'Not only that. She respects our judgement. Maybe we can use that to help free her? We've got to stop her, you know.'

They shouted, calling her.

'She can hear you anywhere under the cloud,' Piex informed them.

A moment later Allastassia appeared over the stage. Her visage was truly terrifying. She was surrounded by a nimbus of dark blue light. The magical ring was glowing a golden beam, but it too seemed polluted, and terrible. Her clothes and hair fluttered in the air.

Darrix spoke, his voice commanding. 'Allastassia, stop. What you are doing is wrong. You are taking away these people's freedom to choose. If you don't stop, you are going to endanger the king!'

For a moment Allastassia just stood there.

Kialessa knew he'd failed.

Suddenly the ground rose up around Darrix, and a moment later he was gagged with stone.

Kialessa screamed, and tried desperately to reach out to Darrix. But the people held her back.

Darrix fell over. He must have been in terrible pain, and was probably having a hard time breathing.

'Allastassia, what are you doing?!' Kialessa screamed. 'Stop it, set him free! You're hurting him.'

Just like he hurts me, Kialessa, every time I smile, and he doesn't notice. Every time I dance to impress him, and he is talking to someone else. He never listens to me. He spends so much time praying, how will he ever learn to love me?

Kialessa was astounded. Did she somehow think listening to her automatically meant obeying her? Was this the depths of Allastassia's perverted desires; to force people to love her?

'This isn't right,' Kialessa told her. 'You can't make him *love* you…'

Allastassia paused, thinking. *Sleep then*, she told him, and the stone snapped from off Darrix's bleeding mouth. But he did not get up.

Kialessa tried to stand, but it was useless.

Allastassia was preparing to begin the second half of the play. More guards arrived. Soon, it would be the king's councillors, and she would make them bow too.

Then it would be the king, and she would make him give her the sceptre and the crown.

Then there would be nothing to defend him.

'Allastassia!' Kialessa screamed. She looked down at Piex, calling as much magic as she knew. *Ponio*, she told Allastassia, but her nascent wizardry was completely ineffective against the terrible blue nimbus.

There was nothing she could do, unless… somehow… if there was still the desire to be loved inside Allastassia. If that somehow could be used to get through to her...

'Hypocrite,' a deep male voice whispered from behind Kialessa. She jumped with fright.

It was Posk.

Allastassia smiled. 'So glad you're here too, Posk. Come, take a seat with the rest of them. Take it easy, I'll do the curtains now.'

'Hypocrite!' he roared. 'You told me you knew what love was?! Then what is this! This is tyranny! This is *lies!*'

Allastassia looked at him with a smile. 'Ah, little boy. You will soon learn there is much more to love than a pretty face. Sit down.'

Posk didn't wait. He swung around and punched the two people who'd tried to grab his arms and knocked them out in an instant. Taking a single step, the blacksmith and his dear little wife met the same fate.

Kialessa rubbed her now free arms, and stood with Flower.

'You see, you did this, in the name of love!!' Posk roared.

Allastassia was silent, and did not smile, 'I'm sorry you feel that way,' she said. An instant later, the earth beneath Posk rose up and swallowed him whole.

'Posk!' Kialessa screamed.

Was there no stopping her? Tears flowed freely, for her friend, for her king. For the unreachable heart of a lost enchantress.

Suddenly the ground bulged where Posk was buried, then again. Allastassia reached out, yet in the next instant Posk erupted from the earth like some kind of primordial godling. His shirt was torn clean off, and his skin scratched with countless abrasions. But what worried Kialessa the most were his eyes.

Two pools of molten black.

He was entering the troll rage.

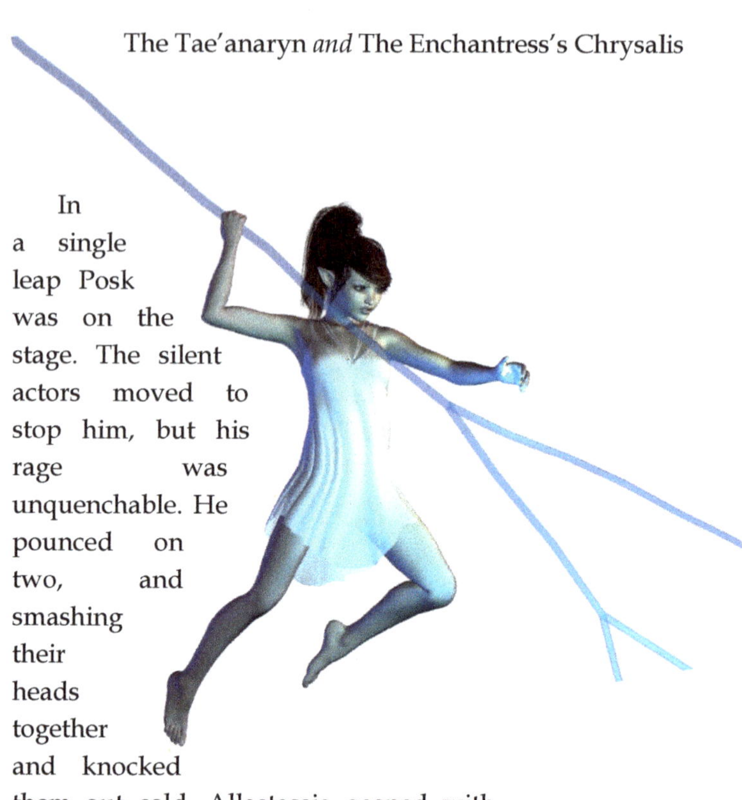

In
a single
leap Posk
was on the
stage. The silent
actors moved to
stop him, but his
rage was
unquenchable. He
pounced on
two, and
smashing
their
heads
together
and knocked
them out cold. Allastassia gasped with
indignation. The actor playing the prince drew his metal
sword, but Posk reached down and snapped off a board from
the floor. They lunged at the same time. Posk deflected the blade
with his makeshift shield, then head-butted the poor man right
off the stage.

Allastassia held out her hand, and lightning danced down
from the sky. For one glorious, threating moment, Allastassia
was holding a bolt of lightning.

She looked down at Posk.

He looked back.

And with a roar he ran up the stage wall, leaping high off it
to reach out toward Allastassia.

The lightning struck him right in the chest, flowing all
around him.

But it did not stop him. Lightning burns, but it doesn't push.

And it burnt Posk brutally.

　　　　By Dr Joseph Ireland "Dr Joe"

Yet ignoring it all, and his many smoking wounds, he grabbed Allastassia by the ankle and pulled her from the sky.

She shot downwards and crashed into the stage, standing unharmed, but landing knee deep in splintered wood.

Less than a breath later Posk stood before her.

She glared at him.

He roared in her face.

Dark lightning crackled in the sky.

And then he slapped her.

The crack sounded across the entire audience, from one end of the field to the other. Allastassia was clearly unharmed, but she was anything but impressed. She glared at Posk with her glowing eyes, her mouth wide open in indignation and surprise.

'You…' she stuttered.

He roared again, as if to say, *Stop this! Now!*

'You…' she repeated, getting angrier.

He roared again, and raised his hand. But he could not bring himself to strike her again. He stepped backwards and beat his fists down on the stage with such power the hardwood splintered and went flying everywhere. He grabbed the curtains, and tore them one end to the other.

He grabbed up a metal sword from the ground, and

8 Alli v's Posk

bit it in two.

Allastassia glared at him with equal power and rage.

For a moment they just stared.

Then, incredibly, Posk started to walk away, his eyes regaining their normal colour.

He just turned away, and hopping down from the stage began pushing his way right through the centre of the audience.

'Posk!' Allastassia called after him.

He kept on walking.

'Posk!' she screamed, her voice thundering from the sky.

He stopped, but didn't turn. When he spoke, it was a whisper almost too soft to hear. 'I cannot stop you. I care about you too much. So if you're going to insist on destroying yourself, this castle, and everyone you ever cared about then go ahead. I'll be waiting here to help you pick up the pieces.'

He turned, and looked at her, his face full of sorrow and compassion. Then he turned, and kept walking.

Thunder rumbled in the sky.

Allastassia looked around, as if seeing the stage and its silent audience for the first time.

A single tear floated down her cheek, and turning into sparkles floated away in the air. 'Please…' Allastassia begged, 'please, don't leave me.'

He kept walking, but there was no denying he could still hear.

She whispered, the dark light dimming around her, 'I just wanted to make something people would love. Something so beautiful, they would never forget it. They would never… forget me.'

Posk did not turn around, but they could all hear his sigh. 'Live, or die tonight. *I will never forget you,* Allastassia Greens'holm.'

With a sudden leap was gone from their sight.

Suddenly the oppressive feeling lifted. People began to blink as though coming out of their daze.

　　　　By Dr Joseph Ireland "Dr Joe"

Kialessa heard Allastassia crying from the stage. She looked incredibly tired.

Kialessa stood, and dragging Flower with her ran towards Allastassia. She was still glowing with terrible blue light, still wreathed in unnatural power. But now she trembled. Now, it finally seemed she was fully aware that she was surrounded by a broken stage of fallen backdrops and unconscious actors who could no longer stand.

Allastassia held out her hand, the one with the ring. And without a sound, she allowed Kialessa to try and remove it. It resisted, and Allastassia winced in pain.

Lights and dire magic flowed around the ring. But then Flower took hold of it. Something she did, or was, dissolved the magic before it could even touch her. Dark whispers, like demon threats, echoed in the night, but the young acrobat acted like she couldn't hear. Bending all her concentration to the task, Flower removed the ring.

A demonic shriek echoed in the night, yet the ring turned to ash as soon as it was off, and Allastassia fell into their arms weeping. Starlight began to stream once more through the clouds, and the magic slowly ended.

Then, one at a time… the audience began to applaud.

The Enchantress's Chrysalis

When soft the caterpillar,
Spins her cocoon,
Patience waiting not amiss.
Soon the butterfly,
Will emerge,
From this sacred chrysalis.

Lady Annadaria Greens'holm, 294 CY (Allastassia's mother)

Kialessa stood, not sure of what to think. For slapping Allastassia, the king had put Posk in the stocks for an entire afternoon. Allastassia was sitting by him, offering encouragement he didn't seem to need. He just grinned, and hadn't stopped grinning since she'd sat there. It was clear he would have been glad to spend a whole week there if it had been by her side.

　　　By Dr Joseph Ireland "Dr Joe"

So she sat, looking glorious and dignified. A stranger passed by and might have said something, to which Allastassia replied, 'No. For sure it is I who belong in these stocks, and not he.'

9 At the stocks

Kialessa heard Ugly, Flower and Darrix walking up to stand beside her.

The young paladin had his squire's armour on, his blade Defender in the hilt at his side. 'I wonder,' Darrix seemed to think out loud, 'if the guilt of seeing Posk suffer is her true punishment.'

'He doesn't seem to be much put out by it,' Flower muttered.

Ugly grunted with agreement. He still wasn't speaking to

anyone, though why it was so was anyone's guess.

Posk was still grinning, but perhaps that was because Allastassia was patting him on the cheek again.

'And that,' Darrix ensaged, 'is perhaps the most terrible burden for a good person to carry.'

It was true. The king had blamed the intruder, he had blamed the ring. He had blamed everyone but Allastassia. The priestess had claimed the ring cursed, and thus all blame was alleviated from Allastassia once and for all, or so it seemed. No injured soldier or damaged property was recompensed. It was all counted to the account of the enemy of the king.

But slapping a young woman?

To the stocks!

***

The next two weeks flew by.

Kialessa waited with great excitement. The long delayed night of the enchantress's play had arrived. The stage was repaired, and wounds healed. For some reason the king had insisted the play be performed, and that he be in attendance personally. Kialessa could only guess at his reasons, but perhaps it was just for Allastassia's benefit; so that she did not come to fear her own wishes. So that she would know that she could, indeed, do anything she wanted with good friends and hard work, and *without* the help of magic that threated to turn the world inside out.

Kialessa waited with the others backstage. Allastassia, at the king's orders, was back in her dream role as princess. She looked glorious in the distinctly non magical dress they'd made for her. The senior students were back in there too, including Aolith, Federach, and Natasha. The choir had almost doubled.

For her part, Kialessa was back in the choir. But being the princess, even for a little while, had been *fun*. She'd enjoyed the attention, and found she knew the whole entire play by heart

        By Dr Joseph Ireland "Dr Joe"

and back to front, unlike most people. Kialessa now almost *wished* they had a role for her to play.

The king arrived, with a substantial contingent of his royal guard. It was a show of force, and of confidence. No one could intimidate her king!

Suddenly Kialessa heard shouting from behind the stage. Piex ran up, and Allastassia rushed to meet him.

He stuttered at her.

'What is it, wizard!' she demanded.

'You're not going to believe this,' Piex began, then continued with a noticeably nervous stutter. 'Federach, see, was caught with several students … she's wrote "Tyrant" on the high king's statue – she's accused of defacing the property of the king!'

Everyone gasped in horror.

Piex continued, 'She's seeing the town guard now. I think they have her in the lock up… I don't think she's coming tonight.'

'Surely the king can forgive that, just for one night!'

'Not before the preliminary council,' Piex explained. 'Not according to the law, anyway.'

They looked at Allastassia, perhaps hoping she would conjure up a solution to this last moment disaster, or fearing she might.

'I… I don't know what to do,' Allastassia admitted.

Kialessa smiled, and walking up, picked up the spiked pitchfork Federach had used as a prop to establish her evilness.

But she left the fake horns still sitting there.

'Well,' Kialessa announced, 'I guess it's time I got to work as well.'

***

Patsi went on, and in a bold, unwavering voice announced the play in perfect rhyme. The musicians hit their cue without fail, and the scene began. On danced Allastassia, as proud as sunshine, all guilt and fear forgotten. She danced so beautifully, it was clear no one loved, or needed, this role more than her.

Darrix came on next, and sung his song. It was beautiful. It was a magic all of its own, and for a moment it felt to Kialessa as though he was singing just to her, or at least, just to someone… like her. It ended too soon.

The princess announced her interest in the carpenter's son, and the scene ended as Posk rolled up the pit from hell. Thunder rolled from the musician's pit, simulated by students striking great sheets of metal.

And Kialessa smiled.

It was her turn.

Wrapping shadow from her hidden collection around herself, she ran up the skirting. She was supposed to come up from the floor. *But every performance benefits from a little… improvisation,* she thought. She hid in the shadows near the roof, and causing her eyes to glow, hissed menacingly.

The audience screamed, and the musicians stopped dead as the silence held the audience in rapt attention.

Kialessa held on to the awning with her tail so that, from most of the audience's point of view, it must have looked like she was floating.

She almost whispered her threatening verse, so soft the entire audience held their breath to hear it.

'Each day in burning I am pained,
By wrath of gods most pure,
And though I suffer, it is clear,
A greater pain I must endure,'

'For to know love unanswered, it is known,
A greater pain there can be none,
And I will die before I see,
A princess marry a carpenter's son!'

     By Dr Joseph Ireland "Dr Joe"

'For he is mine! I do declare,
From earth to hell below,
That he I'll wed, and death to all,
Whom my love will not bestow…'

The last words ended in a whisper, and time seemed to pause. Then the musicians caught their cue and burst into sound, and the audience erupted in applause. Many stood.

Kialessa slunk from the stage, the last part visible most likely her still glowing eyes.

She dashed off to her position while the audience still clapped. With a beaming smile she ran to the others backstage.

But they weren't smiling.

They looked aghast.

Kialessa stopped short, not understanding what she could have possibly done wrong.

'You said, "he",' Patsi burst out in explanation.

For a moment Kialessa was confused. Then she remembered. She'd said 'he.' She'd said, "For *he* is mine!"

Her hands leapt to her face, and she pressed down the sobs that wracked inside her. The perfect play they'd almost died for, and she'd ruined it!

But Allastassia was smiling, and patted her shoulder, 'Don't worry, I got this! Every play improves with a little *improvisation*. Dancers, on stage now.'

Kialessa apologised with tears in her eyes, but Allastassia just smiled, and went on to dance.

Kialessa watched with fear in her stomach, but it somewhat faded as she watched the dancing. They were very good this time. All that practice was finally paying off. But there was something more. They were really trying this time.

They were giving it their all.

Even more than in combat training, Kialessa thought.

The ballroom dance ended, and the suitors presented

themselves to the princess with a suitable mix of humour and wit. Everyone was really impressed with Darrix, and shouted him encouragement.

Then it was the "king's" turn to speak.

The Rude Boy.

For a moment, there was silence. It was as if he'd forgotten his lines. When he spoke, it wasn't in his usual voice. He sounded, well, like he was actually trying to be a king.

'Am I the king?' he asked them.

Everyone froze.

'Am I **the king**!' he roared, sounding threatening. He was really… improvising here. No one had any idea what he was trying to do, but one thing was clear, he was really trying very hard. For the first time ever, it actually looked like he was acting.

Allastassia played along, keeping in character, but Kialessa could feel the tension in her voice. 'Yes, your highness.'

The rude boy paused, 'Yes, and so I am. But did you know that if I force you to choose, I cannot force you to **like** what I choose. Did you know that?'

He asked, and for just a moment, he seemed to be talking to Allastassia. Not the princess. 'It's something I've only just realised,' he muttered, tapping his head almost as if thinking was a new experience for him. 'So, I guess what I'm saying is… in the end… the choice is up to you. You have to make it for yourself.'

Allastassia was astounded.

So was the audience. They stood up to applaud the honest and thoughtful king.

He bowed, and sat back down.

'Well, in that case,' the Princess said, 'I choose…'

She paused, and in that instant, Kialessa realised it was her cue. And she knew just what to do about her little mistake before.

She hissed, and gathered as much shadow around her as she could. She raced to the pit where the demon was supposed to

　　　　By Dr Joseph Ireland "Dr Joe"

rise and made it only just in time. She rose up like a shadow from the underworld. Kialessa spoke,

'Foolish king, your power fails!
You think to let her choose?
Then I my claim will gladly take,
In this, I'm sure, you lose.'

'For this young man will soon be mine,
For what other choice has he?
In burning deaths of endless pain,
Where my love, only, sets him free.'

And Allastassia, standing protectively in front of Darrix, boldly proclaimed;

'Touch him not, you fiend of hell!
Speak not of love, you cannot tell,
A prisoner of him you shall not make,
A prisoner you are, of your own mistake.'

Kialessa replied, matching her rhyme.

'Peace forever will be denied,
From my love you cannot hide,
Each day a loved one will be slain,
Until my prisoner he remain!'

Roaring with indignity, Allastassia shouted:

'You cannot force a love so true,
But choose to love, and soon will you,
Find love again, but not through this,
To force a love, and steal a kiss.'

Suddenly Allastassia's voice choked up, and for a moment, she broke character. It sounded perfect, as though the princess was experiencing real fear when challenging a demon's love, and perhaps, in a certain way, that was exactly the war that was going on within a young woman.

Kialessa stood there a moment till she remembered to hiss, and say;

'He will be mine, oh, you will see,
For this written, in destiny…'

Kialessa then lashed out, Allastassia falling melodramatically backwards. Then Kialessa literally climbed onto Darrix's shoulders. 'You're coming with me!' she told them all.

It was the line she was supposed to deliver to the princess.

But Darrix was clever, and had worked out what was going on already. He took Allastassia's place, and with a cry of terror all his own descended into the stage trapdoor.

The princess screamed.

The choir screamed.

The audience applauded.

Darrix made his way to the backstage, where the assistants fitted the manacles that were really made for Allastassia. He had to hold them in place.

Kialessa couldn't hear what the princess was saying, but she could tell the people were cheering.

'She's working them into a fervour of passion,' Darrix smiled.

'Just like the princess she is,' Kialessa agreed, getting a little worried at the violence of one cheer. 'I hope she doesn't set them on me for real.'

Darrix smiled, and Kialessa's fears disappeared.

Almost.

A moment later the dancers were moving off stage,

Allastassia in the lead. Kialessa was just beginning to gather shadow for her next big entrance when Allastassia ran up to her, and shoved Flower's fire ribbon into her hands.

'Kialessa, you have to dance.'

'What?' Darrix and Kialessa said at the same time.

'Dance, Kia. Dance like you do when you play with your ribbon. Just like that, no more, no less. You have no idea how beautiful you look. Besides, we need the time to change my outfits.'

Kialessa looked down at the ribbon, excited enough to try just about anything right now. 'But what about the music?'

'I got this,' Allastassia smiled.

Kialessa grinned. Yes, it was a good time for some magic.

The curtain opened to Darrix chained to a pillar, something he'd never rehearsed for, except perhaps in real life. He tugged at the chains, doing a fine job of struggling without ripping them out of the thin wooden post.

Kialessa walked on wearing her battle armour.

She pointed the ribbon at his heart, and twisting it snapped it like a whip at the very moment she unleashed the only wizard spell she really knew. The ribbon burst into flames.

Everyone gasped.

Music started from the pit, but Kialessa didn't have time to admire the instruments floating up in the air on their own. They were playing a strange song; one made up of the melodies Kialessa had occasionally heard Allastassia hum one time or another.

But it was great music to dance to, with a heavier beat than their people were no doubt accustomed to.

Kialessa spun around, dancing completely impromptu. The ribbon seemed to grow, flowing with fire and light.

The audience was silent, and Kialessa spun around Darrix with all her energy. The ribbon obeyed her every wish, dancing with the magic. She was having the time of her life, teasing Darrix with the fire so that he cringed. Kialessa laughed from among the flames, spinning them around her head, wrapping the ribbon around her unburnable ankles and wrists, making pictures with it in the air.

She lost track of all sense of time and place simply enjoying making a dance.

Then the music began to slow, and with her frantic breath Kialessa brought the dance to a close. The beautiful flames spun one more time around her head and then, without her effort at all, they turned into a black ash that settled down to the ground. There, they formed a perfect circle, a fitting end to a wonderful dance.

The audience erupted in applause, and all stood. They cheered her with thunderous noise.

Kialessa grinned, and turned to look at Darrix.

His eyes were wide open with astonishment. She'd never seem him look so… speechless. For a moment she just stared at him, and it seemed like there wasn't anything else he wanted to look at.

She felt her face blush red, and the applause continue. They begged her to do it again, but Kialessa shook her head. That magic was for once, only.

Kialessa shared the rhyme once more, telling the imprisoned man that she would keep him here till he learnt to love her.

The audience roared their disapproval and Kialessa hissed at them with glowing eyes. They cheered even louder.

The scene changed again.

Darrix and Kia quickly ran backstage.

He was breathing heavily, 'Kialessa… that was… that was…'

She smiled.

'Come on you two,' someone muttered, slapping Darrix on the shoulder in preparation for his next scene.

They waited out the next twenty moments as the princess and her assistant fought their way into the hellish prison. Kialessa was just beginning to think how clever Allastassia was, to be making all this up on the spot, when the boy who was supposed to be playing the carpenters son's companion went to stand up next to her.

'Ahh, shouldn't you be out there?' Darrix asked.

'Well, yes… but just as I was getting ready, you'll never guess, as soon as Patsi realised you two had changed gender roles on the rest of us she just grabs my false legs and puts them on. She's out there now, making it all up on the fly like the rest of us.'

'I wonder how she's doing?' Darrix asked.

As if in answer the audience burst out laughing. Allastassia's reply, though it could hardly be heard, was met with laughter as well.

'Apparently, she's doing all right,' Kialessa said.

'If that's one thing Patsi knows,' the boy grinned, 'it's how to make us all laugh.'

They smiled, and waited for their turn back on for the finale.

They ran back on at their cue, Darrix setting up the shackles with Kialessa pretending to feed him some poisoned food.

When to their surprise Posk began to roll up the wrong backdrop.

They were about to be stuck in front of hillside scenery where the princess had sung her first song.

Kialessa froze; she had no idea what to do.

'Shadow,' Darrix whispered.

Suddenly he roared, and snapped the chains on his pole.

She covered him in darkness, and he crawled up from the ground. It must have looked like he'd just fought his way up from hell.

'I escaped,' he told the audience, falling to his knees.

They cheered. Then someone shouted, 'No! The princess is looking for you! You have to go back!'

'Go back, go back!' they shouted.

Darrix nodded.

But Kialessa had other ideas. Cuing the musicians from the

side she walked in.

People screamed.

They waited in silence, and Kialessa walked up to the still kneeling man. He looked tired, and defeated.

'Why?' she asked him.

He made up the poem, right there and then, on the spot.

'Love… is a choice, of who we choose to be,
But it just isn't love if that choice isn't free,
You cannot claim love, I know,
Until you are free to let someone go.
While fire and lightning turn the sky black,
And with all your will wish you might hold me back,
Though your heart begs me, forever to stay,
My heart bids me knowing, I must turn away.
Release me, I beg you, fair demon,
In eternal loves name,
Already in knowing you, I am forever changed.
Release me, and you too will be set free,
Unrequited obsession, unfulfilled need.
Set love free, and in doing,
You too will know…
Show love, I beg you,
By letting me go…'

The audience fell silent. Kialessa was moved, and for the first time let her tears flow openly. For the first time in her life, Kialessa really felt like something she was doing was good, and it was loved. And she was perfect for the role.

Then Allastassia walked on the other end of the stage. She gasped, and was silent. She reached out to the carpenter's son, but said nothing as though she feared some demon reprisal.

Everyone waited on Kialessa. She didn't know what to do, or what to say. There was no script for this part.

'Set love free!' someone shouted from the back of the

     By Dr Joseph Ireland "Dr Joe"

audience.

'Set love free, set love free!' They began to chant. They got louder and louder.

It was hard to stop from smiling; they just loved this show so much.

But she wasn't going to let them tell her what to do. So she called her father's whip from the chest at the foot of her bed and snapped it. The sound thundered through the crowd and brought them all to silence.

She couldn't seem to think of a poem, so said nothing. But walking up to the manacled prisoner and knelt before him. Saying nothing she tenderly took the chains from his wrists.

The crowd held its breath.

And then he hugged her, in front of the entire audience. For just a moment, she forgot she was acting, and let his arms wrap around her. In that embrace she suddenly realised that she had never been hugged by anyone but the king before. Not since she was a child, and only by her parents. No stranger of another race, no friend… not even her brother would ever admit to touching her in public though they shoved each other all the time.

No one said anything.

He pulled back and looked at her from much closer than he ever had before.

Then, without almost any warning at all, he kissed her.

On the lips.

The audience was absolutely silent. She knew why. That was more than an act. Darrix had just… shown some very public affection for… a tae'anaryn.

She was just so grateful, and so embarrassed. She just put her head down on his chest, and he held her in his arms.

Then, the entire crowd went "aww" and a moment later Kialessa felt another pair of arms slip around her. It was the princess, Allastassia. Kialessa could not believe it, and felt more loved right then than any other time in her life.

Then, just as the moment was about to pass, Patsi went to

join in the hug and ended up falling flat on her face. Never had she heard such laughter from a crowd.

Somehow the musicians realised it was time to start the finale music and they stood up to dance. Kialessa wiped the tears from her eyes, and clapped her way right through the scene change to the wedding. One of the flower girls ran passed and shoved a bouquet in her hands too. She joined them in the procession and cheering. Allastassia and Darrix acted out a pretend wedding, and she wrapped her arms around his neck, dragged him sideways and downwards, and smooched him squarely on the lips.

For an instant, just an instant, Kialessa felt her heart pricked with envy. Then she cast her glace sideways and saw Posk. He looked away into the shadows of as though allowing his unrequited love the privacy she desired from his gaze.

Darrix stood up and smiled, looking embarrassed, and the people cheered. Oh, how they cheered!

It was by far the most interesting night of her life.

***

'I have decided,' the wrinkled old lady who took care of the students announced, 'that while you may be a tae'anaryn girl, you have the heart of a human.' She said it with such romance and kindness it made Kialessa smile. It wasn't much acceptance, but it would do for a beginning.

Kialessa and Darrix were at the shrine the next day. People still teased him about that kiss.

Kialessa was offering hugs all around the next day, and receiving many more than ever before. It was nice.

Late evening found her, sitting alone, on the hill where they'd first met Flower. As if on cue, the performer and her minotaur arrived with Allastassia. They'd only talked a moment before the boys joined them, it was clear they'd been in some sort of conference with each other all morning – Posk still had a lot to catch up on.

They sat in a circle to listen to Flower as she sung to herself, Allastassia humming some kind of improvised harmony. A compassionate breeze cooled the warm day, while the occasional dandelion seed, the fairy parasol, wafted by them.

'I suppose we'll be going soon to catch up to my parents,' Flower suddenly decided.

Ugly grunted his agreement.

'Once they hear how I didn't destroy the kingdom,' Allastassia tried to smile.

Posk sat cross legged, wearing leggings and a shirt Kialessa had never seem him in. He was chewing on a grass stem in, well, exactly like Darrix was actually. The half troll boy looked at Allastassia, eyes narrow. 'What I would like to understand is what happened. Why'd you all of a sudden become this demanding, dangerous, freak?' he asked without any tact.

Allastassia did not look at him when she answered, speaking to them all. 'I woke up one morning, just before the circus arrived, and found my body was changing, my whole world was changing. I was not a little girl any more. I needed to become a woman, and I wasn't really very sure what that meant. Everyone loved me as a little child; I just needed to be cute and charming. But to become a woman, like mother … I needed to be different. I think I was too afraid people wouldn't love me anymore or that… I wouldn't deserve their love.'

They were silent a moment. It was a deep admission that they were all painfully aware of, except, it seemed up until that moment, Allastassia.

Then Darrix spoke, 'And what did you learn?'

She sighed, and looked up at the sky. 'That the world is actually quite full of love, more especially when you don't try to force or prescribe what form that love should take. But when you help people, and serve them with your talents, it will bring out some the best love in you. I have never felt more loved than when helping others with what I can do,' she confessed.

Kialessa grinned. How she'd wished she could have just told Allastassia that a few weeks ago! But then she realised that even if she had, it wouldn't have stopped her. Allastassia had to go through this for herself. Kialessa just had to love her, let her figure it out for herself, and in a certain sense simply keep out of the way.

And aside from a wonderful play, word would surely soon spread: The kingdom held the most powerful enchantress this generation would ever see.

But what was best, perhaps, was that Allastassia was finding her own way to be good, and helpful. Kialessa found she had to admire that, it was really tough to find yourself like that.

'I love you folks,' Allastassia suddenly told them.

'We love you too,' Kialessa replied.

And even Posk was allowed to join the ensuing group hug.

       By Dr Joseph Ireland "Dr Joe"

Appendix

10 Despite all claims to the contrary, Flower's unique pose did *not* appear to help her defeat Darrix in the game of Knights and Knaves

Points to ponder by chapter

The chrysalis

Have you ever had a friend, or perhaps you yourself, who has had to face change? Was it easy? What made it more difficult? What kind of friends did you wish you had during this time?

The circus

In this chapter, Kialessa has to deal yet again with the consistent bullying in her life. How do you think she did? Can you see how hard it was for her to not lose her temper at times? Would you have done differently?

In this chapter I'm very proud that, while she is aware of injustice and other people's faults, Kialessa is not blaming other people or focusing on things she cannot change. Instead, she is using this as a chance to learn from her own actions. How one defines a problem has a very big influence on how that problem will be approached. How do you think it will affect her life to see this as everyone else's fault, rather than a chance to become excellent and outstanding?

Individuals of various minorities sometime mention how they feel they must be *exceptional*, simply to *fit in*. Does this seem fair to you? How can you show better appreciation and understanding of someone whose race, religion or beliefs are very different to your own?

The play

What clever trick did Allastassia use to get the ringmaster to agree to put on the play? At times, how does acting like a certain decision or course of action will make you happy work better than directly asking for it? Or is this tactic unhelpful and maybe even unkind?

There's an old saying, "It's amazing what you can achieve

   By Dr Joseph Ireland "Dr Joe"

when you don't mind who gets the credit for it." Whose idea was it to put on the play? Who did Allastassia encourage to think it was their idea?

Mild herbs

What was Allastassia doing, and not doing, that makes her change more difficult and challenging?

How did Allastassia react when she felt people weren't listening to her? Do you think there might have been a more effective way to express her anger and frustration?

The plan

Allastassia again uses a clever trick of getting other people to offer what she wants, by being very coy and enthusiastic about it – by showing them that their help would make her very happy. Is this a useful way to get others to help out? Or is this the very heart of cruel sedition?

At this point, her friends are suggesting to Allastassia that now might not be the best time to take on such a big project. Should she take their advice and chill out, or is this exactly the kind of distraction and challenge she needs to bring out her best during this time of change in her life?

Realisation

Allastassia gets the news that she does not get her dream role in the play. How does she react? How would you react?

As expected, the play is a very stressful time for a young enchantress who has been told she should be taking things easy. What would you have done; fired Allastassia? Or helped out even more? What could anyone do at this point?

Imagine having as simple a solution as a hat that allows you to concentrate and makes you twice as smart. What would you use such a device to achieve?

The clock

With the help of a wizard's hat, Posk's innate love of mechanics and machinery really comes out.

Having talents and pursuing our interests is an important skill in living, learning and becoming. What things do you love to do? What compels you, and what would you like to be excellent at?

Allastassia, not to be upstaged, shows off her own talents and demonstrates a power not even the wizards have uncovered. The ability to see the very small has a big influence in science, and will have a big hit on society. What difference does seeing the very small have on a society? (For one, they will discover germs.)

Dress rehearsal

Sometimes life, like some dress rehearsals, will be disasters compared to the images we have in our mind of how it should all work out. Do we give up? Or try again, maybe try something new?

Is Allastassia being kind or fair towards Piex at the end of this chapter? Do you think he should help out and loan his powerful wizardry headband to this project?

Special training

With the new headband on, Posk can converse normally. Do you think some physically disabled people have totally normal thoughts inside?

Kialessa is also selected for some intense special training, which she accepts without question. Imagine getting into elite, special training, and then treating it like a burden; a chore. Do you think you would do well at it? Do you think some of the hard things we have to do in life might be easier if we looked at them, at times, as 'elite training'.

Dreamdancer and Shadow weaver

In this chapter we begin to see how extraordinarily powerful Allastassia is, and how she is exerting her power to keep her own conscious mind unaware of her stress and confusion. The idea here is that the moon goddess Lumos steps in and is trying to help Allastassia calm down, but Kialessa is too worried to trust her. Why do you think Allastassia doesn't want to listen to Kialessa's concerns about the event?

Allastassia does, however, help Kialessa develop her own special talents, with good advice and by sticking up for her in front of others. By showing everyone that she's not afraid of Kialessa's shadow weaving she makes it OK for Kia to keep practicing. What kind of a friend is Allastassia trying to be?

Improvisation and fire

Is it all right to make it up as you go sometimes? How much skill and practice does it take to be confident at improvisation and spontaneity?

Kialessa is learning how to keep fit through dance, drama and acrobatics. I think that some of the fittest people in our society are dancers, what do you think?

To faraway places

The captain of the king's guard is commanded to give Kialessa a weapon, and she chooses one of her own to keep. Many cultures value weapons and their responsible use, what do you think about arming an 11 year old with a magic, flesh eating dagger? Is it something you would do?

This hidden trove of weapons at the castle of Lenmer'el will probably be very useful at some point in the future...

The Shadowrealm

Where is the Shadowrealm? What did Kialessa think of a place no one else could see? If you had a unique talent would you use it to help others?

Flower is very sympathetic toward Kialessa because she sees in her a similarity – they're both very different to the other children their age. Also, Flower likes Kialessa because she's friendly, clever, and confident. Do you think Flower would make a good friend to Kialessa?

Confessions

Why do you think Allastassia and Flower got into an argument? What does Flower think of Allastassia, and what does Allastassia think of Flower? What should you do when two close friends are arguing?

Do people sometimes use criticising a mutual friend as a way to strengthen their own relationship. Is this backstabbing?

Liber de Nocte Tenebrosi

AKA: "The book of the dark night". Another special gift from the king, this chapter also focuses on Piex's skills in wizardry and his desire to help Kialessa.

Kialessa uses her privilege of seeing the king to encourage Allastassia. How does this make Allastassia feel? What questions did the king ask, and what do you think he really wants to know?

Ever training

Kialessa is finding the circus training very difficult, but she's in the top 5 students in the entire college for dance and acrobatics. We use this chapter to demonstrate Posk's continued love of mechanics – for better or worse. What is Kialessa learning at this point? Who can she count on as her friend, and as an acquaintance who will still help her. Some people assume that if others don't actively like them, it must automatically indicate they hate them. I have learned that most people don't mind you either way, and will generally be polite and kind simply for their own protection. What do you think?

Existential

Why do you think Allastassia is fixated on Posk's ability to open the curtains and backdrops? Is it really that important?

The new headband allows Posk to access his abstract and existential thoughts. He dwells on several of the very important, and very deep, issues of philosophy. Some such questions might not even have an answer, what do you think?

Posk expresses his love for Allastassia. What do you think of what she said to turn him down? Was it kind, or cruel? Did she make it clear how she felt, or did it drag him out with a false hope?

Do you think Posk is really in love with Allastassia, or is it just a huge, immature, crush?

Presenting problems

When you ask someone what is wrong, they will sometimes give you a false answer – instead of telling you the real problem they might tell you a similar, or even unrelated, problem they are having. This might be to throw you off from finding out what's really wrong, because otherwise this will force them to confront problems they don't feel ready to confront. What do you think? Did Kialessa help Allastassia, or was this more about distracting Kialessa from the deeper problem of Allastassia not feeling loved as she changes?

Dreamtime

At what point do you know a trouble or concern is getting out of hand? What lengths can even good people sometimes go to in order to cover up their unravelling world?

Can dreams help us reinterpret our waking world?

The news

Here, the four closest advisors to the king express their concern that the situation with Allastassia is getting out of hand. What do you think they should do at this point?

When the show must not go on

Not waiting for a solution, the circus decides to pack up and leave before things fall apart. Rather than leave things be, Allastassia again insists on ploughing through despite the apparent danger to her and her friends. Do you get the impression Allastassia enchanted her friends to keep going with the play? Does Flower's behaviour, considering Flower is immune to most magic, indicate that some enchantments were defiantly going on at this point? Do you think the circus was right to flee the impending danger?

Uninvited guests

Flower and Ugly once more arrive to help out, risking everything to protect Kialessa. However, it seems another uninvited guest has arrived, and may have been working behind the scenes for some time now. The assassin of kings, Jerik, whom Kialessa calls Dog, has returned and is trying to lure the king out of the safety of his castle. Allastassia is just a pawn in his plot to destroy the king. What will happen if Dog succeeds?

Why do you think Allastassia took the magic ring from the satyr, despite all the warnings of her own heart, and from her friends?

From the heart

How did Posk stop Allastassia, or to be more precise, what did he say that helped Allastassia stop herself?

Why do you think Allastassia feels such an overwhelming need for love, acceptance, and even fame – especially considering that she is rich, famous, beautiful and powerful already?

The enchantress's chrysalis

Why did the king put Posk in the stocks, and not Allastassia?

What did you think of the final version of the play? Was there a bit you really liked? Do you think you could improvise as well as these talented students did?

Here Allastassia confesses that her body is changing and that scared her. She felt uncertain of how to meet the future now that new expectations would be placed on her as a woman. What did it take for her to accept the love that surrounded her, that for a time, she seemed to have become entirely unaware?

The Tae'anaryn *and* The Enchantress's Chrysalis

 By Dr Joseph Ireland "Dr Joe"

The Tae'anaryn *and* The Enchantress's Chrysalis

By Dr Joseph Ireland "Dr Joe"

The Tae'anaryn *and* The Enchantress's Chrysalis

Choice, set free   247

By Dr Joseph Ireland "Dr Joe"

The Tae'anaryn *and* The Enchantress's Chrysalis

The Tae'anaryn *and* The Enchantress's Chrysalis

 By Dr Joseph Ireland "Dr Joe"

Spear of the Troll Prince

War breaks upon the peaceful kingdom of Lenmer'el. The troll hordes are massing at the edge of the Broadwaters River. Uniting them for the first time in three hundred years is an ambitious new warlord who wields the Greenflame Sabre, a powerful troll artefact which was supposed to be hidden in the deepest vaults of the magical castle at Emerel. Now all he requires is the Spear of the Blood Lord and all troll fealty with it, and an army half a million strong will sweep across the Great Kingdom in less than a year, destroying all in their path.

And the first obstacle in that path is Kialessa and her closest friends…

Place the date and your personal mark here each

time you read this book – libraries included!

Why not share your experiences and thoughts with the

fandom! Get a grownup's permission and visit

www.DrJoe.id.au

for fan art, sequels, competitions and more!

 By Dr Joseph Ireland "Dr Joe"